¿Eres tú?

¿Eres tú?

A HISTORY OF LONQUIMAY

Frank H. Tainter, Ph.D.

Copyright © 2024 Frank H. Tainter, Ph.D.

All rights reserved. No part of this book may be used or reproduced by any means, graphic, electronic, or mechanical, including photocopying, recording, taping or by any information storage retrieval system without the written permission of the author except in the case of brief quotations embodied in critical articles and reviews.

This is a work of fiction. All of the characters, names, incidents, organizations, and dialogue in this novel are either the products of the author's imagination or are used fictitiously.

Because of the dynamic nature of the Internet, any web addresses or links contained in this book may have changed since publication and may no longer be valid. The views expressed in this work are solely those of the author and do not necessarily reflect the views of the publisher, and the publisher hereby disclaims any responsibility for them.

Any people depicted in stock imagery provided by Getty Images are models, and such images are being used for illustrative purposes only. Certain stock imagery © Getty Images.

Interior Image Credit: Frank H. Tainter

Contents

Dedication

This book is dedicated to *Ramón Rosende*. He was my Chilean counterpart when I served in the Peace Corps from 1964-66 and was a good friend and a true Chilean. Shortly after the military coup in 1973 he shared confinement in the national soccer stadium with *Víctor Jara* and was to be executed because he was a socialist. However, his life was saved by the intervention of a retired army general named *Jorge Beroíza*. Mr. *Beroíza* was the fiscal agent at the *Instituto Forestal* where *Ramón Rosende* was employed. Mr. *Beroíza* was not sympathetic to the cause of the military coup but because of his military experience, successfully argued on behalf of *Ramón Rosende, Oscar Wetling, Germán Tamm,* and other former employees of the *Instituto* who had been arrested and were to be executed.

After three months in the national soccer stadium, *Ramón Rosende* was released, now reduced to skin and bone, and infested with lice. When he arrived at his home, his wife, a medical doctor, informed him that she had arranged for safe passage, and work, for the both of them in Venezuela. *Ramón* stood in the door, crossed his arms and declared, "I am a Chilean, I was born here, and I will die here." He lived several more years but had a fatal heart attack at the wedding of one of his sons. In the final analysis, he loved Chile more than his life. He didn't know it but he shared much of that love with me.

The price that some people have to pay for being a good citizen in their country of birth can be a strange thing. *Ramón Rosende's* father had been an ambassador to Italy and was later a candidate for the Chilean presidency. He ran as a popular socialist. Just before the election he was poisoned and killed by unknown members of the opposition.

Ramón Rosende,
with his sons, *Ramón* (left) and *Pablito* - Christmas, 1964.

This novel would have not been possible without the support of my wife, *María Magdalena*. And, she would want the reader to know that this is not how we did it.

Appreciation is extended to Jennifer Metcalf for her valuable editing of the first edition.

Prologue

This novel is fiction and most of the characters in this story are fictional. However, many of the individual events described herein actually happened, either to the author or to members of his immediate or extended family. The major historical events are true and provide a backdrop around which this story is woven. The timing of a few historical events was changed to better fit the narrative.

A born and bred true native Chilean might have preferred a different slant on the history and examples than what the author has chosen to present and may wonder about the strange assemblage of adventures that are presented. Suffice it to say that the *gringo* author has attempted to present this narrative as seen mainly through the eyes of Robert, our hero, and, to a lesser extent, through the eyes of our heroine, *Rosa*, and later through the eyes of their daughter *Paulina*, though, it is part of a much larger saga about how the *Pehuenche* medicine women, or **machis**, came to be and their important role in early *Pehuenche* development as human beings.

This novel is written primarily in English and is printed in normal font style. All Spanish and Latin words and phrases are printed in italics. There are a few words from the dialect of the native Chileans living in the area of the story, the *Pehuenches*. These are presented in italics and in bold font style. An example is **foye**, a medicinal plant that in Spanish is called *canelo*.

This novel makes considerable reference to medicinal plants and includes a list of many of these plants and many of their supposed remedies. The reader should be aware that most medicinal plants have not been rigorously tested for their efficacy by modern scientific techniques against neither disease pathogens nor illness. However, any potential critic must consider that, while modern medicine has only been in existence for a little over a century, medicinal plants have been used by countless individuals on several continents for many thousands of years. Would these people have continued to use medicinal plants if they had no positive effect? The answer to that question makes a strong argument that perhaps medicinal plants with historical usage do have some authentic medicinal value. More is said about this in the introduction to *Paulina's* notebook printed near the end of this novel.

At any rate, anyone contemplating the use of medicinal plants should first consult with their doctor. As recent research has shown, many of the medicinal plants listed in this novel have been found to have extremely powerful medicinal effects. When the hero of this novel began his exploratory work in the 1960s, general public interest in medicinal plants was only local at best. By the time the first edition of this novel was published (2015), there had been an incredible upsurge in the acceptance, use, and commercialization of medicinal plants, and subsequent scientific testing has revealed efficacious chemical components in certain plants.

At the beginning of most chapters there is a title, or short verse, of a piece of music from Chilean folklore that the author has chosen to help convey a sense of the emotion that the reader might experience during the reading of that chapter. If the reader wants to expand on that emotion, it would be helpful to listen to that suggested music. The listener will gain an appreciation of the tremendous variety and beauty of Chilean folklore music.

The inspiration for this novel came literally during a night flight from *Santiago*, Chile on October 23, 2013. Sleep came in fits during that night. The plane was nearly full, and the uncomfortable seats allowed only short periods of fit-full sleep, and then joint aches from sitting in one position or other caused the author to awaken in a stupor. During those moments of stupor this entire story came to the author almost as if he were reading it from memory and with such clarity that months later he could recall each and every detail.

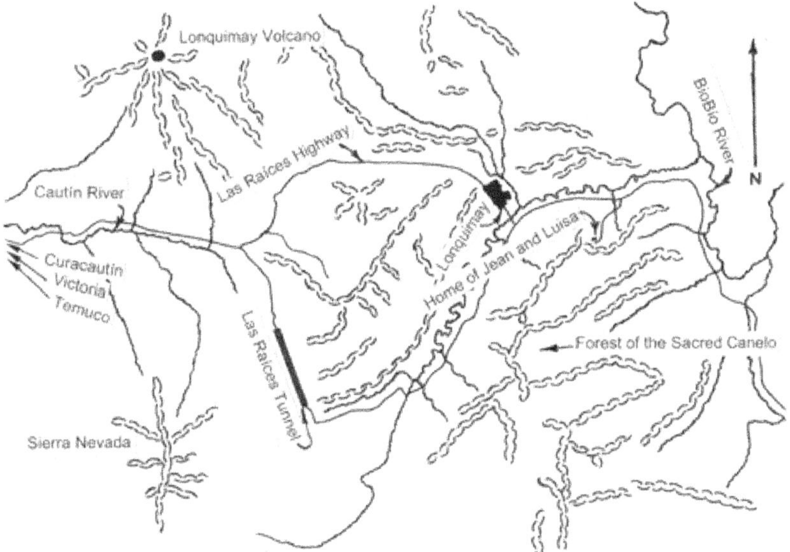

The Area of Our Story

CHAPTER 1
Lonquimay Valley, Chile – November, 1980

"Rosa colorada, quién te deshojó:
Por qué no esperaste, mi vida, que llegara yo:"
(My red rose, who stole you from me?
Why did you not wait, my love, for me to return?) Verses from *"Rosa*
colorada."
(The red rose.) – Song from Chilean folklore.

This story is centered near the small village of *Lonquimay*, in south-central Chile. The name *Lonquimay*, or *Lonkimay*, has two possible meanings. In the original native tongue the name means " *bosque tupido*" (dense forest) or "*cabeza del rio*" (river basin). Either could be true since both describe the area in near-prehistoric times. Before illegal logging and uncontrolled wild-fires in the mountains surrounding the village destroyed most of them, extensive and dense forests of *Araucaria* pines blanketed the region. The village is also just downriver from the source of the *Naranjo* River that is a tributary to the *Biobío*, a major river of Chile, and, that for many centuries served as a physical border protecting these natives from the onslaughts of the invading Incas and the later invading Spaniards.

The village of *Lonquimay* is near the head of a valley of the same name. It is a long, broad valley that begins about halfway between the cities of *Victoria* and *Temuco* and follows along the *Cautín* River upstream as it meanders its way down from the Andean Mountains. The valley crosses the Andean *Cordillera*, becoming an inter-mountain plateau, and then forms another valley that winds back down into Argentina on the eastern side of the *Cordillera*. More will be said later to describe the area and the people living there.

It was a bright, crisp, spring morning in the valley, covered with an intense blue sky and, although the nights were still cool, the days had begun to warm quickly. The landscape vegetation was in early full bloom. It was mid-November and the intense-scarlet flowers of the *fosforito* trees formed large and small splotches of intense color in the view from the road. Along fences and the edges of fields there were individual trees with their bright scarlet flowers and large patches of the same trees in the native forest on the hillsides on either side of the road. The most plentiful tree component of this forest was *ñirre*, one of the deciduous southern beeches, which was just beginning to leaf out and its new leaves lent a light-green color to the landscape.

The globose witches' brooms of the bright yellow/gold-colored parasitic plant called *misodendrum* were just beginning to be partially obscured by the unfolding leaves of the *ñirre*. This combination of colors produced splotches of dark green, light green, and bright scarlet against the massive dark, green-cloaked mountains. A light dusting of black volcanic sand drifted across the road in the morning breeze and several condors lazily circled overhead.

A closer examination looking westward down the valley revealed that a car was traveling eastward up the valley road. The car wove its way along the crooked gravel road and finally came close to the crest at the upper end of the valley, raising a faint trail of dust as it putted and bounced along. The main character of our story, Robert, had rented the green 1947 Jeep station wagon in *Santiago*.

Oddly, it was the same vehicle he had used almost ten years earlier during his medicinal plant hunting forays. Older vehicles were difficult to find now that the Pinochet military regime had outlawed them from service. They were thought to be an embarrassment in an advanced country like Chile. Trucks older than 10 years of age were removed from the road almost immediately after the coup, but automobiles were only beginning to be subjected to the new ruling. The owner said this would be the last time that Robert could use this car and after this trip he would not be able to renew the license.

It felt good to be back in Chile and, as Robert drove along, a flood of disjunctive memories flashed through his mind, each occupying only a second or two of his thoughts. Some he didn't want to think about but they forced their way into his head anyway. Each time he shifted gears, though, he had to leave his reverie. The clutch and standard transmission had caused him considerable discomfort as he had not previously driven in a standard transmission vehicle with his newly acquired artificial left leg.

After six years in a coma his physical rehabilitation had been extremely difficult and any physical exertion caused extreme discomfort and very quickly developed into a general debilitating fatigue. He could will his leg to depress the clutch pedal but repeated clutch work made the left leg muscle seem to have turned into jelly. Then he reminded himself as to why he was here and he willed himself to ignore the pain and move on.

After he left *Santiago* he had taken a hurried trip down the Pan American Highway to *Victoria*, although he stopped at nearly every service station to sample the fresh fruits and juice drinks. He particularly liked fresh strawberry juice, and there was a lot of it at each stop as the strawberries had begun to mature a few days before his arrival. During his earlier time in Chile, he had also enjoyed watermelon juice but on this trip it was much too early for watermelons. At *Victoria* he had turned eastward onto the secondary road that penetrated approximately 125 kilometers up the *Lonquimay* Valley and toward the Andean *Cordillera*. Nearing the head end of the valley the road came to a junction.

Either road led to the village of *Lonquimay*. Robert chose to take the *Camino Las Raíces* road. In the winter season this road was impassable because of heavy snow but now, in spring, the road had been recently plowed and was free of snow. During the winter the only road passage to *Lonquimay* was through the *Túnel Las Raíces*, at that time the longest tunnel in South America. It was constructed for a railway line during the 1930s but it had been abandoned for that purpose and now was the only all-weather road to *Lonquimay* from Chile.

As the terrain rose in elevation, he entered the zone of pure *Araucaria* pine forests and he recalled the majesty and beauty of these trees, each with dark green foliage forming an umbrella-shaped crown that complemented the tall, nearly black branchless trunk. These, in turn, contrasted with the deep blue sky above them with scattered white cottony clouds. *Araucaria* pines dated from the time of the dinosaurs and the larger trees were several hundreds to over a thousand years of age. Although many had been logged or burned, some areas still retained many of the majestic pines.

The *Araucarian* pines were considered to be sacred by the *Pehuenche* natives. However, after the military coup in 1973 the new military regime had encouraged land grabbing on the *Pehuenche* lands and many of these sacred trees were being logged by illegal land colonizers. Along the road, Robert passed several teams of oxen, each team slogging along pulling a wooden-wheeled cart, each cart carrying a single, large *Araucaria* pine log. Some logs were over a meter in diameter. Further along several drovers herded a flock of sheep and Robert waited as they passed by on the road.

The drive up the valley was nostalgic for Robert but as he began to relive the memories of some of his work and experiences there, he also began to feel more emotional. He recalled the last time he was here in this valley, about the joy he felt performing his work and his medicinal plant collections, about the *González* family, *Claudia* and *Juan*, descendants of *Pehuenche* natives and who had helped him a great deal with his collection of medicinal plants. He also thought about their daughter, *Rosa*, who hadn't seemed to like him very much, except for those last few days he had been with the family as he packed his plant materials and prepared to leave Chile. The *González* family, *Rosa's* mother *Claudia* and her father *Juan*, and her older brother *Miguel*, had a small sheep and cattle ranch that had been in the family since their grandparents had fled to the valley from the Argentine side of the Andes Mountains during the *Rojas* campaign to exterminate the native aborigines.

The *Gonzálezes* were probably a little more well-to-do than many of their neighbors, partially because of the moderate wealth of some of their ancestors, and because they also supplemented their subsistence ranch income by preserving and singing folk songs at various events and celebrations around Chile. They were well known as folk singers and respected because they made great efforts to seek out and preserve Chilean folk music, especially that of the *Araucanian* natives of all of southern Chile. They had even gone on tour in Europe and had cut a number of records.

Claudia was also a respected **machi**, a person with a great knowledge of medicinal plants. She was not a practicing **machi** but, rather, spent her energies preserving ancestral knowledge of those remedies. Robert really enjoyed the time he spent with the *González* family and now he was recalling, when he was in a coma, the vision of *Claudia* imploring him to return to

Chile and help *Rosa.* He could think of no reason why he should be needed.

Robert's thoughts were abruptly interrupted again by another vision of *Claudia* and he didn't want to think about jumping into the cold, muddy river to save her life, but he could not put that thought out of his mind. He remembered the little dog that heroically jumped into the water and tried to save his mistress but was caught in the swift current and dragged under some floating branches and drowned. He reflected at the extreme emotions they all felt after the team of oxen had pulled the tree off of *Claudia* and many hands pulled both of them out of the river and up onto the bank and everyone realized that she would be all right. That happiness was severely tempered, though, by the loss of their faithful dog.

Shortly before that day, in mid-1973, he had received his draft notice and had only a few weeks in which to settle his affairs and return to the States. So, several days later, after he had bid farewell to the family, and as he was driving down the valley he passed through a street fair in *Curacautín* and saw a vender with several puppies for sale. Following an impulse, he stopped and watched the puppies for a long time.

As they rolled and wrestled around, one, a yellow Labrador, looked up and saw Robert standing there. The dog sat down and continued to watch Robert for a while and then tried to walk toward him, pulling on her little leash in the little cluster of tumbling puppies. She again sat down but kept wagging her tail to her right side as she watched Robert, for some unknown reason very interested in this *gringo.* Robert finally walked over, pulled out his wallet and asked, *"¿Cuánto vale?"* The man answered, *"Cinco escudos."* He handed the money to the vender, who was surprised when Robert didn't even try to negotiate a lower price.

So, he put the dog in the back of the Jeep and turned around and headed back up the valley. Two hours later he again turned into the driveway and pulled up to the *González* house. As he opened the car door, the surprised family came out onto the porch and he heard *Rosa* say, "Uh huh, so the *gringo* can't leave his Chilean family, huh? He wants to steal more of our magical plant remedies."

Robert put the puppy under his arm and walked up to the porch and handed it to *Claudia.* "Here," he said, "A little something to remember me by." As he left for the second time he noticed that this time everyone had tears in their eyes. As he got into the car he heard *Rosa* say with a choked voice, "Hurry back *gringo*."

He was finally able to push that thought out of his mind but it was immediately replaced by another day, in late 1973 in Vietnam, when he thought he saw, and heard, the vision of a much younger *Claudia* imploring him to save the Vietnamese family trapped in the middle of a fire fight. He often relived both of these visions and would awake with his heart pounding and his clothes drenched with sweat. He couldn't understand the significance of that experience or why he thought he had seen her there. Today we might conclude that he suffered from a type of post-traumatic stress syndrome.

It took him quite a while to recover from his experience in Vietnam and dealing with the loss of his leg plus getting used to the prosthetic limb. He also still had some pretty brutal trauma that made his transition back into a somewhat normal life very slow at times. After awakening from six years in a coma he had worked on his physical rehabilitation with a passion as he recalled the dream he thought he recalled of *Claudia*, telling him that *Rosa* needed help.

Robert could have lived a relatively decent life on his disability pension, but he wanted to get back to his plant work and renew the joy that he had experienced earlier as a plant explorer and collector, especially in Chile. His former partner at Pharmtec had urged Robert to return to Chile and resume some of his collecting attempts, at least on a trial basis. If it didn't work out he could still return to the company and work at the desk or at a laboratory job.

As he pushed these thoughts out of his mind, he looked out the open driver's window at the *Lonquimay* Volcano on his left and deeply inhaled the fresh air with just a hint of the odors of the last of the melting snow on the volcano's flanks, and *cilantro*, a common herb used as a food flavoring. He thought about some of the plants he had collected, some of the medications extracted from them, and the day when he had stopped at the *González* farm to ask for permission to collect on their land. They had certainly helped him a lot and, when he was in Vietnam, his partner had subsequently developed a plan for a *Pehuenche* cooperative to compensate them for their help. He wondered if they would remember him, if *Rosa* had married and moved away, if the little dog he gave them was still around. Was *Rosa* in some kind of trouble as his vision of *Claudia* had intimated?

His heart beat a little faster as he turned south onto the winding secondary road into their ranch, and then he stopped as he saw that the bridge crossing the creek was washed out. He could see their house a kilometer or so up the side road, nestled in the base of a narrow valley. He parked and climbed out. As he walked along the road toward the washout he inhaled the familiar scents of the land, the earthy odor of new plant growth, the dried sheep manure, and the faint spicy scent of dried plants from last year's growth. Overhead, the perpetual condors circled and wheeled around in an air updraft.

As he approached the washout and began to walk down into the ravine, he noticed that the house and yard in general seemed to be in terrible repair, far worse than when he had left. He noticed someone, a woman perhaps, on the shed roof pounding on the sheet metal roof with a hammer. He could see that she had long, black hair but he couldn't see well enough to determine if that was *Rosa*. He saw her suddenly drop the hammer and then heard her curse, *"¡Ay, miércoles! ¡Me pegué en un dedo!"*, (Oops, Darn! I hit my finger!) and put her finger in her mouth. Could that be *Rosa*? He had never heard her swear!

He crossed the creek by jumping from rock to rock and just as he had begun to climb back out onto the far bank, a young girl came running from the back of the house into the front yard, throwing a stick for a dog to fetch. As Robert approached, the dog suddenly saw him and started barking and began to run towards Robert. He wondered if it was the same dog he had given to *Rosa's* mother on that day when he had left the valley. This dog was grown up and the same color but this one was missing a hind leg.

The girl abruptly stopped when she saw Robert and called for the dog as it ran toward Robert. Then she dropped the stick and ran over to the shed and shouted to the woman on the roof, *"¡Mamá, Mamá, alguien viene"!* (Mommy, Mommy, someone is coming!). The woman turned to look, and looked for a few long moments, still with her finger in her mouth. Then she climbed down the ladder and stood by the girl.

As Robert got closer, noticeably limping as the stump of his missing leg was hurting a great deal, the woman's hand went to her mouth, she gasped and hugged the girl closer. His heart started to pound! It was *Rosa*! She was a little thinner than he remembered but still had the long, black hair and the aquiline features that he had grown so fond of although he never did find the courage to tell her. And, her brown eyes were certainly flashing at him now! Robert could see those flashing eyes very clearly now. She, the girl, and the dog just stood there, watching Robert hobbling toward them with his one good leg and his other, artificial leg.

As Robert approached, the dog ran up to him barking fiercely as if its jaw were going to fall off. Then, she suddenly stopped several meters away and just sat down and looked at Robert, panting, tilting her head, and with her tail wagging, toward her right side. Robert again wondered if this could be the same dog he had given to *Claudia*. The dog tilted her head from side to side and whimpered, and seemed to be questioning herself as if it might have recognized him. *Rosa* and the girl walked up behind the dog. Robert noticed that *Rosa* held the girl's hand very tightly.

Robert's gaze briefly flashed over to the *Lonquimay* Volcano over his right shoulder, then his eyes began to mist over as he heard the girl ask, "*¿Mamá, por qué estás llorando? Por favor no llores. ¿Qué pasa?*" (Mommy, why are you crying? Please don't cry. What's the matter?). Robert's heart sank as he realized that *Rosa* must be married and that this young girl was her daughter. *Rosa* and Robert just stood looking at each other for several longer seconds.

Then she placed her hands on her checks, gasped, and asked, "*¿Eres tú? ¿Roberto, eres realmente tú?*" (Is it you? *Roberto*, is it really you?) Then, as tears began to roll down her cheeks, she looked down at the girl and said, "*Paulinita, este hombre desgraciado es tu papá!*" Robert remembered enough Spanish to understand what she had said. "*Paulina*, this nasty man is your father!"

After that shock, he thought that perhaps he should just turn around and leave, but then she said as she started to sob, "*¡Y estoy tan feliz de verlo nuevamente!*" (And I'm so happy to see him again!). *Rosa* and Robert just stood looking at each other again for another long second. Then, she, and the dog, ran toward him, jumped on him and they all fell down in a wild embrace of arms and legs, dog paws, her long black hair, and their tears.

Robert was back in Chile, and alive again!

CHAPTER 2
To a New Land – At Least 13,400 Years Before the Present

"Soy de la sangre Araucana."
(I am of *Araucanian* blood.)
– Song verse from Chilean/*Mapuche* folklore.

The history of human involvement in what was to eventually become known in the present day as the *Lonquimay* Valley began at least 13,400 years ago when people arrived on the American continent. The ancestors of the modern-day *González* family were part of a small band of men, women, children, and dogs. They had trekked southward in a mountain valley, approximately 220 kilometers north of what is now Yellowstone National Park in the present state of Montana. We know this today because they left traces of their passage.

They carried weapons with a characteristically shaped stone head that would later become known as the Clovis point. The Clovis point was a well-crafted and beautiful stone spearhead and arrowhead. It was designed for killing large animals such as the wooly mammoth and the American mastodon. However, this particular projectile point style was used for only a relatively short time, appearing suddenly with the Clovis people as they would later become known as, and then disappearing from history just as suddenly, for reasons which we will soon see.

The story of this band actually began around 80,000 years before, when their ancestors arrived in Europe following a long trek from Africa. That journey had even begun 200,000 years earlier, by which time modern *Homo sapiens* had evolved. Around 160,000 years ago, climate conditions had deteriorated, leaving inland Africa dry and uninhabitable. By the time those people arrived in Europe they were true *H. sapiens* and thrived there after they had become accomplished invasive predators. We know nothing about how they communicated with each other, nor of their value systems.

Those early humans had formed a symbiotic relationship with the wolf ancestors of modern-day dogs. Many large animals such as cave bears became extinct at about that time in Europe and it is believed that their demise was a direct result of these new, highly efficient hunting partners. There has been some speculation that another race of primitive people, the Neandertals, became extinct at this same time because they could not compete with these new, more efficient, hunters.

Genetic and archeological evidence indicates that around some 32,000 years ago, these humans had moved from Europe, into Siberia, and then into northwestern Beringia. Subsequently, between 26,000 and 18,000 years ago, they went into eastern Beringia, ready for the trek across the land bridge. There is some archeological evidence that a few may have migrated as early as 32,000 years ago, during one of the inter-glacial epochs before the Pleistocene when the land bridge would also have been exposed. However, subsequent genetic mutations in the later and larger group (our group) left unique DNA markers that were found only in what were soon to become Native Americans. There is also some evidence that there were human visitors to ice-free Pacific coastal areas approximately 16,000 years ago and they left stone tools that resemble those found in Japan from the same time period. Genetic evidence to date suggests that they did not remain here although they did visit often.

A nagging question among paleontologists was raised by the observation that skeletal remains discovered in the Siberia area prior to the great migration into the Americas was that those people had strong oriental features, yet after the migrations that began about 14,000 years ago, those features had been lost. What is know known, based on genetic sequencing, is that beginning about 33,000 years before the present, several groups of people migrated into the Siberian area, and mixed genetically for the next 20,000 years. When their descendants departed from Siberia and crossed into North America across the Beringian land bridge when it opened about 14,000 years ago, those people had the modern genetic makeup of what are today recognized as native Americans even as they migrated into what is now Alaska.

Based on the evidence gathered from archeological, genomic, mitochondrial DNA, and Y-chromosome DNA, there were only three major migration events into the prehistoric Americas. Our group was among the first arrivals. Two later migrations from Siberia peopled the northwestern regions of what is now Canada and part of western North America. These migrants concentrated in northern Canada and are the ancestors of the Intuits. Another group migrated into west-central Canada. All the groups came with their dogs. The dogs, which were becoming more and more domesticated, continued to give early humans a great advantage for survival because they allowed them to track smaller animals such as deer, and to corral and harass big-game animals, and then kill them with their spears. For a time they may have served as food for their masters, but they also probably helped carry meat of recently killed animals to the next camping site.

All of these immigrants came during the time of the Pleistocene glaciation, traveling along the Beringian land bridge, created by lowering of the oceans as a great deal of the ocean water was tied up in the form of glacier ice. This land bridge connected Siberia with Alaska. The frigid climate was quite inhospitable to humans and the newcomers traveled quickly southward mainly along the coast of western North America. Genetic evidence also suggests that perhaps less than a total of 5,000 individuals dispersed across the bridge and then southward. It was during this trek that this particular group of individuals obtained their first primitive sense of their humanity.

The new arrivals were constantly on the move. The harsh climate precluded gaining much sustenance from the meager plant life, mainly from tundra species, and so they were forced to depend exclusively on hunting animals for their food. At the time, the vegetation was arctic in nature and not very diverse. Later research would reveal that much of arctic vegetation consisted of dry steppe-tundra type dominated not by grass but by herbaceous vascular plants. By the time of the glacial maximum (25-15,000 years before the present), plant diversity had declined markedly. When the later moist tundra appeared, it was dominated by a more diverse assemblage of woody plants and grasses that promoted a different group of herbivores.

One of the earliest medicinal plants they undoubtedly encountered was horsetail (*limpia plata*), a very primitive plant that was useful for polishing objects because of its high silica content. It had some medicinal properties as well.

Small animals did not provide enough sustenance for a group of hungry people constantly on the move although small animals, and fish, undoubtedly supplemented some of their food needs. Large animals were needed to provide the considerable amount of fresh meat needed to survive in the frozen environment. In the tundra the new immigrants hunted the large animals already mentioned, the wooly mammoth, the typical tundra elephant, and farther south, the American mastodon, a spruce-eating elephant that also lived at that same time but in a different, and slightly more favorable environment.

As each successive generation of migrants passed farther south, and eastward, into their new home, they pursued the larger animals and were quite successful in causing their scarcity. In only a few generations they caused the extinction of the large animals, and the Clovis point, which was designed to kill these large animals, was no longer useful on the smaller game animals. Then the Folsom point was developed for hunting the smaller animals and especially the American bison.

The members of this group had not eaten in several days and were hungry. Today they were following the trail of an American mastodon, as they had been doing for the past several days. The mastodon knew it was being followed and was succumbing to their hunter/gatherer strategy. The dogs were constantly harassing the animal. They would worry the animal or wear it down physically until it would finally make a stand. Then they would attack the animal from all sides, with the men, women, and older children attempting to spear the lower parts of the mastodon with their Clovis-tipped spears. The animal was pushed to further frenzy by the dozen or so barking and snarling dogs nipping at its heels.

If one of the hunters was successful, he was able to sever one of the hamstrings in the lower leg. This reduced the animal's mobility and, as it became fear-crazed, the animal started making mistakes in its defense. This was when it was most dangerous. Another method of attack was for a person to run underneath the animal and stab it in the belly. If the hole was large enough, the animal's intestines would burst out of the hole and trip the animal, or it would slowly bleed to death, or become weakened or slowed enough to be dispatched by other means.

Attacking a large animal like a mastodon was a risky business and seldom was there an attack event that did not result in injury or death to at least some of the hunters. On the other hand, if a hunt was successful, the enormous quantity of fresh meat that resulted ensured that the band would survive for several more weeks.

In the colder weather, the band would load up as much meat as they could carry and continue their southward trek. Somewhere during their southward trek they learned to dry the meat during the drier summers to produce jerky, which then also allowed them to survive longer periods between hunts.

Hunting of large animals such as mastodons was relatively easier in one sense as these large animals were not able to run very far for long distances and they could be successfully pursued and eventually stopped. The mammoths and mastodons, the wooly rhinoceros, and the wild horse all fell to the Clovis points of their spears and arrows.

As these larger animals became scarce so too did their predators such as the American lion and the saber-toothed tiger. There simply wasn't enough large game for both the humans, and the other large predators, to hunt and survive. The hunt by the Clovis people for other more plentiful smaller animals such as deer or antelope was successful but required more time spent in chasing and stalking, or cunning, and it provided less food for the amount of time invested in the hunt.

Later the hunters also used the bow and arrow, the atlatl, and still later when in South America, the bolas. Deer and elk were particularly desired as so many tools could be made from the antlers and bones, and clothes from the hides. Grizzly bears were often encountered but were not killed unless the migrants were forced to by the enraged bear. The migrants were efficient killing machines. As big game became sparse in a particular area, they moved on, usually southward but sometimes eastward.

The sharpest extinction of mammals occurred at the end of the Pleistocene glaciation. Over 39 genera of large animals disappeared in less than 3,000 years, including mammoths, mastodons, camels, llamas, two genera of deer, woodland musk oxen, two genera of pronghorns, stag-moose, shrub-oxen, horses and giant beavers.

We know that our group passed through what is now central Montana around 13,000 years ago, because one of their members, a 1-year-old baby boy died and was buried where he died, on land now belonging to the Anzick family. The grave was discovered by accident in 1968 by construction workers.

The distinctive spear points and other items buried with him show that the boy belonged to the Clovis people who arrived in the area of present-day Montana roughly 13,000 years ago. This Anzick boy, named for the present-day family that owns the land, is remarkable as it is the only known Clovis burial. Clovis culture was widespread between 13,000 and 12,600 years ago and within a few generations the only presently recognized relics from their culture, the finely crafted Clovis spear and arrow points, ceased being made and, except for the genetic trail of their makers, left no other trace.

Analysis of the child's DNA revealed that the boy's family members connected the Anzick boy to his widespread American relatives and to the Mal'ta boy who lived in Siberia about 12,000 years earlier. This evidence strongly suggests that Native American populations have a common Asian heritage as about 80 percent of native Central and South Americans were the direct descendants of the Mal'ta and Anzick boy family groups and, thus, are the true ancestors of Native Americans. For a while, it was erroneously thought by some that European migrants (the Solutrians) had entered North America and had mixed their gene pool with those from Siberia.

During the next 1,000 years, or even in as short a time frame as several hundred years, this little band grew in size, not too much, but enough to consist of several dozen closely related families. As they traveled south, and east through what is now North America, they lived as true hunter/gatherers, but probably mostly as hunters as the variety of edible shrubs and herbs was limited at that time during that cold climate, although as the climate warmed significantly, more southerly plant species migrated northward. As these plant species grew in numbers and as individual plants, they were undoubtedly harvested and consumed by the migrants. Perhaps some were noticed as having beneficial effects on health or well-being and this knowledge was passed on orally from generation to generation.

Concurrent with the arrival of these people into the New World, the European bison migrated with them. It was a much larger animal then, having a horn spread of over two meters. However, as this bison spread eastward, its size diminished somewhat as it adjusted to the changing climate and food availability. It prospered and immense herds resulted. Bison later provided a rich source of food and materials for the descendants of these first human immigrants.

The first Americans, though, were never able to exterminate the bison as the bison reproduced faster than they could be killed by arrows, spears or associated weapons. It was not until the late 1800s that the bison were nearly exterminated by single-shot Sharps and trap-door Springfield rifles in the hands of recently arrived European settlers. At one time only a dozen or so bison remained.

We now know that this band of hunter/gatherers passed through what is now the Yucatan Peninsula within the same 1,000-year time frame. The climate in Yucatan at that time was dry and as a 15- or 16-year-old girl was searching for water in a cave in the limestone terrain, she tumbled into a 30-meter-tall chamber, or *cenote*, breaking her pelvis. She died and her bones remained there for the next 12,000 years.

She had died among piles of bones of saber-toothed tigers, giant tapirs, and bears. The scientists who discovered her bones in 2007 named her Naia, after a water nymph of Greek mythology. Her mitochondrial DNA showed that she was directly related to the other early Americans who arrived across the Beringian land strait.

Another early group had passed through a site now known as *El Fin del Mundo* in Mexico's Sonora Desert and they also hunted with Clovis points. Bones from a gomphothere, a large, now extinct elephant-like mammal with two tusks extending from its lower jaw and two from its upper jaw, but smaller than mammoths and mastodons, were found at this site adjacent to four Clovis points. A date from 13,400 years ago makes this site one of the oldest and southernmost Clovis sites known. This date and the finding of these Clovis points led some scientists to conjecture that Clovis points actually were developed in the Mexico area and then the technology moved rapidly northward.

The story of how the ancestors of what would eventually become the *González* family, in what is now Chile and Argentina, is the continuing object of this and the following chapter. Their migration had been swift and in only a few generations a part of this small band of intrepid explorers had migrated as far south to what is now known as *Monte Verde* in south-central Chile, and eventually even as far south as *Tierra del Fuego* on the southern tip of South America.

Other people from Polynesia had arrived in Chile at about the same time and had begun to extend some explorations as far north as present-day *Puerto Montt*. They had brought the potato with them. While not particularly flavorful, the potato produced tubers that could be stored for long periods of time. The two groups had met in the area around *Monte Verde*. There, the two groups enjoyed a somewhat uneasy existence, doing some trading, but each keeping their distance from the other to a degree. During this period there was also quite a bit of volcanism in the Andean *Cordillera* and this helped maintain a sense of unrest between the two groups.

Eventually the Polynesian group remained on the island of *Chiloé* for some time but eventually were forced either to retreat or were exterminated by the Chilean natives now becoming more dominant and protective of their newly acquired territories. The genetic record would eventually show that the Polynesian invaders, while frequent visitors and early colonizers, never attained permanent residence status in the area. Evidence also suggests that the potato may have originated in *Chiloé*, or at least certain cultivars of it may have. The large variety of potatoes in present day Peru also suggests that the potato could have originated there. It is possible that separate varieties of potatoes originated in both areas and were actively traded for a time until the later Incas became belligerent and invaded the Chilean lands to their south. The large variety of habitats in Peru, and the intensive cultivation practiced there, may have been responsible for the rapid development of so many varieties.

These early peoples undoubtedly conversed by some means and probably had a spoken language. Present-day evidence of a major language developed by these early people as they spread into South America was *Amerind*. As the Americas were populated, this basic language evolved into dozens of regional dialects. Today the major Andean dialect extends down the western coast of South America from present-day Ecuador to *Tierra del Fuego*, and consists of about 20 separate languages.

The Southern Andean portion that contains the **Mapudungún** ("*lengua de la tierra*" or "language of the earth") (*i.e. Araucanian*) accounts for, along with the Aymara and Quechuan speakers in the northern Andes, over half of the entire Amerind population in both of the Americas.

As these native Americans, later to be generally known as the *mapuches* (which means "*gente de la tierra*" or "people of the earth"), spread into South America, they developed use of the bolas that allowed them to hunt large animals, including horses, that were abandoned by the Spaniards after some of their early explorations. Later the *mapuches* learned to use the horses for rapid mobility. These early colonizers thrived in the Argentine pampas and after the arrival of the Spaniard *conquistadores*, they were driven to the high-altitude intermountain plateau that was rather isolated from both the east and west. The Spaniards called these people "*araucanos*" which means "*guerreros rebeldes*" or "rebel fighters". It was also a term used by the Incas in *quechua*.

This region was forested with *Araucaria* pine forests and it was upon the edible nuts produced by these trees that the sub-group that became known as the *Pehuenches* **"Pewenche"** (of the **Mapudungún**) thrived. They were people of the *pehuén* **"pewen"**, or pine nut. The nuts were collected in great quantities and served as a reliable food base from which they learned to prepare a variety of foods and drinks. The pine nuts also had a great advantage in that they could be buried in the ground and would stay sound for months, thus allowing the *Pehuenches* to survive the long, cold winters in the region.

Prior to conflicts with the Incas, and later with the Spaniards, and still later with the Chilean government, these people became concentrated in the *Lonquimay* region of present-day Chile but some also remained in Argentina where at an earlier time they had occupied all the land from the Atlantic coast to the Pacific coast. The long journey of these people had taught them a very important survival trait – that of family! Each member of the family had a value and, that if the family acted as a group, they were better able to survive an inhospitable environment. That trait survives to this day in the modern *Pehuenches*. And it was during that long trek to their future homeland that they learned much about the medicinal values of certain plants!

Postscript - Discovery of what became known as the Anzick child led to an important career choice several years later by one of the family members on whose land the remains were discovered. In 1968, when the remains were discovered during a road construction, a young Sarah Anzick was only 2 years old. After their discovery, the remains were stored by archeologists for 30 years and then returned to the family in 1998.

At that time, Sarah was working as an undergraduate student on the Human Genome Project, later specializing in cancer genetics. She realized that an examination of the child's bones might reveal important genetic secrets. The team she worked with reconstructed the child's entire genome, indeed, revealing that the Anzick child's family were ancestors of eighty percent of all Native Americans alive today. This finding finally settled the question as to where the first Americans originated.

On a rainy day in June 2014, a group of people including scientists and representatives of North American tribes gathered for a reburial ceremony as Sarah Anzick returned the remains to the control of tribal leaders. Not only were the child's bones among the most important discovered in the Americas, they were reinterred in the place where his people had originally placed them.

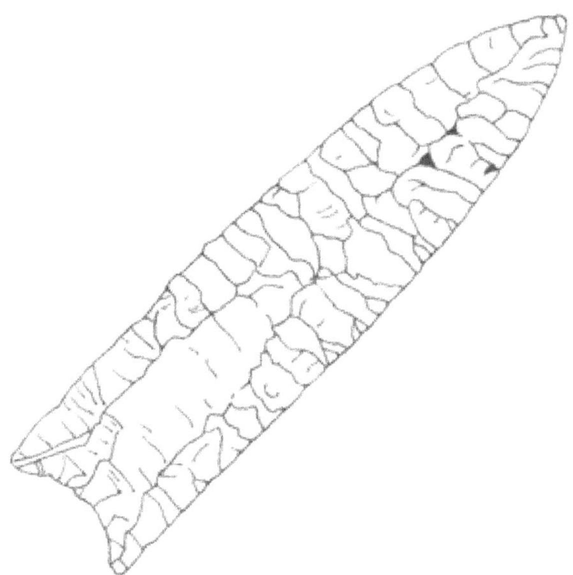

The Clovis Point
(redrawn from Sloan, 2005)

CHAPTER 3
Near *Monte Verde*, Chile – 37 A.D. – The "Gift"

"Amor se nos va la vida, ven vamos a buscar entonces, toda la ternura, toda hermosura,
tesoros del alma, Volcan es mi pecho ardiente, su lava insolente cura las heridas."
(My love, our lives are slipping away, then come, let us seek all the affection,
all the beauty, treasures of the soul.
The volcano is my ardente passion, its insolent lava cures all wounds:) –
Verses from *Hijos de la Tierra* (Sons of the Earth) – Song from Chilean folklore.

It was near the present-day site of *Monte Verde*, Chile, that this group of individuals experienced the arrival of a great gift, one that helped them develop their modern-day sense of humanity. This chapter explains the manner in which they received this gift.

Several dozen individuals were crowded around a large pile of freshly cut shrubbery. On top of the pile lay the body of a young girl. A woman was standing next to the body, working furiously with her hands. She was hunched over with sorrow as she twisted another hand-full of wild-flowers into a sort of wreath. She was so filled with grief that her **fëtawen** (husband) had stayed by the bier since yesterday constantly waving a branch of **magthun** (*maíten*) to remove the fever, and now he also waved branches of crushed **triwe** (*laurel de campo*) to cover the growing odor of putrefaction. He was fearful that she would lose her humanity and become crazy from her grief. Then their tribal group would be lost as they had no one else to help cure them from the various injuries and illnesses that seemed to always present themselves just when they thought that life was going pretty well.

Their ancestors had come to this area, near to a place that would two thousand years later become known as *Monte Verde*. It was an almost idyllic site, in a wide valley with a meandering stream flowing through it that provided plenty of water for their needs. The climate was mild throughout the year, and there were plenty of plants and animals for food. A severe series of earthquakes many years ago had caused their original home site in the valley to become flooded and the group was forced to move nearby to somewhat higher ground. But they always tried to stay close to their home area.

The woman's husband glanced up and he saw her coming. She had finished making her flower offering and shuffled distraughtly as she approached and laid the bunch of wildflowers on top of the bier where her daughter lay. They were dried *copihues* but she did not know them by that name. To her they were known as **kodkëlla**. It was her business to know all the plants, especially the ones that had some medicinal value to the people of her tribe. She was the group's **shaman** or **machi**. She had used roots of the *copihue* plant to promote sweating to push out or expel the fever caused by some unknown demon. She tried it yesterday, but the cure did not work with her daughter as it had previously worked with many others that she had treated in her lifetime.

And now her daughter lay there - dead! She had loved her daughter so much and had trained the girl in the knowledge of healthy attributes of certain plants and she had come to know nearly as much as did her mother. Yesterday the mother and daughter had been collecting plants in the foothills of the mountains that stood like a great wall far off in the direction of the rising sun. There had occurred a series of great tremors and the volcanoes in the mountains had spouted great volumes of smoke and pumice all day. It became so dark that they could hardly see. The earth continued to shake into the night. The mother and daughter rushed home but shortly after their arrival there, the daughter had fallen seriously ill.

And now her daughter lay there - dead! Although the mother tried not to look, she did anyway, and she could see that her daughter's face had become darkly colored, her eyes were sunken into their sockets, and there seemed to be a foul odor emanating from where she lay. She picked up the flowers she had just put on the bier and placed them over her daughter's face, she could not stand to look at it any more.

In her heart, something had told her that these flowers would not work this time but she had tried them anyway because of their beauty. They matched her daughter's fading beauty, and now, like that of the flowers, the last vestiges of her beauty would soon fade as well. Her group stood around the bier from which her daughter's body would soon be taken and buried. Some were murmuring in sympathy, some touched the woman's hands or arms, and some touched her cloak, out of love, respect, and sympathy. Yet, no one would make the first move to pick up the girl and carry her over to where she would be buried. They would not hurry the grieving woman because each of them had experienced a similar loss at some time in the not-to-distant past.

The woman thought about her daughter, the laughter they had shared, the grueling work they had shared, and the simple joys they had shared as the family struggled to survive in this land. She could almost not handle her sense of grief and she wanted to scream, and keep on screaming! Her people had been here at the place that would some day be known as *Monte Verde* in a country called Chile for many, many generations now and it felt like home to them.

As her ancestors had trekked southward through the Beringian land bridge, they had learned to utilize many of the plants they encountered to heal their ills. And now, after so many generations had preceded this present generation, and with the knowledge they had so painfully acquired, she felt as though she now had the right to carry the name of **machi**, as one respected amongst her people who had a certain skill to heal some ills. But her magic had not worked yesterday to cure her daughter!

For many generations now her people had a large body of knowledge regarding the various attributes of wild plants, acquired as they moved quickly southward along the corridor between the returning glaciers as a minor cold-spell began about 14,000 years ago. Some of the attributes were bad, but most were good and they helped improve the quality of life for her people. Her people looked upon her as someone of power, as someone who knew all of the useful attributes of certain plants.

They now had a language, but it was only an oral language and its survival depended on responsible persons, usually women, the **machis**, who had the necessary interest, and a certain sense of responsibility, to acquire and maintain their knowledge of plants. These women were not worshiped as deities, but rather respected as very responsible members of their community and as someone crucial to the group's survival. In this culture, the close relationships between mother and daughter, and mother and granddaughter, were especially crucial. But, now this connection between her and the future well-being of her people was in jeopardy. And, her daughter was dead!

Suddenly there was a shout, and one of the men in the group standing by the bier raised an arm and pointed to the top of the nearby hill. There was someone standing there – someone in a gray garment! Even from this distance they could see that the garment was well-woven but of a pattern strange to them! As the stranger began to walk down the hill toward them, most of the men ran to their huts, brought out various weapons and began to form a perimeter around the grieving family group. The stranger disappeared from their view!

Suddenly he was standing in their midst! All were shocked and so surprised that no one made a move to attack him. He took several steps and stopped in front of the grieving woman with his forearm in the air and his palm pointed toward her! Several of the men raised their weapons as if to strike, but the woman said, "No, look at his eyes, do you see the love, compassion, and peace in them? He will do us no harm today!" Then the stranger spoke to her, in her native **Mupudungún**, "**Mari, mari lawentu**. (I salute you, medicine woman.)".

She replied, almost overwhelmed in shock, "Who are you? Where do you come from? What are you doing here? Where did you get that strange garment? And is that a fresh blood stain on your cloak?" She pointed toward the stain on the side of his garment. The wound underneath seemed to be oozing fresh blood. The stranger paid her no attention.

"**Mari, mari** (Peace to all of you)", he said as he turned and showed them his open hands. The group, likewise, was stunned, and they lowered their weapons.

Then he spoke to all, but focusing on the woman he said, "I come from a distant place. You do not know me, but my father has been watching you and he knows that you are grieving for your lost daughter."

The people did not know what he was talking about and only starred in disbelief.

He continued, "As a people you have been blessed. My father has followed your progress as your ancestors left the dark continent on the other side of the world long ago and came to this new land, all full of hope and wonder. Many other groups left that place after my father placed them there. Most have not fared well or they have behaved very badly, and now they are mistreating and killing each other. They are also abusing the land and its inhabitants."

Then he pointed at them and said, "Many years ago, your ancestors wiped out many of the beautiful, large animals that inhabited that place. Their demise then changed the beneficial interactions of the smaller animals, plants, and other vegetation. The group that preceded you through the path between the mountains of ice and arrived here to this same land many years before your ancestors came here did not survive. They fought and killed each other and now there is little trace of them, only a few stones, bones, and pieces of rotten wood."

He continued, "In many aspects, the history of your family group has been much more pleasing to my father than the history of the groups you left behind. Unlike them, you have maintained a sense of dignity and wonder toward the natural world. You have developed some faults but you are basically an innocent people and he feels that you are deserving of his pleasure. He is pleased that you have maintained contact with the natural world. You do the natural world no harm but use its resources wisely, as my father intended. He has asked me to give a special blessing to your people. In the past, he has given you a series of small blessings on your sojourn as you developed your humanity. You probably did not recognize them. The blessing I will give you now is a small blessing, but one that will place you at an advantage as you face an uncertain future."

Then he turned back toward the woman and, pointing his finger at her, he said, "From this day forth, the one whom you call *machi* will be somewhat more privileged among you, even a little more than she is now."

He turned back toward the crowd but continued to point at the woman and said, "She and her descendants will have the ability to fore- tell the future. They will not be able to abuse this ability but it can be used on special occasions to see what the future might bring if a certain path is followed. My father will be watching to see how you use this power. He may eventually give you other powers."

He paused and then said, "Most of what I say and what you have seen here today will soon be forgotten, but a spark of that knowledge will be retained by the **machi** and her descendants."

He waved his hand over the group and continued speaking, "Soon this part of your land will spill over with war and much blood will be spilled. First, invaders, some of your ancestors, will come from the north, and later more invaders, some of your more distant ancestors, will come from across the sea. They will try to take your land and subjugate you. However, you will be safe if you follow my advice. You must go back north to the land between the mountains where grow the mighty **pehuéns** and where your ancestors lived for a long time. There you will find shelter and you will be safe from most of the coming dangers. Your life will be harsh, but at least you will survive."

For these few moments the woman had forgotten her intense grief, but it returned now as the stranger stepped up to the bier and looked at it for a few moments. He turned his face upward and seemed to be muttering words that she could not clearly hear or understand. He then removed some of the flowers covering the dead girl's face. As he stretched his arm to remove the flowers, the woman noticed a fresh wound that had pierced through his wrist. As he raised his other arm to remove the remaining flowers, she noticed a similar wound on that wrist. Even though the wounds had begun to heal, he must have felt much pain as he removed the flowers. And she could see that they were both freshly bleeding.

She cried to her husband, "Quickly, go to the hut and bring me a few crushed leaves and stems of **keltri lawen** (*limpia plata*) from my medicine bag."

The woman asked the stranger about the wounds and if she could give him something to help the healing. The stranger ignored her and began to touch the girl's forehead with both of his cupped hands. But, then he hesitated for a moment, removed them and allowed the woman to examine the wounds and wipe away some of the fresh blood. Her husband arrived with the crushed leaves and stems and she formed a poultice that she then pressed on each of the bleeding wounds. This stopped the bleeding. When she glanced up at the stranger, she saw him looking at her with much compassion and she felt a great love emanating from him.

He reached up and touched the side of her face, saying in a very gentle voice, "Even though you are distraught with the death of your daughter, you still find energy to care for me, a stranger. Indeed, you are a powerful woman and worthy of respect!"

He then turned back to the dead girl, and placing his hands on her forehead, he said, "***Wenulen*** (arise) little girl."

The woman could not believe what she had just heard! Was he playing games with her? How cruel of him! How could he have such a mean spirit as to play such a trick on her? Her daughter was dead! Could he not know that?

The stranger turned to the woman and, ignoring her surprise, said, "Please give your daughter something to drink, she is thirsty."

Then, as he turned away and waved his hand in a salute, he said, "Now I must leave you and go to my mother, for she is grieving for me this very day just as you have grieved for your daughter."

Then the stranger turned and walked briskly away from them. As he walked up the hill, he gradually disappeared from their sight. Several of the men ran toward him but when they arrived where they had last seen him, there was no trace of him, not even footprints. The men did not see the few drops of blood on the ground, and if they had they would have seen them disappear also.

The woman did not care, she stepped up to her daughter as she sat up and began to cough. Her color had returned and she was breathing. Her daughter was alive! She was alive! The woman hugged her and gave her a drink of water and all the people cheered for her and for her daughter.

For many years after that day, descendants of those people recounted stories of their encounter with the stranger. After two thousand years the stories lost some of their drama, but for this line of *Pehuenches*, the story was as vivid as ever, and from that day forward, this group continued to be blessed, even if in only a small way. They never abused that blessing.

CHAPTER 4
Fleeing from European Colonialism – The 1800s

"Con certeza y con razón va cantando una canción, huinca, tregua, me robaron mi potrillo,
mi ruca y el ternero:"
(With certainty and knowledge I go singing a song, a foreign devil stole my cart, my hut, and the heifer.)
– Verses from song of Chilean/*Mapuche* folklore.

These first Americans had quickly migrated southward into what is now South America, and then into southern Chile and Argentina. They led a harsh life during this migration. Hunger and injury were likely constant companions. However, after they had occupied the lands where they were to eventually stay, they led reasonably comfortable lives. But if their lives had been harsh up to this point, in one sense it was to eventually become much harsher after they clashed with European settlers.

These people had developed a complex language prior to their encounters with the Spaniards and certainly had developed a rich heritage during the past 10,000 plus years in the Americas. Unfortunately, they had been able to communicate and transfer knowledge down the generations only orally. It wasn't until after they met the first European settlers that they were able to adopt a written language, Spanish. So, most of what we know of their knowledge of medicinal plants stems from their collective knowledge starting from that time period.

At some point these early Americans were referred to by the Spaniards as *Araucanians* and this is the name by which they are generally known today. They were immortalized in the poem, *"La Araucana"* by *Alonso de Ercilla*, a Spanish *conquistador*. But the term *Mapuche* is another name the natives have used to describe themselves. Both terms will be used somewhat interchangeably in this novel. *Pehuenche*, conversely, is a more specialized sub-group that refers to those who settled in and now live in the inter-mountain plateau at the head of the *Lonquimay* Valley in Chile.

How these first early Americans came to be concentrated in the *Lonquimay* Valley was foretold by the stranger who visited them centuries before in *Monte Verde* and was the direct result of incursions by the Incas prior to European settlement. These incursions, aimed at enslaving them, pushed these fiercely independent people southward and eastward, and then later westward during the nearly successful extermination of natives by the Argentine military in the 1800s and to some extent somewhat later by the Chilean military on the *Pehuenches'* western range.

The Argentinian war of attrition against the *Pehuenches* was well underway by the time a young Charles Darwin visited southern Argentina in 1833. At that time, the wandering tribes were called horse Indians. They had adapted swiftly to the horse, abandoned by the retreating Spaniards after Argentinian independence in 1816. At first the horse was a source of food, but it soon gave them great mobility and allowed them to steal from and harass the outlying *estancias*. The warfare to exterminate them, though, was brutal and bloody, prompting Charles Darwin to observe that, "The warfare is too bloody to last."[1]

Darwin noted that it was sad to trace how attitudes toward the natives had changed. In 1535, when *Buenos Ayres* was founded, nearby villages of native Indians contained several thousand inhabitants. But, friction soon increased between them and their new Spanish neighbors until the Indians became more barbarous to match the intolerance of their new neighbors.

At the time of Charles Darwin, the government at *Buenos Ayres* had given command of the army to *General Juan Manuel de Rosas* and equipped it for the purpose of exterminating the Indians. The continual persecution soon changed the Indians from being farmers living in villages to wandering the open plains without a home. They naturally tried to defend themselves.

---

[1] Darwin, Charles. A Naturalist's Voyage Round the World: The Voyage of the Beagle, Project Gutenberg EBook #3704 produced by Sue Asscher. August 6, 2008. The e-version is based on the 1890 11th edition. (The book first appeared in 1839.)

Extermination continued during the 1800s until the 1870s when *General Julio Argentino Roca* extended Argentine power into the Patagonian dessert and ended the possibility of Chilean expansion there. A decisive event had occurred in 1872 when the Indian leader *Calfucura* and 6,000 followers attacked several cities, killing 300 settlers and driving off 200,000 head of cattle. These they drove to Chile, where they were welcomed, and they traded the cattle for goods. As early as 1830, Chilean invaders had begun to settle in Patagonia with the intention of laying claim to those lands for Chile. As the war of extermination continued, Chile initially supported the natives because they hoped to wrest those lands from the Argentinians.

In 1875, *Adolfo Alsina*, the Argentinian Minister of War, decisively attacked the Indians and forced them to retreat. He then constructed a 374 km long trench that served as a barrier to the unconquered territories to the west. It was 3 meters wide and 2 meters deep and mainly served as an obstacle to cattle drives by the Indians.

Late in 1878, *General Roca* believed that the only solution to the Indian problem was to finally exterminate the Indians. He started a sweep of the area between the *Alsina* trench and the *Negro* River. After numerous hostile encounters, thousands of Indians were either killed or captured. Large numbers of surviving Indians migrated far westward into the zone around *Curraehue* and *Pucón*, Chile.

The Spaniards and the *Mapuches* had earlier achieved an uneasy truce, with the Spaniards unable to vanquish the *Mapuches*, but the latter were barely able to defend their homeland. In a meeting between the two adversaries in 1641, both sides compromised and a treaty was signed giving the *Mapuches* title to all the lands south of the *Biobío* River. After 1817, however, when Chile won its independence from Spain, the truce was broken as new settlers contested ownership of these lands. The Chilean government's official program of pacification began in 1861 but this was interrupted by the War of the Pacific (1879-1883). By 1883, however, the *Mapuches* had been vanquished to the extent that the lands were declared pacified. This period covered a long process of stepwise military occupation as the Chilean government constructed a series of forts across southern Chile, from the Pacific coast to the Andean *Cordillera*. The last fort was built at the village of *Lonquimay* and that area was opened up to European settlement. Like their ancestors in North America, the *Mapuches* were duped with treaty promises and handshakes.

The first wave of European immigrants arrived between 1883 and 1884, reaching the northern part of the area. They came with the promise of a great economic future. To some extent, they were also duped by the economic incentive as few of them had agricultural backgrounds and they contributed little or nothing to the region. After this first largely unsuccessful arrival, later introductions proved to be more successful and the area was eventually colonized by immigrants who had the skills necessary to not only survive on the frontier, but to thrive. Five hundred families of Spanish, French, Swiss, and German origin were among those arrivals. At the beginning of the 20th century, there were also colonists from Holland and Italy. At the end of the 19th century the government constructed a network of railroad lines to help tie the region together. The first rail-line united *Victoria* with *Temuco*, and later with *Curacautín*, and then with *Malalcahuello*, and finally with *Lonquimay* via the tunnel at *Las Raíces*.

Arrival of the railroad marked the beginning of forest exploitation in the zone and, over a period of only forty years, most of the formerly vast expanses of *Araucaria* forests were lost to sawmills and uncontrolled fires. Lumber cut from trunks of *Araucaria* pine trees was eagerly sought after by builders of clipper ships. The straight branch-free masts and hull planks 30+ meters long sawn from them were of superb quality. Many of these trees were hundreds to thousands of years old and would be almost impossible to replace in a human time scale.

Sometime before the arrival of Europeans in this part of South America, after most of the big game was long gone, including the giant ground sloths, the *Mapuches* began a shift in their diet to include the domesticated *guanaco* and smaller wild animals such as rabbits and birds. After the introduction of Spanish animals, they also ate cows, sheep, horses, and pigs. As European colonization encroached on their territory they were forced to rely less on hunting and shifted to cultivation of such plants as potatoes, corn and other native plants including beans, cloves, and *quinoa*. They also collected fruits of *copihue*, *boldo*, *peumo*, *maqui*, *luma*, and *cocos* of the Chilean palm. They collected wild honey. Excavations at the *Monte Verde* site in southern Chile found potatoes (a 13,000-year-old specimen of *Solanum maglia*, a wild potato species).

Subsistence farming forced them to move closer together into cooperative family units to share work, trade, and defense and they tightened their grip on their land. This closeness to the land forced them to develop an intimate knowledge of the various plant species and whatever edible or other beneficial value they might have. Their survival depended on it. And, they did this pretty much on their own, except for some contact with their neighboring families. As they mutually explored their environment, they tested every plant to see what value it might have for them. Nutritional value was relatively easy to determine, testing for beneficial effects on health was quite another task, which took millennia to perfect as some plants had no beneficial affect or were poisonous.

By not spreading themselves too thinly geographically they were able to resist domination by the Incas and the later attempted extermination by the Spaniards. They might have preferred to live mainly in the climatically more agreeable Central Valley of Chile, near to what would later be named *Monte Verde*, but when the Incas began their conquest southward from what is now Peru, this small group of families remembered the stranger's advice and decided to migrate back up into the *Andes* mountains and over into what is now near to the Argentine/Chilean border to escape the Incas' raids, yet still survive with an initially meager source of food.

They developed an almost symbiotic relationship with the native *Araucaria* pines that were abundant in the valley. An *Araucaria* pine, when mature, is a large tree with a single, straight, and usually branchless trunk topped by an umbrella-like crown of downwardly hanging curved branches. The female trees produce cones with large nuts that are quite nutritious and were a valued food to the *Pehuenches*.

At the time of human arrival in the valley, vast *Araucaria* pine forests covered most of the region, from Argentina to the Chilean coast. By adjusting to this treasure house of pine forest they were able not only to survive a dramatic change in diet, but, in fact, actually thrived by collecting large amounts of the nutritious pine nuts, thus ensuring plenty of food for consumption in the winter season. Just prior to European contact, the *Pehuenches* lived a harsh life but were able to produce all their own food and clothing. This trait allowed them to more or less survive the first onslaughts of European invasion.

CHAPTER 5
The War of Pacification

"La cordillera alta me espera, sobre las nubes vuela el aliento, sobre las nubes vuela el aliento:" (The high mountains await me, over the clouds blows the wind, over the clouds blows the wind.)

Verses from *Canción del Sur* (Song of the South) – Song from Chilean folklore.

All Spanish conquests in the southern third of Chile were successfully repulsed by the *Mapuches*. That resistance was so effective that Europeans did not return to try again until late in the 19th century, long after Chile freed itself from Spanish domination. Prior to the arrival of *Pedro de Valdivia*, the natives had even occupied the land far north of where he established *Santiago* in 1540. But, several centuries before arrival of the Spanish, the Incas had successfully driven the *Araucanians* southward.

The natives were initially very gullible to the Spanish invaders and did not recognize their intent and this eventually led to their downfall in the north. Some tribal groups even welcomed their new neighbors while others resisted. This resistance grew fiercer, however, as the invaders moved southward. But, the farther south the invaders marched, the further away they were from their supply sources and the more vulnerable to attack they became. Eventually, the main border between the Spanish and the *Araucanians* was the *Bíobío* River. This prolonged period of war was known as the War of *Arauco* and was immortalized in the epic poem *"La Araucana"* by *Alonso de Ercilla*.

But the situation was not only that of constant war. An uneasy truce between the two antagonists encouraged trading and interchange. But this relationship deteriorated quickly after Chilean lands began to be colonized both to the north and south of their homeland in the southern central provinces of *Arauco, Bío Bío, Malleco, Cautín, Valdivia, Osorno,* and *Llanquihue.* By the mid-1800s, the natives were largely defeated by the European invaders, and an active colonization program had been initiated by the Chilean government.

Several factors were responsible for the initiation of this colonization effort. Firstly, as stated above, the areas to the north and south of these central provinces had been largely populated by European settlers and there was increasing public pressure to open these provinces to colonization. Secondly, there were fears that Argentina would claim that this area was part of their national territory. The Argentine government was certainly encouraging the *Mapuches* on both sides of the border to pillage Chilean landholders and sell the pillaged resources to them.

The rest of the world, and Europeans especially, were aware of the problems confronting Chile in this regard. So, in 1858, a French adventurer and lawyer named Orelie Antoine de Tourneus came to Chile and lived in *Valparaiso* for several years where he learned Spanish and the rudiments of the *Mapuche* language.

In 1861, he appeared in *Araucanía,* near the village of *Curacautín,* and began to take advantage of the natives' dis-satisfaction and some settlers who despised the Chilean government. He convinced more than 50 *caciques* to proclaim him the "*Rey de la Araucanía*" (The King of *Araucanía*). He quickly named an aboriginal government, with ministers and even sent to Paris ambassadors to negotiate with the government of Napoleon III to convene a new kingdom under the protection of France (at that time the Falkland-Malvinas belonged to France). He was very active for several years in consolidating the natives against the government. In 1870, he was captured by Chilean troops and was eventually sent back to France, where he died in 1878. The activity of Orelie was a significant factor encouraging Chile to take some kind of aggressive action in the South.

The first colonization act had been passed in 1873. A major effect of that, and a series of subsequent laws, was that the native lands were declared to be the property of the Chilean State and, as a result, were auctioned off to wealthy owners of the ruling class. The most fertile lands were the first to go into private ownership. Of a total of 10 million hectares of their original lands, under the new ownership rules, the *Mapuches* received less that 500,000 hectares, or 6.1 hectares per capita. The new *huinca* owners received an average of 500 hectares per person. But, before the new owners could colonize the region and obtain their land grants, the area had to be pacified.

In 1873, President *Aníbal Pinto* began the war against the *Mapuches* in earnest. The increased sustained level of activity in that effort can best be described by summarizing the military conquests of *Don Gregorio Urrutia Venegas. Urrutia* was born in 1830 in *San Carlos*, beginning his military career as a standard bearer, and then rising through the ranks to become brigade general in the national guard. He had earlier fought the *Mapuches* in 1859 and then led various campaigns on *Arauco* from 1862 to 1865, 1866 to 1871, 1878 to 1879, and then from 1881 to 1883. In the 1862 campaign he assaulted *Mapuches* in the swamps along the *Cautín* River. Between 1877 and 1879 he founded the city of *Traiguén* and established military forts at *Mirador, Lebuluán*, and *Adehuencul.* In 1881, he founded *Nueva Imperial* and established forts at *Carahue, Galvarino, CholChol*, and *Freire.* He then directed his army toward the northeastern part of the region and in 1882 built a fort at *Curacautín.* In 1883, he founded the city of *Pucón* and built forts at *Villarrica, Nilquen, Palguin*, and *Cunca.*

He had previously been called into service during the War of the Pacific against Peru and Bolivia, and served there from 1879 to 1881 and fought in the battles of *Lima, Chorrillos*, and *Miraflores.* He retired as general and after retirement, fought to depose the legally elected President *José Manuel Balmaceda.* This led to a civil war that resulted in the death of 10,000 Chileans and the suicide of *Balmaceda* in 1891. *Urrutia* died September 10, 1897.

Mapuches, each family with 6.1 hectares, or less in many cases, could not make a living on such a small tract of land and many sold their tiny parcels to European settlers. So, unable to obtain meaningful employment, each generation sank lower and lower in the economic chain. Their mortality rate was high, their children were segregated beginning with their first year in school, and would never have the possibility of finding a decent job due to a lack of education. The communities were becoming overcrowded and many left to seek a life in the north, where they continued to face prejudice, or moved to Argentina where they tried to start a new life.

So, most of the *Mapuches* did not fare well under the new land redistribution. What was even worse was that they could not move around as they were formerly able to do in the days when the lands were jointly owned. They had to stay on their little parcel and try to scratch out a living. Previously, when all the land was collectively theirs, each family could move around as they wished to harvest the natural resources of the land.

Many of the *huinca* settlers did not do all that well either, at least in the first few decades after settlement. The winters were harsh and the variances of the land and weather took time to figure out to the settler's best advantage. This required several generations of trial and error.

An example of a *huinca* who did exceptionally well was that of *José Bunster*. He was the son of an English sailor and began work at the age of 19. He went south to *Araucanía* and beginning in *Mulchén*, started a series of small shops that sold agricultural supplies and various other sundries. In each town he moved to he established these small shops, most of which he later sold. He followed the construction of the new forts. In 1869, he built a mill in *Angol*, in 1877 a mill in *Collipulli*, in 1883 a mill in *Nueva Imperial*, and in 1884 a mill in *Traiguén*. In each location he produced wheat on land that he purchased, to such an extent that he became known as the "king of wheat". He produced more wheat than there was available storage room and so then he built storage sheds. He also purchased large tracts of land and then resold them after they were divided into small parcels. In the mountains he built sawmills and began harvesting the bounty of the forests. In 1882 in *Angol*, he founded the first bank. He also provisioned the military in its expedition to the zone of *Cautín*. He took advantage of the situation, and he did well.

With the initiation of the war of pacification, and into modern times, the *Mapuches* have been increasingly forced into the background of society. They simply could not compete with capitalists like *Bunster* and the thousands of other *huinca* settlers that colonized their usurped lands. To this day they are still treated as an inferior social class by Chilean society. The Spanish they speak is imperfect, their skin color is different, many are illiterate, few are permitted to enter universities, and they are discriminated against in many of the factories now extant on their former lands. In many aspects they are far worse off than their prehistoric ancestors in North America who faced, and still face, similar serious hardships.

Today, the region of *Araucanía* is generally prosperous if one ignores the situation of the natives. Agriculture has done well under the toils of the European settlers and there are several factories that manufacture or process agricultural products. Exploitation of the valuable and unique native forests has been replaced by harvest of plantations of exotic tree species that grow rapidly and produce wood and fiber that has also been successfully incorporated into the Chilean economy. Tourism is bringing in badly needed funds, some of which trickle down to the pockets of the natives. There has also been a resurgence in the use and sale of medicinal plant products, many of which are unique to the region. They are being increasingly offered on the international market.

CHAPTER 6
La Rochelle, France – 1919

"Más allá del abismo sin fondo, más allá de la cumbre estrellada, más allá centinela del mundo, está:"
(Beyond the bottomless pit, beyond the starry summit, there is the sentinel of the world, there it is).
– Song verses from *La Centinela* (The Sentinal)
– Song from Chilean folklore.

Jean Piñon was born in France, into a wealthy family. As a young boy he was fascinated by machinery, and especially with the new fangled airplane then becoming popular. His parents supported his interests as they minimized his interaction with the Bohemian crowd then blossoming across Europe. In 1913, when he was 19 years old, his parents hired Alberto Santos-Dumont to teach him how to fly an airplane. If he successfully learned to fly, they promised that in the coming year they would purchase an airplane for him. So far, although there had been quite a few accidents, not many deaths had resulted from flying. So, his parents encouraged his growing love of flying.

Jean quickly developed his flying skills and it appeared that he was becoming what would later become known as a natural-born aviator. He excelled at flying and had a number of ideas of how small engineering aspects of the flying machine could be more efficient and/or safer.

Jean's world began to change quite a bit in 1914 when Archduke

Ferdinand was assassinated! In a complex series of relationships, European countries quickly aligned with the two major antagonists, and World War I began. Jean immediately volunteered for the newly formed Lafayette Escadrille as the French Army tried to quickly adapt airplanes for use in warfare. At first, airplanes were used for reconnaissance over enemy territory to determine troop movements, *etc.* Then, someone had the bright idea that bricks, and later bombs, could be dropped from the airplanes. That was quickly followed by the idea that the pilot of one plane could shoot at the pilot of an enemy plane. Not to be outdone by each new technological development, both sides quickly adopted each new technology.

Jean flew quite a bit during the first years of the war, adapting quickly to the idiosyncrasies of each new model of airplane as it came into service. His officers tried to take advantage of his quick mind and ability to improve not only the mechanisms of airplanes, but also the increasingly complicated developing tactics of aerial combat.

His last flight, however, was on June 17, 1916. While returning from a mission, a spent artillery projectile struck his engine. The projectile jammed between two cylinders of the rotary engine powering his plane. As the projectile was flung off in one direction, the force of the impact knocked the engine off its mountings and it flew off in the opposite direction. Although Jean didn't think it was a blessing in that moment, it was, as the engine was blown away without striking the plane and causing damage to it.

The fuel line was ripped off and the gas/castor oil mixture dribbled away without igniting. Otherwise his plane was undamaged. But, the center of gravity had changed significantly and the plane began to flutter to the ground in a series of wide spirals. When the plane struck the ground, Jean was thrown free and landed in a freshly plowed field. He had been thrown perhaps 15 meters. Except for a broken arm he did not appear to be badly injured. But, the blunt force trauma to his head caused parts of his inner ear to swell and he suffered terrible vertigo. As the swelling went down, he experienced much less vertigo but it was obvious that he could not fly again.

After he recuperated, he volunteered for service in the infantry. He saw brutal fighting at the Somme where he was involved in much combat, some hand-to-hand. He saw first-hand the tragedies of war: the mass killings, the thousands of wounded, the victims of gassing, and the obvious insanity of it all. He did not like army life at all and as one result, developed several nervous tics. He also began to not trust his social interactions with other people. Sharp noises startled him and he would often dive for cover. Although he tried to control this behavior, it was apparent to his doctors that he was suffering from some kind of "shell-shock". Today we would probably call it PTSD (post-traumatic-stress-disorder).

He was released from military service just before the Armistice in 1918. While recuperating in the sanitarium he began a relationship with one of his nurses, a beautiful young American volunteer from the state of Minnesota in the United States. Her name was Margaret. As they got to know each other, Jean's outlook on life began to turn around and he again looked forward to living and to planning a life with Margaret. She loved her "little Frenchman".

Then Margaret contracted influenza. It was the so-called 'Spanish flu' and it swept around the world, killing millions of people. Jean's parents hired the best doctors to care for Margaret, but she died, as did Jean's father. Jean and his mother also contracted the virus but they survived. But, now he had little reason to live and he settled into a deep depression.

He could not fly again either as he still suffered vertigo whenever he moved too quickly. He tried to help his mother manage her estate but he became more and more depressed. Neither he nor his mother had any idea of what he might do to regain his mental health. Then, several months later a faint glimmer of hope began to emerge.

Jean's mother had received a letter from a cousin who migrated to Chile nearly a half century earlier. That side of the family was descended from Palestinian-Arabs who had migrated to Chile as the fledging wine industry began to flourish. She described life there and how she and her husband were managing a large vineyard south of *Santiago* in a town called *Talca*. She was aware of Jean's depression and suggested that he come to Chile to visit them. Perhaps he might even decide to live in Chile as it was far away from the battlefields of Europe and such a change might help him to recover his health. The climate was very agreeable, similar to that of southern France, and the Chilean government was encouraging immigration and land was inexpensive.

CHAPTER 7
The Rise of Communism

"Si tuviera un martillo, Golpearía en la mañana, Golpearía en la noche, Por todo el país,
Alerta el peligro, Debemos unirnos, Para defender la paz:"
(If I had a hammer, I would hammer in the morning,
I would hammer in the night, to alert all the country of the danger, in
order to defend the peace:)
– Song verses from *La Canción del Martillo*
(The Song of the Hammer.) made popular by Victor Jarra.

The rise of Communism formed a significant movement during the first part of the 20th century. Rather than the ideological movement in the czar's Russia, the movement in Chile began as an act of almost pure desperation that quickly gathered momentum. The stage had been set beginning half a century earlier with the commencement of the War of Pacification and gathered a full head of steam about the time of World War 1. At the close of the war, German technology developed a technique to extract nitrogen from the atmosphere. Nitrogen was used in the manufacture of ammonium nitrate fertilizer and explosives. Prior to this time, most of Chile's foreign exchange had depended on the exportation of saltpeter and bird guano for the manufacture of these two significant products.

But, during the 1920s the large Chilean exportation industry slowed substantially and this had a stifling effect on the Chilean economy. So, by the time the worldwide depression started, coinciding with the 1929 stock market crash, the result was that there was little money available for public works projects. Construction of the *Túnel Las Raíces* was completed at about the time of this economic slowdown but, fortunately, the Chilean government retained some workers for maintenance on the railroad, tunnel, and access roads. This moderate influx of money had a very beneficial effect on that area but could not prevent the Communist movement from continuing and even growing.

Between 1900 until 1930, the Chilean Ministry of Lands and Colonization had tried to complete its mission of land redistribution. That mission forced the poor *Mapuches* off their land. The major result was that they moved up into the mountain valleys where the soils were even less productive and the climate was even more limiting for most agricultural crops. The immigrants who took over the land of the displaced *Mapuches* were unable to earn a living on that land either, thus creating a new class of poor Chileans who were just as poor as the natives they had replaced.

In response to their condition, these poor settlers formed the "Agricultural Sindicate of *Lonquimay*" to help expand their holdings in the locality of *Nitrito*, an area to the north of *Lonquimay*, that had been recently occupied by the *Mapuches*. The "Puelma Tupper Society" demanded a judicial order to throw out the inhabitants because they had no legal title to the lands.

As these negotiations were underway, *Carabineros* began to harass the settlers, both immigrants and *Mapuches*. Just as the unusually harsh winter of 1934 was beginning, they destroyed fences and burned buildings, forcing their inhabitants out into the cold. North of *Lonquimay*, in the villages of *Nitrito*, *Ranquil*, *Quilleime*, *Loso*, and *Truful*, the farmers, along with the *Mapuches* from *Maripe*, united to help those forced from their homes.

Terrible atrocities resulted. The *lonko* from *Maripe*, who had 15 years earlier lost his lands at *Ralko*, was tortured. His eyes were punched out, and his tongue and ears were cut off.

With the advance of this winter, in June, several thousand farmers and *Mapuches* armed with antique firearms assaulted the food storage rooms of nearby *fundos* and stole their contents. This insurrection quickly spread as far away as 150 km.

The government mobilized police from *Temuco*, *Victoria*, *Mulchen*, and *Santa Barbara*, and with support from the Chilean Air Force, moved on the rebellion.

By early July the rebels had fled to the mountains around *Llanquen*. The women, who had been left in the former camps, were raped and many were killed. Of the nearly 500 persons taken prisoner, most "disappeared". Survivors, including both *Mapuche* and *huinca* settlers, escaped across the *Cordillera* and dispersed in small enclaves of *Neuken* and *Rio Negro*. At that time, Argentina was receptive to these immigrants.

CHAPTER 8
Into the Modern Era – 1920

"Pucha que es linda mi tierra:"
(Gosh, my country is beautiful!)
– Verse of music from Chilean folklore.

The main character of this story, Robert, whom we met in the first chapter, and will not meet again for some time, might never have met the descendants of the *Pehuenche* group of Native Americans who came to Chile so many years earlier if it had not been for the Frenchman who arrived in the valley in 1920. It was the young Jean Piñon, a recent veteran of the Great War in Europe. He had somehow survived four years of brutal war and was so disenchanted with life in Europe, and the death of his fiancé, that he decided to go as far away from civilization as he could.

He was typical of many Americans at that time whom had also been disenfranchised by the war. But, instead of turning to a life of alcohol he decided to do something with his life and go far away. He had distant family members living in *Talca*, Chile who had migrated there to work in the vineyards and so, at the invitation of his cousin *Juana*, he decided to go there for a visit.

At that time, many Chileans still had strong memories of their connections with the earlier frontier life and it was easy to strike up a conversation with strangers regarding memories from their past. Soon after

Jean arrived in Chile, he became enchanted with stories of the *Araucanian* natives who lived in the south and who were never subjugated by neither the Incas nor the Spanish nor the Chilean government. He was impressed by how they had surmounted their hardships and so, he decided to visit some of these people and get to know them on his way to Argentina.

Jean planned to make a trek from the frontier town of *Temuco*, right on the border of the old frontier where a lot of Germans had subsequently settled and go up into the interior of Chile toward Argentina. He didn't want to stay long in *Temuco* as he had just had enough dealings with the Germans in the war. He thought he might like to eventually settle in southern *Argentina* and buy a ranch in the *pampas* where there were not many people and he could isolate himself from humanity's cruelty to humanity.

He took the train from *Santiago* to *Talca* and then to *Temuco* where he purchased two horses to begin the trek up the *Lonquimay* Valley toward Argentina. Although automobiles were just beginning to become common in the area, he felt that horses might be a more reliable form of transportation. He was told that the roads were not very passable for motorized vehicles. After several weeks of moving from village to village along the *Cautín* River, he finally arrived at *Curacautín*. After resting there for several days, he purchased more supplies and continued his trek up the valley. The only road to *Lonquimay*, the next village, if it could be called that, was over the "*Camino Las Raíces*", a seasonal road over the *cordillera* and through the heart of several extensive *Araucaria* pine forests.

Lonquimay was less than 100 kms away and he thought that a leisurely ride would help to clear his head of recurring memories of the agonies he had suffered in the recent war and the death of his beloved Margaret. As he rode along, and camped wherever he wished, he marveled at the majestic *Araucaria* pine forests he passed through. And, the sky was such an intense cornflower blue that it seemed to pull at his eyes as if it were magnetic whenever he glanced upward. He was actually beginning to like this valley as there were few people living there and the solitude felt wonderful.

Jean stopped and talked with *Pehuenches* herding their cattle and sheep along the way, moving them into the fresh grazing in the high country. He learned that outside interests were threatening inroads into the *Lonquimay* Valley. An outsider, a white cattle rancher, had settled in the valley and was now claiming ownership of most of the land along the *Biobío* River to the east of *Lonquimay*. He was so sure of his claim that in that same year he had begun negotiating with a sawmill owner to log some of the *Araucaria* pine forests north of *Lonquimay*, claiming them as his own. The *Pehuenches* began to resist but had little hope of proving their ownership of the land to the government in *Santiago*. At that time, *Araucanian* natives were still considered as second-class citizens by many Chileans and were prejudiced against much as were the Negroes in the United States.

Jean had traveled down out of the mountains and was just entering the *Lonquimay* Valley. As he descended the last little hill he could see scattered houses ahead and suspected that he was getting close to the town of *Lonquimay*. He thought he would camp one more night before entering town and as he was preparing camp late that afternoon along the *Naranjo* River, he thought he heard someone arguing in a loud voice. The argument quickly rose in crescendo and then was punctuated by screams. He thought that the screams were of those of a young girl!

Jean ran in the direction of the screams. As he came around a bend in the river he saw three men who appeared to be assaulting a young woman. As her screams continued, he grabbed a large stick lying on the ground and charged the group. Jean felt no fear, he had faced far worse in the trenches of the Somme. When the men saw him, one pulled a small pistol from his pocket and aimed it at Jean. Jean hit the man's arm and the pistol went flying. Jean hit another man over the shoulder and the third on the side of his head, each time with a crunch as the stick broke off, leaving a shorter piece.

Jean thought it was quite a sight and chuckled as he watched the three men run away with all three missing their pants and shoes. Jean then turned toward the sobbing and partially naked girl. She came toward him and melted in his arms as she sobbed even more forcefully. Being the gentleman that he was he immediately removed his coat and placed it around her shoulders.

"What is your name?" he queried in French, and then again in his broken Spanish as he realized she probably didn't understand French. "*Luisa*," she whispered between sobs.

"Who were those men?" he asked.

"*No sé, pero creo que trabajan en el aserradero nuevo. Son huincas, como usted,*" (I don't know who they are, but I think they work in the new sawmill. They are foreigners, like you.), she replied and then realized that she was in his arms and drew away.

Jean realized that she was probably almost as afraid of him as she was of those men. "Do you live near here? Let me take you home." *"Gracias,"* she said. "I was down here picking some herbs for my sick father. I live just down the valley along the river." So, Jean led her back to his campsite, helped her mount his horse, and then he walked beside the horse as they went to her home.

When they entered the yard and a dog began barking, Jean was afraid that he would be blamed for her disheveled condition, but as soon as her mother came out, *Luisa* assured her that this strange man had, in fact, probably saved her from a certain rape and, perhaps, had even saved her life. By this time several neighbors began to show up and surrounded the trio, at first in a rather hostile manner, but that quickly changed as they began to treat Jean as a hero. Each time a new neighbor joined the group, the story was retold, and Jean began to relax a little.

Luisa's mother could not do enough for him. He was offered numerous drinks of *chicha* and soon was barely able to stand. *Luisa* took him in to see her sick father. The man sat up in the bed and looked deep into Jean's eyes as *Luisa* related what had happened to her. He extended his hand and grasped Jean's with a firm grip and Jean knew the man was deeply grateful for what he had done.

Then, as Jean prepared to leave, *Luisa's* parents insisted that he remain there for a few days as their guest. So, Jean spent the next few days getting to know the family and *Luisa*, and perhaps it was no surprise that he agreed to stay there a while longer.

Later that summer, Jean Piñon and *Luisa Melinir* were married in the little church in *Lonquimay*. Jean didn't know what he would do for a living but he helped the family with their livestock and expanded garden. In the fall, he helped harvest very large quantities of *pehuenes*, which they sold for cash, and they passed that first winter very well. As they passed one of the first cold winter evenings sitting by the stove and discussing just about everything, Jean felt very contented with his life and he somehow knew that he would never make it to the Argentine *pampas*.

In the following spring Jean and *Luisa* traveled to *Talca* and stayed several days at a house at *3y4 Sur Poniente 818* to visit Jean's relatives. They then took the train to *Santiago*, to *2266 San Alfonso*, very close to the *Estación Central*, where some of *Luisa's* relatives lived, and Jean made arrangements with his family in France to send some money from his mother's estate and some of her extra furniture to Chile. The money and furniture came within a few months and he and *Luisa* planned the construction of their new house.

The site for their new house was on land Jean had purchased from *Luisa's* father and was located several kilometers or so up the *Naranjo* River near to the intersection of that river with the *Biobío* River. The location was at the mouth of a little valley, which would provide shelter from the heavy winter snows. The house site was bordered on the south by a series of small ranges and the *Lonquimay* Valley on the north. The entry road was adjacent to a small stream and the area was fairly isolated yet within long walking distance of the village of *Lonquimay*.

Their house was completely unorthodox for the area and it was patterned after the style then common in the Swiss Alps. It had a steep roof with wide overhang to help withstand the heavy snows that were frequent in the valley. The roof and exterior walls were shingled with *alerce* shakes. The interior walls were covered with vertical boards of *ciprés de la cordillera*, sawn from logs harvested on forestland Jean had purchased from *Luisa's* parents. Some boards were nearly a third of a meter wide. The wood frame construction walls were filled with dry saw-dust, providing much needed insulation against the cold winter months. The house had indoor plumbing, with an inside bathroom, kitchen, and all the latest amenities then common in France among the upper class.

The front of the house faced the river and had large glass windows that Jean had to have brought down from *Santiago*. The entry road turned off the public road, crossed a bridge over a small stream, and then curved around to the east side of the house and then around to the back where the main entrance was located. Several outbuildings and a large barn comprised the little farm site.

The story of Jean and *Luisa* became a legend in the valley. *Luisa* became a respected **machi** (shaman) and she and Jean were loved and respected by all. Their only child, a daughter, *Claudia*, continued work that her father had begun to protect the interests of the *Pehuenches* as land grabbing and logging interests became more powerful. Jean eventually became the community **lonco**, an elder responsible for administering community affairs and gatherings. He was instrumental in helping the valley residents to form cooperatives to sell sheep, cattle, and handicrafts. Although life was always harsh there, the formation of cooperatives led to somewhat better economic conditions for many of the valley's residents.

Claudia married *Juan González*, another *Pehuenche* but with much Spanish blood in his veins that originated during the Spanish Conquest of Chile. He was born near the coastal village of *San Antonio* to where his grandparents had relocated following the War of Pacification when they lost ownership of their tribal lands. *Juan* and *Claudia* had two children, a son, *Miguel*, and a daughter, *Rosa*. It is with the family of *Juan* and *Claudia* that our story will eventually continue in more detail.

Luisa Melinir, when she was 8 years old, had a dream that she was going to be a **machi.** Her grandmother had been a **machi** also, but *Luisa's* mother had not had the calling, or gift, if one wanted to think of it in that way. *Luisa's* daughter, *Claudia*, had been trained by her great grandmother to be a **machi** but had never pursued it when she was a young woman. She had met *Juan González* and they spent several years collecting and researching folklore music. After *Juan* and *Claudia* became very successful as folk singers, *Claudia* returned to her training as a **machi**, but rather than becoming a practicing **machi** who diagnosed patients and prescribed medical treatments, she and *Juan* became dedicated to seeking and recording for the sake of posterity, plants and whatever medicinal remedies or benefits those plants might have. At the time that Robert first visited them, they had spent about ten years in that endeavor and had built quite a reputation in Chile and Argentina, and even around the world. They also had a large garden and greenhouse where they propagated many medicinal plants.

CHAPTER 9
The Tragedy of *Las Raíces*

As early as 1886 it had been the joint plan of the Chilean and Argentinian governments to construct a southern trans-Andean railroad system to link access between the Pacific and Atlantic oceans. In 1898 the Argentinian government authorized an extension of the railroad to *Pino Hachado*, a village on the western border with Chile. By 1912 the Chilean equivalent arrived to the east at *Curacautín*, but several mountains in the Andean *cordillera* lay further to the east and these presented a formidable barrier to conventional railroad construction. The only practical path through this barrier was to construct a tunnel, itself being a formidable task. This tunnel became known as the *Túnel Las Raíces*.

Construction of the tunnel project was initiated in 1929. It was initially planned to be 1,000 meters in length, but later the length was re-calculated to be at least 4,545 meters. Construction began with the access roads, a first-aid station, a church, a hydroelectric plant, a ventilation system, an administrative office building, and barracks for the workers. All of this construction was located near the north entrance of the proposed tunnel.

Construction on the entrance began a year later with the employment of 282 men and 125 women. Holes were drilled in the rock face and dynamite was placed in these holes and detonated. Jackhammers were then used to break up the rock fractured by the dynamite. The broken rock fragments were placed by hand into railroad cars and these were extracted in cars pulled by either of two electric narrow gauge locomotives. Three shifts of 8 hours each were performed daily.

At 11:00 AM on May 17, 1932, at a distance of 440 meters from the north tunnel entrance, a portion of the tunnel ceiling collapsed just as a locomotive pulling 15 loaded cars was leaving the tunnel. All the train was buried except for the locomotive and the first three cars behind the locomotive. The material that fell into and blocked the tunnel consisted of unconsolidated rocks, mud, and trees. The crater that formed on the surface of the mountain was 18 meters in circumference and 73 meters deep. A small lake began to form immediately in it and water began filling the blocked tunnel and, as the water level rose, it began pouring out of one tube of the ventilation system.

Excavation started immediately in the tunnel entrance to remove debris but more landslides occurred and that work was quickly abandoned. In order to avoid more landslides from the mountain above, rescue activities were diverted to a small gallery 1.4 meters in diameter located at an angle off to one side of the main entrance. It was laid out at an angle such that it would intersect the main tunnel gallery in an area more interior to the collapse.

At the time of the collapse, 45 workers were inside the tunnel and, except for the two train engineers, nothing was known about the safety of the remaining workers. As water began to pour out from one of the ventilation tubes, a sense of urgency gripped those outside and the rescue was begun in earnest.

The rescue efforts were carried out around the clock, in 4-hour shifts, and were extremely fatiguing as the rescuers were working at maximum speed. At this time, no one yet knew if there were any survivors. In the early morning on Friday, the excavation efforts in the gallery broke through into the main tunnel. The situation appeared to be far worse than expected, as water depth in the tunnel was 2.3 meters. Later it rose to 4.5 meters. The water had to be pumped out and then the debris of mud, rocks, and tree trunks and branches were removed before the rescuers could enter the tunnel to search for survivors.

However, the next day (Saturday) was much more positive, because at four-o-clock in the morning, five days after the collapse of the tunnel entrance, the first survivors came staggering down the tunnel toward the gallery to meet their rescuers. Soon, all the workers were located and led out of the tunnel. The reunion was met with crying and screams of joy as the workers left the tunnel and were reunited with their families and loved ones. Every man had survived! Most, though, were completely fatigued after being in water the entire time and suffering from various degrees of hypothermia. But, they all survived!

For some unknown reason, this episode in the history of Chile soon became known as *"La Tragedia del Túnel Las Raíces"*, although, ironically, not a single worker lost his life as a result of the accident. It was a tremendous example of not only good luck, but also the positive results of a well-organized and conducted rescue effort.

CHAPTER 10
Juan Fernández and the *chonta* palm – 1938

The *Juan Fernández* Islands is a group of three islands located about 414 miles west of the coast of Chile, almost due west of *Valparaiso*. The major island is named Robinson Crusoe Island (*Isla Más a Tierra*) and is closest to the Chilean mainland, the second island is *Isla Alexandro Selkirk* (*Isla Más Afuera*), and a smaller island, *Santa Clara*. This group of islands is well known as being the home of marooned English sailor, Alexander Selkirk, who is believed to have been the inspiration to Daniel Defoe for his novel, Robinson Crusoe.

The group of islands is a geological treasure. They were formed over a period of millions of years when a hotspot in the earth's mantle broke through the Nazca Plate to form the islands through a series of volcanic eruptions. The islands have a subtropical climate that is influenced by the Humboldt Current that flows northward along the South American coast east of the islands, and the southeast trade winds. There is much variability in precipitation due to the influence of the *El Niño*-Southern Oscillation but in general rainfall is higher in the winter months and on the eastward side of the islands.

The islands are also a biological treasure. They are recognized as a distinct eco-region and have a high percentage of rare and endemic plants and animals with many close relatives found in the Valdivian temperate rain forests. Of the more than 200 native species of vascular plants, about 150 are flowering plants and 50 are ferns. Many plants are related to plants found in South America, New Zealand, and Australia. Jean Piñon met Martin Schwope quite by accident! It was on May 17, 1932. They were two of the dozens of workers who had been trapped by the roof collapse of the *Túnel las Raíces* being constructed between *Curacautín* and *Lonquimay*. Jean had been requested to observe the tunnel construction because of his past engineering experience and Martin was a worker, employed to break and load rock in construction of the tunnel.

How Martin happened to come to Chile was the result of a very interesting series of events. Martin was a German veteran of World War I and had been on the battleship Dresden when it was scuttled during the war in the harbor of the *Isla Más a Tierra*.

The Dresden was a light cruiser that saw action at the Battle of *Coronel* on November 1, 1914, near the coastal city of *Coronel* in central Chile. As what was to soon become known as the Great War got underway, the East Asia Squadron of the German navy was attempting to dominate the Pacific Ocean and the British Navy was attempting to eliminate that dominance. The British entered the battle with seven ships of varying age and with crews with virtually no experience. During the engagement with six German ships, two armored British cruisers were sunk, with a loss of nearly 1600 of the crew, and the effectiveness of the British force was virtually eliminated. Only a total of three of all the German crews were wounded.

Approximately one month later, on December 8, 1914, newly assembled British forces caught the German ships near the Falkland Islands, off the eastern coast of Argentina. The German ships had expended much of their ammunition during the Battle of *Coronel* and were returning to Germany to restock their munitions and coal. In a quickly moving game of cat and mouse, the now-superior British force systematically attacked, and sank, six of the German ships, most of which had run so low on ammunition that they could not effectively resist. Unlike the Battle of *Coronel*, this time the British forces virtually annihilated the German forces. British losses were 10 killed and 19 wounded - German losses were 1,871 killed and 215 captured. Two armored cruisers and two light cruisers were sunk, and two transports were captured and subsequently scuttled. Only two ships escaped, the auxiliary Seydlitz and the light cruiser Dresden.

The Dresden headed toward the *Juan Fernández* Islands in a desperate run to replace its depleted coal stock. The auxiliary had been sent to *Valparaíso* to find possible sources of coal. On March 14, 1915, the Dresden was discovered near the islands by the British ships: Glasgow, Kent, and

Orama. After a brief battle, the captain of the Dresden ran his ship into the harbor at *San Juan Baptista* and scuttled it by detonating the main ammunition magazine.

Martin and Jean soon became good friends in spite of being enemies during the war. Martin recounted the scuttling of the Dresden and how the 3-man detail he was with had been ordered to set the explosives to scuttle the ship. On their way down into the hold to set the explosives, they broke into the captain's safe and stole a box of gold bars and coins, which they hid inside a vent on the forward deck of the ship during the confusion which resulted as the rest of the crew was abandoning the ship.

Their intention was to recover the gold as they were leaving the ship, but the explosive devise they had set detonated sooner than they had expected. The rope supporting one end of the lifeboat Martin and his crewmates were on broke as the boat was being lowered and Martin fell out and was saved but the other two men were badly injured and died shortly after they reached the shore. They were buried on the island and their marked graves are still there.

Martin was taken prisoner by the British, but after the war migrated to Chile, joining the already substantial German community in the *Curacautín* area. He worked here and there, finding work wherever he could. Being German, he was often employed by other German immigrants living in the area. Most were farmers and they felt a strong kinship with him.

A group of earlier German immigrants had done some gold mining on the *Sierra Nevada* several kilometers southwest of *Lonquimay*. They found some gold, not a great deal, but enough to inspire other schemes or ways of making more money by not working so hard. They eventually came in contact other German immigrants living in *Valparaíso* who had been making a living doing commercial salvage work. Over many bottles of wine a scheme was hatched! All of this was done over a period of several years and on the sly as they wanted no potential competitors to become aware of what they were planning. They were going to recover the lost gold on the Dresden!

The Dresden, after all, was lying in relatively shallow water. Its line and some deck features were easily visible when the sea was calm. Several local residents using simple diving gear had actually dived into the wreckage and retrived dishes and some other memorabilia. But, none of them knew about the gold or they could have easily retrieved it as well!

Martin persuaded Jean to go along with them. Jean initially wanted no part of the scheme but he was aware of several medicinal plants that grew on the island and nowhere else. He could use this as an excuse to visit the islands to look for some of these plants. *Luisa* knew of a very effective medicinal plant that could cure several forms of cancer. It was the *chonta* palm that grew only on the *Juan Fernández* Islands. So, Jean reluctantly went along with the group.

The salvage expedition initially went very well, but soon met with a series of setbacks. The diver used a canvas suit and copper helmet and he entered the vent of the sunken ship and found the box containing the gold. He placed it into a basket attached to a separate line. He then signaled the crew in the boat to raise him and the basket. Unbeknownst to them, a seaquake (*maremoto*) had occurred about an hour earlier just off the Chilean coast. As their bad luck would have it, it produced a tsunami that arrived on the east coast of the island just as the crew was preparing to bring up the diver and the gold.

The water level in the harbor dropped suddenly, so suddenly that the little boat they had rented actually smashed down against the deck of the Dresden and broke into two large pieces. The crew helped the diver clamber into the wreckage of the boat, and they observed the box containing the gold slip over the edge of the ship's deck and disappear into the black water alongside, with a long rope trailing behind it. In the long minute that passed afterward, as they were realizing what had just happened, they suddenly became aware that the water around them was rapidly rising and they began to cling to the boat wreckage to save their lives.

The tsunami washed all of them up onto the shore and deposited them in the center of the main street in the little village of *San Juan Baptista*. Fortunately, none of the party drowned but as they began to realize that they were still alive, and still poor, they thanked their respective saints for their good fortune. As they stood there in the street and began to be surrounded by island residents, they started laughing at their good fortune. None of them ever dreamed again of easy riches.

When the *Carabineros* questioned them as to what they were doing diving on the sunken ship, they honestly stated that they were simply looking for treasure. None of the police officers believed them and they were not charged. Incidentally, that same tsunami caused the Dresden to shift somewhat where it rested and it slipped off of the relatively shallow water covering the undersea cliff and slid into much deeper water, water so deep that it could never be reached again with conventional diving gear.

A lobster fishing boat would arrive there in another week so they would be able to obtain passage and return to the mainland, chagrined but still alive. Jean was not too surprised. *Luisa* had told him that something bad was going to happen but that no one would be killed. He decided to continue with the project that had been his excuse to go along on this little adventure.

He eventually found a little grove of *chonta* palms growing on the opposite side of the island, on the western slope on the other side of *El Junque*, near a little trail going down to the beach. Earlier conversations with island inhabitants indicated that this grove was, indeed, the only one still in existence. Jean collected some of the fruits and brought them back to *Lonquimay*. *Luisa* used steeped extracts of this supply for several years and had great success curing various kinds of cancers in the area around *Lonquimay*.

But, the supply of *chonta* eventually ran out and she had to shift emphasis to other medicinal plants, none of which were as effective. Jean always wanted to go back to *Juan Fernández* but various interruptions prevented him from doing so for many years.

CHAPTER 11
Upper Kintla Lake, Glacier National Park, Montana, July 1962

"This is no shit."
– Usually the first sentence in any story told by smokejumpers. It means that they tell only the truth, never lies or exaggerations.

Robert awoke instantly when the pilot of the DC-2 throttled back and entered the slow seesaw motion of the plane as the pilot and spotter took the first look-see over the fire. Robert had been sitting in a cramped position for over an hour now and was beginning to feel drowsy. He had taken off his helmet as soon as the plane cleared the runway but that did not offer much relief. The harness, which was comparatively loose an hour ago, was now digging into his shoulders and the strap across his chest prevented him from taking little more than short, shallow breaths.

Added to that discomfort was the weight of the 7.3 meter-diameter emergency parachute on his chest and the cramped harness of the 9.8 meter-diameter main chute on his back, plus being dressed in an insulated nylon jump suit. The jump suit also had a .3-meter-high collar that prevented much air circulation around one's head and within a few minutes after the plane took off he was sitting in a pocket of sleep-inducing carbon dioxide. He lay back on his parachute pack and tried to tell himself that he was comfortable, but he wasn't. The plane was rolling from side to side and he began to feel sick.

The pilot and the spotter began an animated conversation over their radio headsets about the safest place to drop the jumpers and their equipment and the best approach to that site. With that information in mind the pilot throttled up slightly as he swung the plane over to the left and then began to fly back around as he decided the best angle at which to fly over the fire and approach the jump spot.

As the pilot was preparing for the first set of jumpers to leave the plane, Robert tried to keep from being sick by recalling his first day of the four-week training period at the Missoula Smokejumper Base with the other 56 trainees. The training period was rigorous to say the least, but it was also fun and very interesting. Each morning at 5:30 the trainees had to report out on the landing apron in front of the parachute loft for an intense half-hour of calisthenics.

After breakfast, approximately half of the day was spent in the classroom learning fire behavior, fire control techniques, first aid, and the theory of safe parachuting. The rest of the day was spent either out in the woods felling snags, building fire lines, climbing trees with the spurs, or working out on the dreaded training units.

The units were designed to make the training so rigorous and monotonous that each jumper would behave instinctively, without taking time to think about what to do. It was much like military training. In fact, at the beginning of World War II, the military officers of the fledging airborne division of the U. S. Army came to Missoula to observe how the smokejumpers trained.

One of the units was a shock tower designed to acquaint trainees with the opening shock of a parachute as it unraveled from the back-board on the jumper's back. The trainees started jumping off at the 5-meter level to get the feel of jumping into thin air and after one or two jumps graduated to the 10-meter-level. The Canadian swing and "A" frames were used to teach trainees the proper way to perform the Allen roll when landing in order to prevent sprained ankles or a concussion.

The instructors tried to pound the training into the trainee's heads and if they saw a sloppy roll the trainee was required to do 25 pushups in his complete jump suit. Robert recalled spending a good share of his time doing pushups and it wasn't unusual for a trainee to do several hundred a day as punishment for some training infractions.

Since a smokejumper sometimes lands in a tree, another of the units was designed to train a jumper how to get out of a tree without breaking his neck. A 32.5-meter-long piece of nylon webbing called a let-down rope was used for this purpose and was carried in a pocket on the left leg. After landing in a tree, the jumper was to secure one end of the let-down rope to his harness and then, after slipping out of his harness, slide down the rope to the ground. With practice the complete let-down should take less than two minutes.

During the third and fourth weeks the trainees made their seven practice jumps, jumping out of a variety of airplanes. The tiny Travelaire, and later the Twin Beechcraft, were used to carry two or three jumpers to a small fire and the former was one of the first airplanes used for smokejumping. Later, the larger Ford Trimotor was a mainstay on both large and small fires. Its slow speed and extreme maneuverability made it perfect for flying in the mountainous terrain where most forest fires occurred. Faster DC-2s and DC-3s were widely used somewhat later, as was the much larger C-46, especially for big fires where many jumpers were needed.

Robert didn't particularly like jumping out of the C-46. It was a big plane by smokejumper standards, and its glide speed for jumping was a little too fast for him. You had to throw yourself out the door in order to safely enter the slipstream of air rushing by the open door and then when the parachute suddenly opened and filled with air, the shock was so great that you felt as if you were going to be turned inside out. There was really no danger, of course, but it still was a rough opening, especially with the 9.8-meter-diameter parachutes being used more and more now. His favorite planes were the DC-2s, with the DC-3s being a close second. He had always wanted to jump out of one of the Ford Trimotors but had never had the opportunity. He knew it would be his favorite because it had real class and a long history of use in firefighting.

The smaller Twin Beechcraft was okay but he felt nervous flying in a plane that stayed aloft and flew mainly through the power of its two large engines. He had seen the wreckage of one of these planes that crashed at the Missoula airport on takeoff when one of its engines failed. It dropped and veered to the side so suddenly that the pilot never had a chance to react. It was turned into a simple pile of wreckage with little semblance of ever having been an airplane. Fortunately, the two pilots somehow survived the crash.

The other feature he didn't like about the C-46 was that the door was so wide. You couldn't reach both edges when exiting the plane to help throw yourself out the door, and that concern came back to haunt him on what would later turn out to be his last fire jump.

Today, though, as the pilot maneuvered the DC-2 around the mountain and entered the glide path in preparation for the first stick of jumpers, in what was to be Robert's next to-last-fire jump, Robert recalled his first fire jump last year. It seemed like a long time ago now, after all that had happened to him, especially the offer of the assistantship. But he could still visualize everything about that jump.

Suddenly, above the deep, bumblebee in-and-out synchronous roar and vibration of the two powerful engines and the shrill scream of the slipstream past the open door, he heard his name called. He looked toward the rear of the plane and saw the spotter motioning to him. They were at the fire now and he was to jump in the first stick.

After some difficulty, he got to his feet and hobbled to the rear of the plane. Since this was a DC-2, only two men could jump at a time. In the DC-3, three men can jump in a stick because the fuselage is a little wider. The foreman was first and Robert would follow. The spotter helped hook up the static lines to the cable that is bolted across the rear bulkhead and made a final check of all the harnesses and buckles.

Then, as the roar of engines quieted down and became smoother as the pilot throttled back, Robert knew that the plane was entering the glide path. He stepped close behind the foreman with his right foot forward so that when he took one more step toward the door, he would step past the threshold and out into the slipstream which would catch his right leg as it left the doorway and turn him facing toward the rear of the plane.

Robert looked through the door opening and there, only a little over 300 meters below, was some of the most rugged country in the Inland Empire, and very dangerous to jump into. It is covered with a shaggy green carpet of trees and scattered here and there were tall, rotten snags and rocky outcroppings.

The spotter yelled, "There is a 4-kilometer-an hour breeze blowing up the canyon so it will be tricky. There aren't any openings so you will have to tree-up. Keep headed into the wind all the way down." The spotter then snapped his goggles over his eyes and jumped down to the floor. For what seemed like an eternity but was actually only 5 or 7 seconds he lay there motionless with his head half out the door sighting on the jump spot.

When the plane was directly over the jump spot he very deliberately rolled back out of the doorway and then with a "Go get 'um Tiger!" he slapped the foreman on the back of his left leg. The foreman disappeared through the doorway; Robert crouched down, took one step forward and threw himself after him with his right leg leaving the plane first.

This fire, which only involved half a dozen jumpers, was a jumper's dream. It had adequate manpower to control, was not too large to begin with, and the weather cooperated to make it almost a joy to fight. It was easily controlled the first day, and then after several more days mopping up, the jumpers hiked out to the nearest ranger station where they were fed and then loaded onto a bus for the ride back to the smokejumper base in Missoula. As he was sitting on the bus, Robert thought about his life thus far and wondered about the momentous changes that the end of this fire season would bring to his life.

Robert loved smokejumping but knew that this would be his last summer for jumping. It had been a slow fire season so far and he was having trouble saving enough money from overtime firefighting to fund his graduate studies at Montana State University for the next school year. It wasn't like that last year, in 1961, the summer of the Sleeping Child Fire in Idaho. Then, there weren't enough smokejumpers, or even ground pounders, to handle the number of fires burning at any one time in the Inland Empire. He racked up a lot of overtime for his studies that year and still had a little left for the next year.

Also, the excitement and lure of firefighting was fading somewhat and, although he didn't fully realize it yet nor could he understand why, he was developing a real interest in plants that could be useful for health remedies. Then, he met several Peace Corps Volunteers recently returned from Chile and Peru who were now studying at the then Montana State University in Missoula. He visited with them and they tried to answer his many questions about life there.

If all went according to plan, he would graduate a year later, in late spring, from the Dept. of Botany and had already been offered a research assistant position in the Department. The condition was that he be willing to go to Chile, in South America, to study and collect medicinal plants and herbal remedies of the indigenous natives. Robert would have been happy to go anywhere in South America.

The Department had been the recipient of an NIH grant to study medicinal plants in various countries in South America. The study in Chile was to be a pilot study to determine the efficacy of this approach and develop the methodology to be used in future studies. Other graduate students at the university in Missoula and at other universities around the United States would follow-up on the material Robert was to collect and they would extract chemicals and determine their effectiveness in laboratory studies.

After he was offered the assistantship, he studied historical accounts of Spanish expeditions in Mexico, Peru, Venezuela, and Chile. After reading Prescott's classic account of the War of the Pacific, he began to feel a kinship with the people, the land, and the plants and forests that grew there. Through interlibrary loan he borrowed some of the major first accounts by La Condamine, Bonpland, Von Humboldt, and other great plant explorers, and re-lived their experiences in being the first to discover and describe the exotic plant life of South America.

The plant life in Chile was especially interesting because it had evolved in isolation from the other major geographic areas of South America and had a closer affinity to the present vegetation of New Zealand, showing that those plants had co-evolved dating back to before the major split-up of the previous continental landform.

A week after he returned to Missoula he was back at the top of the jump list, and so, it was no surprise when he was called early one Monday morning to prepare for a flight to the northwestern corner of Glacier National Park. Soon, the C-46 was loading jumpers for the several-hour flight. As the plane approached its destination, the now tired and bored jumpers began to get to their feet and stretch as best as they could, loaded down with two parachutes, a personal gear bag, a let-down rope, and compressed into a restraining white nylon jumpsuit.

Robert, too, got up and began checking his neighbor's gear and bouncing around on the floor as the plane settled into the first jump glide path. The spotter had already thrown out the markers on the previous pass and was mentally calculating the drift that the first stick of jumpers would experience. In a DC-2, a stick usually consisted of 2 jumpers, both exiting the plane one after the other. In the larger DC-3s or C-46s, 3-man sticks were the norm. This was going to be a big fire and this C-46 was getting ready to drop jumpers, and a DC-3 had just taken off from the Missoula airport with another load of jumpers. These two planes were especially useful on larger fires when as many as 44 men, or even more, would jump on what would become known as a project fire.

Robert, though, preferred the smaller, 2-, 3-, or 4-man fires. Small fires could usually be suppressed with only a few fire fighters and the whole operation was usually more relaxed. Sometimes, though, small fires blew up unexpectedly and reinforcements were necessary. This might require dropping more jumpers, or dropping a load or two of flame retardant.

Dropping more jumpers was usually an embarrassment to the men already on the fire, but sometimes things happened such as a change in wind direction or wind velocity that could completely and quickly change the fire-behavior situation. Part of that, though, was the shot of adrenaline, which was probably the major reason why young men, and years later, why young women became smokejumpers.

Today, though, this fire, which became known as the Upper Kintla Lake Fire, was the kind of fire Robert didn't particularly like. It was a project fire. The first sets of jumps consisted of 44 jumpers. Later, that number would be increased, mainly because the fire was spreading fast, but also partially because it was an otherwise slow fire season and the jump base could be a little extravagant with the number of jumpers sent to any particular fire. More jumpers, however, meant more confusion and an increased chance of accidents.

The flight path over the jump spot was rather circuitous because the jump spot was in a long narrow valley surrounded by tall mountains and carpeted with huckleberry bushes. So, the plane had to fly around a mountain each time after a stick of jumpers left the plane. Normally jumpers exit the plane at about 300 meters above the ground. This is high enough to allow the jumper to steer for the jump spot, or adjust for occasional malfunctions of the parachute, or to deploy the reserve chute if all else fails. Today, though, jumpers were exiting at about over 1,000 meters elevation. More chance of an accident, but today, for Robert, it would turn out to be to his benefit.

Robert was about halfway back in the cluster of jumpers and equipment. As the first jumpers began exiting the plane, the remaining jumpers stood and began checking their own and each other's gear for the last time. The flight from Missoula to Glacier Park had taken about 2 ½ hours and was rather bumpy in the early morning flight. Several jumpers were feeling a little airsick and would be glad to exit the plane.

Back toward the tail end of the fuselage was a young man who had been partying the night before. He was the last man to board the plane and was almost left at the airport because he arrived just as the plane was leaving. At any rate, the poor kid was sitting on the floor and looking worse and worse with each bump of the plane. After about an hour he upchucked what seemed like gallons of pure green bile.

Fortunately, after a trickle of bile reached the front end of the aircraft, the spotter saw it and grabbed an elongated cardboard box containing climbing spurs and tossed it to the sick jumper. The remaining bile, and it seemed like there was still a lot of it, was upchucked in there. He wondered who would be the unfortunate individual who had to use those climbing spurs. It would be a good reason to avoid treeing up on this fire.

Unfortunately, the rivulet of green bile that had worked its way forward from the tail end of the plane turned out to be pretty slippery. When it came Robert's turn to jump, he found he was the second man in a three-man-stick. There was nothing to hang onto except each other as he and the other two jumpers slipped and slid around each time the plane dropped or rose a few meters with the turbulence.

Robert held himself in place mainly by will power. When the spotter slapped the lead man's leg as the signal to jump, he and the other two jumpers slid out the door as a three-man mass of humanity with gobs of green goo dripping from their boots.

As the three men exited the plane's door and began to fall, Robert was watching the man in front of him and his parachute as it began to unwrap from its backboard. As if in slow motion, he distinctly saw a cluster of shroud lines unfold and realized that he was falling between several of them.

Thankfully, both parachutes fully opened with double jolts, but as they were unfolding, he found that he was entangled among those lines. With his back to the jumper he was entangled with he really couldn't do much because he couldn't see what was happening. But, fortunately, the other jumper had a good line of sight and told him which lines to pull down and then roll over in order to free himself from the entangling mess and then roll free.

As he began to extricate himself from the tangle of shroud lines he had to chuckle as he recalled the words of the jumper who was commanding him what to do, "Robert, you son-of-a–bitch, don't you dare cut any of my lines!" With that thought, he rolled out of the last lines, swung once, and then immediately stepped out onto the ground and onto a nice, soft huckleberry bush. He didn't even have to do an Allen roll when he landed. If they had not had the extra 600 meters of jump time a sprained ankle, or worse, could have been the result.

Robert made only a few more jumps that summer, but no fire jumps. The fall rains started early and the forest fuels were too wet to ignite from lightning strikes. The few jumps he made were to remote peaks to clear off the trees and to convert those mountaintops for use as helicopter landing pads. This was his last fire jump but his smokejumping experience had prepared him well for whatever the future was to bring. The main thing he would miss would be the adrenaline rush when exiting from the open door of an airplane. And, he would always remember the rush of seeing the jumper ahead of him jump out through the open door and instantly disappear and fall away as his parachute was pulled from his backpack and opened, and then, as if in slow motion, see him float away ever more slowly towards earth as the plane pulled away in a gradual left turning curve. To the jumpers who had just exited the plane, the absolute silence was almost deafening.

He had begun his graduate studies with a passion and was ready to face the future! His experiences as a smokejumper taught him that, when faced with a challenge or with danger, one must quickly assess the situation, then act decisively.

CHAPTER 12
The Medicinal Plant Collector – 1970

"Yo curo todos los males, Yo curo todas las penas, los curo con puras yerbas, las curo con yerbas buenas: Yo traigo yerbas fresquitas, de allá de la cordillera, traigo mentas, traigo boldo y hasta la flor de la higuera:" (I cure all maladies, I cure all pains, I cure them with pure herbs, with good herbs: I bring fresh herbs, from high above in the mountains,

I bring mints, I bring boldo and even the flower of the grape.)
– Song verses from *"El Yerbatero"* (The Medicinal Plant Doctor.)
– Song from Chilean folklore.

What started as a small business that Robert was associated with had an interesting conception and proves that even nerds can become successful in the business world. The initiation of Pharmtec began when a small group of upper-class students at the then Montana State University in Missoula met during a drinking party at the beginning of their junior year at the university. It was a strange group - they had a common love for botany, not partying! As the group went through each year of their studies, there were seldom more than two or three students in the group during any given year but this year the group consisted of five dedicated young men and one young woman who all shared an almost religious interest in botany. Two of the five young men were forestry students.

The common thread between all of them was their love for plants of all kinds, from the mightiest trees down to the lowliest herbs. One discussion after another during their senior year led to a sort of comaraderie as they collectively reflected on how they might make a living with their knowledge and love of plants. At that time, two decades after the Second World War, the economy was still booming and the forestry majors could easily find work with the USDA Forest Service, the BLM, or with any of a variety of state forestry organizations. The botany majors had fewer employment possibilities, as there were few jobs except for teaching in high school science programs, none of which paid more than a bare living wage.

One of Robert's forestry friends, Dick Babcock, had an idea – suppose they started a company that sold medicinal plants as remedies for human ailments. Robert had a small estate from his grandfather in which he was willing to invest and Dick had relatively wealthy parents who might be willing to assist them in getting started. If they collected and dried medicinal plants, perhaps they could package them and sell the product to consumers interested in using such remedies. All the students had some knowledge of some such remedies that their parents and grandparents had exposed them to when they were children.

The group discussed the difficulties, and possibilities, and agreed to join in the formation of the fledging company, initially on a part-time basis and then later full-time if the finances of the business would allow it. One of the partners lived in Hamilton, Montana and his retiring grandfather owned a family medical laboratory that he would let the group use for free in order to help get them started. Robert had been born and raised in Missoula, and his parents were happy for him to live with them at no cost, at least until the venture became economically successful. None of the original group could know at that time just how successful their venture was to become. By their good fortune, they were on the cusp of a major revolution in human health care.

During his last years at Missoula, and especially in graduate school, Robert studied Spanish and took as many elective courses in chemistry as he could. Several friends, including Dick, graduated two years ahead of him and began to assemble the fledgling company. They purchased some common dried plants with known remedies and began to process, package, and sell them. Their success was rather immediate, and surprising, and the company soon gained a national following.

Robert felt, though, that their best business opportunity would be to handle medicinal plants that had a long history of human use, acceptance and, therefore, a long history of efficacy. His readings about the plant explorations in South America convinced him that business success lay in that direction. The tropical, or at least temperate, climate during human migration there had guaranteed a large variety of plant species to study.

So, the group collectively chose Chile as the object of their exploratory work. It was a long, narrow country with a good road system and one person could probably do a thorough survey of the complete country. *Muñoz's* book on the identification of Chilean flora had just been published and Robert would be able to verify identifications of plants he collected. So, on that scary December day following graduation, he purchased a Panagra air ticket to *Santiago*, Chile, and loaded with plant presses and a USDA Plant Quarantine Permit which allowed him to send seeds and dried plant parts to the United States, he left for Chile.

Robert planned his survey for native Chilean plants with medicinal benefits by visiting with country folk he encountered along his meanders in the Central Valley of Chile. He left *Santiago* and drove straight south to *Puerto Montt* where he began a northward trek of exploration, planning to eventually finish his work in *La Serena*. His strategy seemed rather naïve - he would visit the open-air markets and see what kind of medicinal plants were for sale there. He would ask questions about what benefits they might have and anything else he could learn about them.

Although he decided to first concentrate his quest in the area north of *Puerto Montt*, he realized that eventually he would also have to explore the less-populated country south of *Puerto Montt*. When he questioned local medicinal plant vendors they often gave him names of local producers and collectors so he had a foot in the door when he sought them out. After he started, he wished that he had studied Spanish a little more, but, he had a strong desire to learn and he soon did very well.

Before leaving the States he had scoured all the interlibrary loan literature he could find on Chilean plant and herbal remedies so he had a good head start on the project. Now he would have to actually identify and collect plant samples and send seeds and tissue samples back to the States.

He actually started his explorations in the *Puerto Montt* region by visiting with members of a native aboriginal tribe known as the *Cuncos*. At first, tribe members were reluctant to speak with him but, as he persisted with his questions, they recognized that he was serious in his goal of learning about the native plants and the remedies associated with them.

During the next two summers of explorations he met with representatives of the *Huilliches* and later with the *Mapuches*. He had not yet sought out the *Poyas* and *Puelches* since they were located on the east side of the *Andes* in Argentina and they were relatively inaccessible from the Chilean side. His plan was to eventually go north to the *Lonquimay* Valley, meet with the *Pehuenche* natives living there, and when that work was finished, cross over into Argentina and return southward on the Argentine side of the *Andes* to meet with members of the latter two tribes.

He had noted that there was a common unity of many plants recognized as having medicinal properties, so in some ways his work became a little easier with each trip. All of these tribes were part of the larger *Araucanian* race, not vanquished by either the Incas or by the Spanish, or by the Chilean government after Chile's independence from Spain.

The indigenous history of the usefulness of medicinal plants was well known when the Spaniards arrived. During the 14,000, or so, years after they arrived in the *pampas*, these people had experienced centuries of trial and error in discovering the efficacious health benefits of certain plants. In other words, many of these remedies worked, and some worked very well.

The purpose of Robert's surveys was to collect as much information as possible about medicinal plants and the health benefits they provided and, where possible, collect the actual plant tissues and also seeds. He had a Plant Import Certificate from the USDA that allowed him to ship a wide range of plant materials to the Pharmtec laboratory in Hamilton, Montana. After their initial analyses, the scientists could request additional materials on which to conduct further tests.

When the NIH grant, which funded their early work, was terminated due to budget-cutting by Congress in order to fund the war in Vietnam, and they could no longer realistically continue significant extraction and expensive testing research, their focus shifted to identifying medicinal plants, growing them in the greenhouse, harvesting, packaging, and then marketing the product. When this shift in focus occurred, Robert's work in Chile became particularly important. He had to know for sure which plants were responsible for alleviating specific ailments.

Robert's new and somewhat shortened responsibility was to survey the southern part of Chile roughly from *Temuco* southward to *Puerto Montt*. If that work produced positive results, he would then expand his surveys to include the areas north of *Temuco*, and south of *Puerto Montt*. Long-range research planning included extending the surveys to Argentina, and then, perhaps, to other South American countries.

As Robert identified plants associated with medicinal traits, he would then visit the *Museo de História Natural* in *Santiago* and examine the herbaria there and piece together range maps of these herbal plants. After he began his work, he found that personnel at this museum had a lot of information that they were eager to share with him. Chilean scientists had a lot of interest in doing exactly what Robert was doing but they lacked financial backing to pursue their interests. A great help to Robert was the recently published *"Sinopsis de la Flora Chilena"* by *Roberto Muñoz Pizarro*, and later *Muñoz's* daughter *Mélica* helped him a great deal in his work of identifying medicinal plants.

CHAPTER 13
The Valdivian Forest

"Por bosques virginales de otra edad, neblinas iniciales vuelven ya, parece que me voy a ir
a buscar,
para alumbrar, iluminar."
(In virgin forests of another time, where young clouds fly, I will go there
to search, to illuminate, to enlighten.)
– Song verses from *Bosques Virginales* (Virgin Forests)
– Song from Chilean folklore.

Robert was fascinated with the vegetation of the Valdivian Forest of southern Chile and Argentina. The huge variety of plant species within the forest was impressive, indeed. And, he would never have suspected the number and variety of parasitic plants on those majestic trees.

His first gastronomic exposure to the marvels of the Valdivian Forest was the first time he had stopped at a roadside stand on his first trip from Santiago to the south. He saw a handwritten sign that said *"se vende dihueñes.* He walked over to the stand and asked what they were. The lady said that they were a form of edible fungus (*Cyttaria espinosae*) that grows on *coigüe* and *roble* trees and explained several ways in which they could be prepared for consumption.

Robert purchased a *kilo* and, during the next several days as he continued his trip south, tried all the different ways of preparing them. Their slightly sweet flavor, their golf ball to baseball size and shape, their initial color of white to tan changing to orange-yellow as they matured, and their internal change to a greenish-grayish gelatinous consistency, made them a good choice to add variety to any meal preparation.

Dihuenes are extremely common at roadside stands from September to November but were sometimes also available dried during most of the year. The fruiting bodies, or galls, at maturity, are full of sugars and a unique yeast fungus (*Saccharomyces eubayanus*) is only present in these galls and it ferments the sugars as the galls mature and then decline.

At the time of writing of this novel, an interesting new relationship had been discovered that added another benefit of these strange fungi. When lager beers were first developed in Bavaria, a hybrid species of yeast (*S. pastorianus*) was used to ferment the lagers. It was long known that the common baking yeast *S. cerevisiae* was the one parent of the hybrid but the other parent was not known until recently. That other parent was the yeast (*S. eubayanus*) found in the *dihueñes* galls and it had apparently been used in Bavaria for many years to brew lager beers. It preferred the cooler temperatures typical of chilly Patagonia, which is the temperature at which lager beers are brewed. It must have been transported to Europe, probably by family members of some of the early German settlers to the Patagonia area.

The Valdivian temperate forest is the second largest temperate rain forest in the world. The Valdivian ecosystem is located mostly in the southern half of Chile, with a long, narrow strip on the Argentine side of the Andean *Cordillera*. The moisture-laden warm air from the Pacific Ocean, which demarks the western coast of Chile, rises into the Andean foothills toward the eastern edge of Chile which is demarked by the Andean *Cordillera*, and as it rises, creates abundant rainfall that is responsible for maintaining the Valdivian forest type.

The Valdivian forest type is comprised of species found almost exclusively in Chile and Argentina. They are closely related to plant species in New Zealand and reflect a time in the geologic past when those two land masses were connected. The Valdivian forest type is considered to be mature as regards to its plant biodiversity. That fact might explain the large variety of parasitic plants.

Most of the species in the Valdivian forest type have considerable commercial value but have been over-exploited during the past century. We shall briefly describe some of the most important tree species in this forest. Many have medicinal properties. The most important coniferous families (the Gymnosperms) include these families and species:

Podocarpaceae - *Uva de cordillera* (**Lleuque**) (*Podocarpus andina*) over 600 meters above sea level in the foothills of the Andean *Cordillera*. **Mañio** *de hojas punzantes* (*Podocarpus nubigena*) prefers shallow, moist soils. **Mañio** *de hojas largas* (*Podocarpus saligna*) also grows in moist areas at higher altitude. **Mañio** *de hojas cortas* or **Mañio** *hembra* (*Saxegothaea conspicua*) grows in moist areas. The wood is yellowish with reddish streaks. It is very lightweight and used for general carpentry, furniture, carvings, and historically for barrels.

Araucariaceae - *Pino araucaria*, or **pehuén**, is the only species of this family found in Chile. Once plentiful, it is now found only in very restricted zones. In ancient times, **pehuén** had a much larger distribution, mainly at higher altitudes with ample precipitation. At higher elevations, this forest type produces majestic, open stands with little understory. At lower elevations, it is commonly mixed with other timber species and shrubs. Before extensive logging removed much of the older forests, **pehuén** was commonly encountered with a height of 27 to 41 meters and a diameter at breast height of 114 to 152 centimeters. These trees were hundreds of years old. Its major disadvantage is its extremely slow growth. The wood quality is superb, it is yellowish in color, fine-textured, and useful for general construction and cabinetry. It also is excellent for production of pulp and paper and plywood. In the time of sailing ships the wood was extremely valuable for ship's masts and planking. The trunk resin is used to cure skin ulcers.

Cupressaceae - *Ciprés de la cordillera*, **Lahuán** (*Austrocedrus chilensis*) grows in drier sites and produces a wood that is very decay resistant and is employed for posts and grape stakes. *Ciprés de las Guaitecas*, **Lahuán** (*Pilgerodendron uviferum*) grows in swampy area at low altitudes and near to the ocean. The wood is very decay resistant, has a fine grain, and finishes to a very smooth surface. It was used for construction of wharfs and boats.

Alerce, **Lahuén** (*Fitzroya cupressoides*) produces wood that is very resistant to decay and weathering. For these reasons it was widely used for posts, poles, shingles, shakes, and siding for exterior coverings of buildings. It typically grows in low-altitude swamps and, at one time, formed dense, nearly pure stands covering thousands of acres. Old-growth trees were very old, rivaling the redwood trees of California. These older trees were 40 to 46 meters tall and about 122 centimeters in diameter. The tree grows very slowly. During much of the early logging, the logs were extremely large in diameter and difficult to transport and so were elaborated on site by splitting the logs with wedges. The wood was so uniform in texture that a single wedge driven on one end of a log could produce a board of uniform thickness for the entire log length. It is now a very rare species, found only in isolated and protected stands.

An interesting event occurred about a thousand years ago in the Central Valley when a series of volcanic eruptions dumped several meters of ash on an extensive *alerce* forest, knocking down trees and completely burying the entire forest. During the 1960s, the downed trees from this period of volcanism were mined just as if they were valuable minerals. Workers would clear away the volcanic ash around each fallen tree, cut the tree into logs on the spot, and then split the log, usually into shakes. The shakes were loaded onto carts, hauled away, and were in such abundant supply that they were used for several years to shingle houses over much of Chile. After such a long time buried in the ash, the wood was still useable, but is easily identified by presence of small white pockets of decay uniformly scattered throughout the wood. Although abundant in the wood, the decay pockets do not significantly reduce its strength.

The remaining tree species are all in the Angiosperms (the largest and most complex group of plants on the earth). These families are present in the Valdivian forest:

Winteraceae

Canelo, **foiye** (*Drimys winteri*) grows more frequently below 1,200 meters altitude in swamps and along rivers and estuaries. Its best growth is on the island of *Chiloé*. This species was considered to be sacred by the *araucanos*. The wood of *canelo* is too soft for construction and is best suited for the production of pulp and paper. The species has many medicinal properties, especially for the treatment of cancer.

Monimiaceae

Tepa, **Huahuán** (*Laureliopsis philipiana*) is found at various altitudes, depending on the latitude where it is growing. The wood, which is of a whitish-yellowish color, is widely used in general carpentry and especially for the production of plywood. Some trees have the defect known as "*mancha* *mariposa"*, which indicates that the wood has a putrid odor that severely limits its use. Logs from these trees are chipped and used for the manufacture of fiberboard, or peeled for the production of plywood.

Laurel, **tihue** (*Laurelia sempervirens*) occurs mixed with *robles* and *lingues*. It has rapid growth and produces a wood with excellent properties that make it valuable for the manufacture of furniture and use in general carpentry. Flowers, leaves, and bark have medicinal properties.

Boldo (*Peumus boldus*) has a wide distribution, mostly in the Central Valley. A small tree, the wood is used mostly for firewood and charcoal production. The leaves and bark contain substances useful for their medicinal properties. They are also rich in tannins that are useful for tanning leather.

Lauraceae

Peumo (*Cryptocarya alba*) is a small tree and is also more abundant in the Central Valley. The wood is very dense and resistant to moisture, which makes it very useful for the manufacture of shoe heels and parts of animal-drawn carts. The bark has medicinal properties and has been used to color leather orange.

Lingue (*Persea lingue*) is a relative of avocado and grows at lower altitudes. It is Chile's most desirable and beautiful furniture wood. However, it has been harvested almost to the point of extinction. The bark was used for tanning leather and to stain leather brown. The leaves are poisonous to cattle. The leaves, fruits, and bark have medicinal properties.

Proteaceae

Notro, *ciruelillo*, *notru*, *fosforito* (*Embothrium coccineum*) has extremely beautiful wood that is used for manufacture of small furniture items. The bark and leaves have medicinal properties and are used to alleviate toothache and help heal skin lacerations.

Avellano, **guevín** (*Gevuina avellana*) has wood with beautiful figure and is used for manufacture of musical instruments, veneer, and cabinetry. Because of its elasticity, it is also used for manufacture of oars. The outer shell of the fruit has medicinal properties. The bark is useful for tanning leather.

Ciruelillo (*Lomatia dentata*) is a small tree and produces wood similar to that of *avellano*. The wood has a similar grain and is considered to be somewhat inferior to the other species, but it is also used for cabinetry.

Fuinque (*Lomatia ferruginea*) is a small, evergreen tree that grows best in shady, humid sites. The wood has a beautiful grain and is used for manufacture of cabinets. The bark and leaves are used to heal injuries and as a purgative and diuretic.

Radal (*Lomatia hirsuta*) usually grows in groups in foothills of the Andean *cordillera* and the Coastal Range. The wood has a figure similar to that of *ciruelillo*, and *fuinque* and is considered to be superior for cabinetry and fine veneer. The bark has medicinal properties.

Mirtaceae

Luma (*Amomyrtus luma*) grows best in humid, shady sites. The wood is extremely dense and has been used to make axles for animal drawn carts, tool handles, canes, police nightsticks, and for firewood because of its high heat value.

Meli (*Amomyrtus meli*) often grows with *luma* in humid, shady sites. It only grows to be a small tree but produces a very dense wood useful for manufacture of tool handles and wheel spokes.

Arrayán (*Luma apiculata*) is a large shrub or small tree, growing larger farther south in its distribution. Its wood is very dense and is used for tool handles and firewood. It is very useful for erosion control.

Petra (*Myrceugenia exsucca*) is a small tree that grows only on very wet sites and is, hence, important in erosion control.

Temu (*Blepharocalyx cruckshanksii*) is a rather scarce shrub or small tree.

Eucrifiaceae

Ulmo (*Eucryphia cordifolia*) is a rapidly growing, large tree, and in old-growth stands, can be as tall as 40 meters and 2 meters in diameter. It is seldom found in pure stands but in association with *roble*, *tepa*, *tineo* or *coigüe*. The wood is very dense and has been used extensively in construction and for railroad ties, firewood, and charcoal. The bark is rich in tannins and used for tanning leather. The flowers are of high quality and are an important contribution to apiculture in the region.

Eleocarpaceae

Maqui (*Aristotelia chilensis*) has a wide range, preferring moist sites rich in organic matter but is also found on dry sites. It is an early and aggressive invader of disturbed sites and often forms *"macales"*. The fruits were used by the *Mapuches* to prepare *chicha*. The leaves have antidiuretic properties.

Patagua (*Crinodendron patagua*) grows in lower moist ravines in the *cordillera*. Its flowers are important for apiculture. Its wood is light in color and used for furniture. Its bark is used for tanning leather.

Cunoniaceae

Tiaca (*Caldcluvia paniculata*) is a very slow growing shrub or small tree that grows best in humid zones, such as in the zone of *Chiloé*. Leaf infusions are used to control catarrh and intestinal infections.

Tineo (*Weinmannia trichosperma*) is a tree of very slow growth that is most frequent in the Andean and coastal *cordilleras*. It is a typical species of the Valdivian forest with its best growth in moist or swampy sites. The flowers are also valuable for production of honey. The wood is extremely dense, with a beautiful dark color and used mostly for veneer, but has been used in vehicle parts, railroad ties, and as firewood. The bark is used to help speed healing of scratches.

Rosaceae

Quillay (*Quillaja saponaria*) grows in drier areas but has become very scarce as a result of excessive exploitation for extraction of its high concentration of saponins that were used for manufacture of detergents.

Fagaceae

Raulí (*Nothofagus alpina*) is a very important and valuable tree, with reddish-colored wood that has very desirable working properties. It has been used for general construction but because of declining abundance, is used mainly for doors, windows, and furniture. Because of its decay resistance it was formerly used for boat construction.

Ñirre (*Nothofagus antarctica*) grows as a small tree and has a very wide distribution but is most abundant where the temperature is cold and slopes are steep. The wood has little commercial value and is used mainly for firewood.

Coigüe *de Magallanes* (*Nothofagus betuloides*) is often found in pure stands, especially in moist sites. The wood is yellowish in color, of good quality and is used in construction, for furniture, and for cooperage.

Coigüe (*Nothofagus dombeyi*) is very abundant with a wide distribution. The wood is yellowish with reddish stains and is widely used in construction, general carpentry, and manufacture of furniture. It is not very decay resistant. The trees are infected with a disease known as bacterial wetwood that causes excessive moisture content of the wood, and upon drying, the wood shrinks excessively, greatly reducing its commercial value. Treatment with steam allows the wood to regain much of its original volume with little resulting degradation and economic loss in product value.

Roble pellín, *hualle*, ***pellín*** (*Nothofagus obliqua*) is most abundant on deep, fertile, and moist sites, usually at lower altitudes. The heartwood is a reddish color, without visible grain and very resistant to decay. It was very widely used for construction of bridges, docks, posts and poles, as well as for manufacture of framing lumber and furniture, doors, and windows. Bark extracts are used as a red dye.

Lenga (*Nothofagus pumilio*) often grows in pure stands and is more abundant at lower temperatures. The wood is of excellent quality and useful for general construction and carpentry, especially in the southern portion of its range.

Celastraceae

Maitén (*Maytenus boaria*) is widespread over the region and is also planted as a shade tree and for ornamentation. The wood is used primarily for firewood. The leaves are used to control fever and as a purgative. The young shoots and leaves are also used for cattle forage.

Anacardiaceae

Litre (*Lithrea caustica*) grows only in the very far northern part of the Valdivian forest region but is included here because physical contact with it can produce serious allergic reactions. The wood is very dense and was used for construction of carts and keels of wooden boats, and also for firewood.

Aextoxicaceae

Olivillo, ***Teque*** (*Aextoxicon punctatum*) is very common and abundant over its entire range. The wood is reddish in color but not very strong and for this reason is not used much in carpentry but mainly for construction of shipping boxes and for firewood.

Araliaceae

Traumén, *sauco del diablo* (*Pseudopanux laetevirens*) has a wide distribution and with a scattered abundance especially along streams. It is important for the control of soil erosion.

Compuestas

Tayu, *trevo, palo santo* (*Dasyphyllum diacanthoides*) grows at lower altitudes mainly in the coastal *cordillera* on both dry and moist sites.

In addition to the trees described above, there are many shrubs and smaller plants that typify the Valdivian forest. One very abundant species is *quila* (*Chusquea quila*) Tribe Bambuseae that is extremely common, especially on moist sites. When grass forage is in short supply, the leaves and young shoots of *quila* serve as forage for cattle. The stems are also used in construction, for manufacture of animal cages and for rustic furniture.

The other notable component of the Valdivian forest is *copihue* (*Lapageria rosea*) Monocotiledoneae, and it has been designated as the national flower of Chile. It is a beautiful flower and there could not have been a better choice. But, it is scarce in the wild as it has been harvested in excess but is now protected by law. Presently, only cultivated flowers may be legally harvested. The beautiful and unique flowers are much used in floral arrangements, and the vines are used in manufacture of baskets and other art works. The roots have medicinal value.

CHAPTER 14
Medicinal Plants – 1972

"Agüita de Toronjil:" (Water of lemon balm, a medicinal plant.)
– Title of song from Chilean folklore

It didn't take Robert more than two or three visits with indigenous people to compile a rather substantial list of plants that had medicinal value for use as home remedies. As the catalog grew, Robert tried to list the cures they produced into categories of the specific afflictions remedied.

The list included: abortion symptoms, allergies, asthma, backache, blood pressure, bronchitis, bruises, burns, calluses, cancers, colds, conjunctivitis, constipation, cough, deafness, diabetes, diarrhea, drunken-ness, earache, facial paralysis, fever, flatulence, flu, fungus, gut ache, hair disorders, headache, heart palpitations (and other heart disorders), hemorrhages, hemorrhoids, indigestion, inflammation, injuries or wounds, insomnia, insect bites, intestinal gas, intestinal worms, kidney and gall stones, kidney problems (general), libido loss, mange or scabies, menstrual pain, miscarriage (prevention of), muscle spasms, nerve pain (and sciatic pain), nose bleed, rheumatism, skin disorders (irritation and rash), liver pain, sore throat, stomach ulcers, stomach ache, and warts.

It was apparent that these remedies did not necessarily cure or eliminate a specific disorder but rather alleviated the pain and suffering the ailment caused. In other words, they improved the quality of life. Some plants had curative properties against a single malady, others acted against several or even many maladies. As Robert continued his survey, he was aware that many exotic plants grown in Chile also had curative properties. Initially he focused only on native plants with medicinal attributes as he wanted to record for posterity those with known remedies. This fast-growing list of medicinal plants and some major remedies are listed in the compendium that his daughter *Paulina* compiled when she was growing up.

The interesting feature about the plants in this list is that each had a centuries-long history of efficacy against some particular ailment(s). There didn't seem to be any obvious grouping of ailments and plant groups. As he conducted later surveys he added to this list. His aim was to only investigate native Chilean plants as a great deal of research had already been done in other parts of the world on other medicinal plants. So, his work in Chile was cut out for him.

His partners at Pharmtec did not initially plan to extract the active chemicals effective against these ailments. However, the initiation of their company coincided with an actively growing interest, not only in the United States in the use of effective medicinal plant and herbal remedies, but in the world in general.

So, to verify the historical efficacy of each plant, Robert collected plant samples and pressed them in a plant press to create museum-quality specimens that could be used for reference purposes in future scientific work. As he collected these plants, he made maps of their locations and followed their cycle during the growing season. Then, in late summer or fall he collected fruits, dried them and then extracted the seeds. These he would either package and send to the laboratory in Montana or take them with him in his baggage when he returned home for the northern summer.

The business in Montana was now doing quite well. Sales in Europe and the United States had increased and all of the former part-time employees were now working full-time. Several were taking special courses to increase their abilities to cope with a growing business. At Pharmtec the seeds were checked for possible pathogens and then germinated. Employees measured germination rates, cultured for possible pathogens, and recorded growth data as the young plants adjusted to the environment in the new greenhouse.

As the plants grown in the greenhouse increased in quantity, tissues were dried or extracted for crude extracts to be used as remedies. They were sold in attractive packaging showing the remedy of interest on the packing with a color picture of the medicinal plant as it appeared in its natural setting in Chile.

These extracts were sold as organic herbal remedies only and not modified. Thus, they were not subject to FDA inspections or rules. The employees at Pharmtec, though, ran a top-notch operation and seldom did a customer complain that the product they purchased had not had the desired effect on their particular ailment.

In early October 1972, Robert had begun working his way east-ward up the *Lonquimay* Valley, starting at *Temuco*, and then moving on to *Victoria*. As he progressed up the valley he began to hear about a *Pehuenche* **machi** who lived further up the valley and who knew a lot about the local plant remedies. She and her husband were rather unusual as her father was a French man who came to the valley in the early 1920s and married a local girl who was viewed as a princess within the local *Pehuenche* tribe.

The family was better off financially than most in the valley and they had never moved away. There were stories about the grandfather who had come from France broken by the First World War, and how he had come to marry into the family. There were now a son and daughter who helped their parents as well. The family spent much of their time searching out and recording local Chilean folklore music, and the wife was especially knowledgeable about medicinal plant remedies.

Several individuals told him to be sure to stop and see these people, but also to be careful of the daughter as she was very protective of her parents and was kind of mean to strangers and especially to people she didn't like.

CHAPTER 15
Lonquimay Valley – October, 1972

"Soy una chispa de fuego:" (I am a spark of fire.)
– Song verse from Chilean folklore.

So, it was with some trepidation that Robert stopped at the driveway to the *González's* house on that bright, early spring day in October. He read the sign on the post that read, "***Lawentu chefe***", and on the second line, Claudia G. He knew that ***Lawentu*** referred to someone who dispensed medicinal plant remedies. Also, the sign showed a symbol of the *Araucanian* flag. He went down the driveway, crossed a small stream, and then followed the road that wound around behind a rather large house that resembled a Swiss chalet. It appeared that the main entrance was in the rear of the house. He stepped out of his vehicle and was met by a little barking dog that didn't bite but had a menacing appearance. The rear door opened and a middle-aged man came out on the porch and cheerfully said, "*Buenos días*" (Good day).

Robert introduced himself and said he was collecting medicinal plants and would he know anyone in the area who knew a lot about these plants. The man said his name was *Juan*. His wife, *Claudia*, he said, was a ***machi*** in the local *Pehuenche* tribe and was very knowledgeable about medicinal plants. He called back through the open door and called, "*Claudia, hay un joven aquí que quiere aprender algo de las plantas medicinales. Creo que es el que hemos estado esperando.*" (*Claudia*, there is a young man here who wants to learn about medicinal plants. I think he is the one we have been expecting).

A middle-aged woman came out of the house wiping her hands with a towel. She did not appear quite as Robert expected. While most of the *Araucanians* that Robert had previously met in his travels tended to be rather short and stocky in build, and although *Pehuenches* tended to be somewhat taller, this woman was quite tall, thin, and with long, straight black hair. She was wearing modern clothing, which included a medium-length black skirt, a white blouse, a flashy necklace of silver and *lapis lazuli* gemstones, and large, matching earrings.

She extended her hand and smiled as she said in perfect English, "Hi, I'm *Claudia. Juan* says you are interested in medicinal plants. Come in, we were expecting you. We have been hearing stories about this crazy *gringo* combing southern Chile for medicinal plants. We were just going to have *herba mate* for *once*. Although we usually drink tea, at least once a day we also drink *mate* because it's good for digestion. Today we might even have a little *guarisnaque* to celebrate your arrival here." Robert wondered to himself, "What is *guarisnaque*?" Later that day he would learn that it was a very powerful rum beverage. And, did *Claudia* say that she and *Juan* were expecting him? How could that be? They must be a part of a pretty good grapevine communications system.

During the next very pleasant hour, which soon extended to several hours, *Juan* and *Claudia* told Robert about their recent tour in Europe playing Chilean folk music. They were going to tour less now that their daughter, *Rosa*, was studying at the University of Chile in *Santiago*. Their son *Miguel*, was now living in *Santiago* and working for *CORFO*, a government department responsible for developing economic programs.

Robert explained his work in more detail, what he was doing in his survey, and what his company hoped to do with the information he collected. During his explanations, Robert thought that *Claudia* seemed to be studying him, but he didn't want to embarrass her so every time he felt her gaze on him he would glance away and talk about some other detail of his work, addressing his attention to *Juan*.

In later years, Robert would remember that afternoon with great affection. First of all, he was impressed that he seemed to be a special guest. *Claudia* served them with her best china and a white muslin tablecloth (or *mantelito*) that she said had been in the family since the 1700s. Each place setting had a monogrammed muslin napkin, not a paper one. Robert also noticed that all the fruits and vegetables served were cut into pieces and served on the finest china. Nothing was served unpeeled or whole. He had first noticed this when he began moving through the south of Chile searching for medicinal plants. Even the poorest country folks had treated him like an honored guest.

As Robert sat there, he reflected on his journey so far in Chile and realized that each time he stopped and had a conversation with someone in the Chilean countryside about medicinal plant remedies, he would invariably be invited to someone's house for *once*, and he was always served as a special guest, deserving of the finest china, silverware, and linen napkin. Never before in his life had he been treated with such hospitality. He recalled some houses he had entered where the floor was hard-packed dirt and its occupants obviously poor, but the houses were always immaculately clean and the floor always recently swept. And he was always welcomed!

He wanted to collect plants in this area and asked them if he could set up his tent down by the *Naranjo* River a hundred meters or so away from their house. He would use it as a base from which to operate as he made his plant collections but not so close that his presence would be a bother to them. When he collected as much information and plants as he felt was sufficient for that area he would move on further up the valley and continue collections there.

Claudia and *Juan* seemed to be happy to have him camp on their land. They seemed to trust him from the start and he hoped that he would not give them cause to lose that trust. During the next few weeks, Robert was delighted with his work with *Claudia* and learned a great deal about medicinal plants and the remedies associated with them. *Claudia* explained some of her work as a **machi**.

She said that **machis** had certain unexplained powers but they were difficult to understand and use. One power that she had come to recognize was a certain ability to see into the future, but it was frustrating because there were never enough details and, so, she almost never recounted her premonitions to any one because neither she nor they would understand what the premonitions might mean. After some event had happened, though, the premonitions usually made perfect sense.

During the last week that Robert was there, camped with his little tent alongside the river, he heard a *Tur* bus drive up and stop at the turnoff road to the *González's* driveway. Their little dog ran toward the bus as a young lady stepped out, carrying a small travel bag. *"Chao Don Eduardo"* she said to the driver, and he replied, *"Chao Señorita, saludos a sus padres."* She walked up the road to the house, not too far from where he was preparing plants that he had collected that day. He had to stop and watch, and thought to himself, "Boy, she is good looking!"

Her aquiline facial features suggested Arabian or Moorish blood somewhere in her ancestry. She was dressed like a university student. It must be *Rosa! Claudia* had said that she was a student at the University of Chile in *Santiago*. It was very unusual for a country girl from such a remote location in Chile to be accepted as a student at such a prestigious university but *Juan* and *Claudia* had used their influence as nationally known folk singers to help her gain admission.

Robert returned to his work, removing pressed plants from his presses, labeling them, and packing them between pieces of cardboard for eventual shipment to the States. He was absorbed in his work and was startled when he heard a young girl's voice say in a rather accusatory tone in English say, "So, you are the *gringuito* who is stealing my mother's medicinal plant remedies? You should be ashamed of yourself. All you *gringos* seem to want to do is come to Chile and steal our resources! First it was bird guano, then copper, gold and silver, and now you come. Humph!"

A startled Robert looked up and was overwhelmed by her appearance and closeness. He had never seen such beautiful brown eyes! Her eyes had such depth that he thought he could look right into them and not see the bottom. All he could do in reaction was to blurt out, "God, you are beautiful!" But, she quickly recovered her advantage and replied, "I know, but you are not talking to God, you are talking to me." Then they both laughed and she extended her hand.

"My name is *Rosa*," she said, "and I guess you have heard of me. *Soy muy guapa! Ten cuidado gringuito!"* (I am very tough! Be careful little gringo!). "But, I guess I will have to accept you for a while as my mother seems to be infatuated with you. She wanted me to tell you to come up to the house and that you are invited for *once*."

Robert had enjoyed *once* at the *González's* house many times in the past several weeks but this one was even more enjoyable. *Rosa* explained her studies at the university. She was a freshman, majoring in economics, and her brother *Miguel* had been studying political science but had married, had two children, and was now working with *CORFO* in *Santiago*.

CORFO, or *Corporación de Fomento*, was a government agency responsible for developing economic programs or projects to assist the growth of the Chilean economy. *Miguel* loved his job and was active with some of his political friends, demonstrating for social justice and welfare. He was a great supporter of the new president, *Salvador Allende*. *Miguel* was a good friend of a university professor and famous folk singer named *Víctor Jara* who was also very active in campaigning for social justice.

What a wonderful family the *Gonzálezes* seemed to be! Before he left to return to his tent, they brought out their guitars, a harp, and sang a series of folklore songs. The singing went on for several hours, along with much drinking of wine.

When Robert got up to leave, he stumbled and almost fell to the floor. He had drunk more than he should have and was a little ashamed. *Rosa* offered to help him down to his tent and as he began to lie down on his sleeping bag he accidently, or perhaps not so accidently, touched her hip with his hand.

She gently removed it and said, *"Gringuito, no señor, tu eres muy simpático, pero yo soy intocable, especialmente por un gringo que quiere robarle a nuestra gente sus riquezas."* (No, Mr. *Gringo*, you are a nice guy, but I am untouchable, especially by a *gringo* who wants to rob our people of our plant health remedies!)

Then she laughed, pinched his now red cheek, and returned to the house. Robert slept like a log that night, thinking about not only about the parasitic *misodendrum* plants but also a little bit about *Rosa*. Now, Robert was a very shy young man and would have never made advances to a young lady, especially to one he barely knew. But, during the rest of his life, and especially during the next few years, he would often and fondly recall that day and realize with much satisfaction that on that day he fell in love with *Rosa González*.

Since the first time that Robert had seen *misodendrum* plants he had been fascinated by them. This was a group of parasitic flowering plants that existed by parasitizing branches of living *Nothofagus* trees. Their natural range is from just north of *Santiago* southward to *Tierra del Fuego* but only at a certain altitude in the Andean *cordillera*. They are found nowhere else in the world. These interesting parasites had evolved in their own small corner of the world in southern Chile and a part of southern Argentina.

When Robert asked *Claudia* about them she seemed a little troubled by his question and initially put him off without a detailed explanation. She said that the plants had some medicinal properties that she did not understand, but that her great grandmother had referred to them as very powerful for certain diseases, but she was reluctant to say much except that they could be very dangerous if not used carefully.

At any rate, Robert collected samples, pressed them, and preserved other tissue samples to send back to the States. The plants of *misodendrum* were very abundant at a certain altitudinal level on the slopes of the *Lonquimay* Volcano and rather rare at lower elevations. They were more abundant at lower altitudes farther south in Chile.

The family of Misodendraceae contains only one genus, and all species are shrubby branch parasites of higher plants, mostly *Nothofagus spp.* The subgenus *Angelopogon* contains four species and the subgenus *Misodendrum* contains seven species. Available evidence suggests that *Misodendrum* may represent the oldest extant genus from prehistoric time that had evolved the mistletoe habit. Most of the *Misodendrum* species have scale-like leaves or very abbreviated linear leaves. Those with scale-like leaves have stems that are usually a golden yellow in color and those with linear leaves are either golden or greenish-yellow in color.

Misodendrum flowers are not very visible until after they are fertilized. Then, each developing fruit produces three long, feathery appendages that grow to be as long as 10 cm or more in length. These appendages are very flexible and, when the seed is released, their increased friction with the air help the seed to be carried long distances by the wind. Then, they help the seed become attached to a susceptible branch by the wind that then also helps wrap the filament around the branch. In function they behave much as a spider's thread spun into the wind, eventually able to carry the weight of the spider some distance simply because of friction with the moving air.

Before seed dispersal, clusters of these long, feathery growths are highly visible from far away. This led early plant collectors to classify *misodendrum* plants as "the feathery mistletoes", *"Barba del Roble"* (Oak's beard) or *"Cabello de Angel"* (Angel's hair) and witches' brooms.

In the Central Valley of Chile and southward into Patagonia, the native vegetation, and even some introduced tree species, are often heavily infected with various species of mistletoes, in addition to the Misodendraceae. Indeed, the abundance and diversity of mistletoes is striking! Recent research suggests that the presence of mistletoes indicate a high degree of biodiversity mainly because of the increased leaf fall and subsequent decomposition that they incite. Some of the mistletoes have medicinal properties, according to *Mapuche* legend. This is probably due to their high alkaloid content. The common *muerdago*, or *quintral* (leafy mistletoe), that parasitizes *alamo* trees in the Central Valley, is said to be effective against cancer when applied by injection, as an infusion, or as drops, and especially when used in combination with *llantén* or *matico*. *Quintral* of *maqui*, also when mixed with *llantén* or *matico,* is effective in reducing cholesterol, thirst, and blood pressure. In the northern Central Valley, there is another fascinating mistletoe (*Tristerix aphyllus*) that infects cactus (*Tricocereus chilensis*). As with many of the leafy mistletoes found in Chile, it has beautiful yellow or red flowers and when in flower adds striking color to the landscape.

Marianne North, a landscape painter in Victorian England, visited southern Chile in 1882, searching for landscapes that contained the famous, and exotic, *araucarian* pine. During her trek to the region, she painted 32 oil paintings, some of which included native deciduous forests (the Valdivian forest type) that were heavily infested with various mistletoes. Some of these included *Nothofagus* species with the characteristic witches' brooms of *misodendrum*.

At the beginning of the Chilean winter in April of 1972, Robert returned for a brief visit to the States. He generally didn't work in the field in winter in the southern hemisphere, especially in southern Chile, because although the winters weren't all that cold, it rained and snowed a lot and camping in a tent could be very uncomfortable. So, he returned to the States to visit his parents and touch bases with scientists at Pharmtec to see how the work was going.

When Robert was a graduate student, he did his thesis research on a species of dwarf mistletoe that was parasitic on the Douglas-fir tree. Dwarf mistletoes are distant relatives of the *misodendra*. One finding of his research was that the dwarf mistletoe converted carbon dioxide in air, and the carbon in sugars derived from the host, to produce large volumes of lipids. He didn't know the significance of this but thought that the plant used fixation of carbon into the relatively inert lipid materials to help maintain a strong nutrient gradient from the host into the parasite. This inert lipid is then mobilized by the mistletoe plant as needed and converted into energy useful for flowering and fruiting.

Scientists at Pharmtec made some preliminary extractions of the *misodendrum* samples he had brought with him and found them to be rich in a certain kind of lipid known as essential oil. This was an interesting finding as many medicinal plants have essential oils as their effective medicinal component. They were going to need more samples and "would Robert please collect a lot more from where he got these, and also from different host species".

And, "oh by the way, his draft number was very high and it was certain that he would have to enter the military as soon he returned". His draft board told him that he would probably get a better deal if he enlisted as long as he returned by February.

Robert returned to the valley that summer in early September to the overture of much unrest in *Santiago*. Wealthier citizens were upset with the rise in food prices and there were public demonstrations almost every day against the *Allende* regime. Rumors were increasing that the military might force out *Allende* in some kind of coup.

Juan and *Claudia* were happy to see him again and *Rosa* was there as well, and not in school. The university had closed because of the almost daily student demonstrations. Again, she was not very happy to see him. *Miguel* had told her that the Nixon presidency was secretly sending money to Chile to help undermine *Allende's* attempts at installing Socialism in Chile. Nixon actually was sending money covertly to Chile to fund much of the social unrest and public demonstrations. Could this be true? Robert doubted it but didn't want to offend her so he said nothing. Many years later he would learn that this was, indeed, true.

Robert was getting ready to pack up his tent in preparation for his trip back to the States the next day. As he was concluding his packing he heard a sharp scream. He emerged from the tent and looked around. The screams were coming from the *Naranjo* River. This was spring and snowmelt had turned the river into a raging torrent, heading toward a much bigger river, the *Biobío*.

Rosa was running along the bank on the south side of the river and screaming, "*Mamá, Mamá*!" Robert jumped up without putting on his boots and ran over near to where she was screaming and shouted, "What's wrong?" She screamed, "*Mamá* was chasing some sheep near the riverbank and the bank collapsed and she fell in. The current is fast and she can't swim well!"

Their little dog, *Quinto*, had already jumped in and was swimming toward *Claudia*. Robert tore off his shirt and ran along the bank as the current bore *Claudia* along. He saw a mass of brush a little farther along and knew he had to reach her before she became entangled in the brush.

He jumped in headfirst and swam toward her. He didn't quite make it before *Claudia* was swept into the tree's branches. Her feet apparently became entangled in the submerged branches and the current pulled her under as the rushing water swept over her.

Robert knew that he would probably not be able to free her feet from the branches but he had to get her head above water or she would soon drown. As he came alongside the spot where she had disappeared, he groped under the water and grabbed her hair. He tried to pull her free and swim away, but all he could do was to hold her head above water and was barely able to hang onto both her and a tree branch.

He had never worked harder in his life as he held *Claudia's* face above the water with one hand and with his other hand, held onto branches to keep from being swept away. The swift current continuously splashed waves over his head and he was not able to see what *Rosa* was doing. And he was quickly becoming hypothermic! *Claudia* was struggling to help him keep her head above the water. He suspected that she was also becoming hypothermic but she was still pretty actively trying to stay alive.

After what seemed like an eternity, and as he began to lose consciousness, he sensed several hands helping him to hold onto *Claudia*. Out of the corner of his eye he saw a man backing a yoke of oxen down the bank and toward the tree. Soon, other pairs of hands were hooking a logging chain to the tree. Years later, Robert recalled very few further details of that day, but for some unknown reason, he never forgot the names of the two oxen as their master urged them to pull, *"Hia, Pajarito, hia Flor!"* (Get going Little Bird, get going Flower!)

As the oxen walked away, they easily pulled the tree out of the water and both *Claudia* and Robert collapsed onto the bank. *Claudia* was immediately wrapped in a blanket and *Rosa* broke down in tears as she hugged her mother. *Rosa* cradled her mother in her arms and sobbed, "*Mamá*, are you okay?" *Claudia* choked a little but soon started breathing more easily and she and *Claudia* began to cry, now out of joy and not out of fear. She choked again and said, "I thought I was going to drown. Robert saved me." And then she looked at *Rosa* as she continued, "What a gentleman he is. Thank you, Robert." But Robert didn't feel too good. He was chilled to the bone, nauseous, and had a terrific headache.

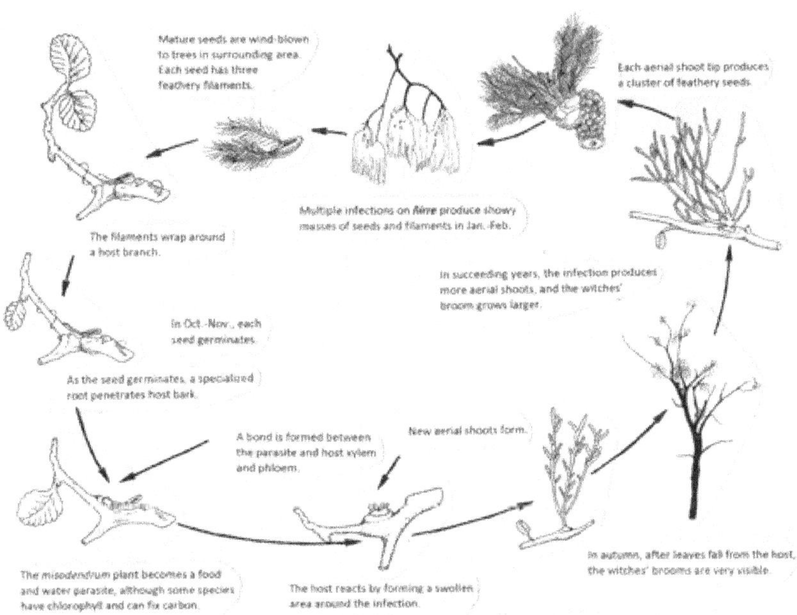

Disease diagram of *misodendrum (Misodendrum punctulatum)* infection on **ñirre** *(Nothofagus antarctica).*

CHAPTER 16
Rosa

"Love of my life, *eres tú, eres tú.*"
(It is you, it is you.) – Verses from "Touch the Wind", the English version of the
popular Latin American song *"Eres tú, eres tú."*

Later that day, Robert developed a fever and felt quite ill. He obviously could not stay alone in his tent. He had probably contracted flu or pneumonia when his body was weakened by hypothermia in the cold water. The *González's* insisted that he remain with them and he was ushered into a spare bedroom. During that night he became delirious.

When he awoke the next morning, the fever was gone and he was aware that *Claudia* and *Rosa* were sitting on either side of the bed. *Claudia* said she had given him an effusion of **Palqui** and that was what had broken the fever. Robert was interested in the plant since he had not yet collected it. He rapidly recovered from his illness that day and he had the name of another medicinal plant to add to his list. And this was one that was actually used on him, so he could speak from experience.

There was a lot of laughter that night at supper. Robert had never felt so satisfied with his life. He was an honored guest for that meal, and a lot of neighbors attended as well, each bringing a little something to eat or drink. He was supposed to leave the next morning but *Claudia* suggested that he stay a day or two longer and that he and *Rosa* should visit the sacred *Araucaria* pine grove on their land up behind the mountain in back of the house. There were some other *misodendrum* species there that he might like to collect. There were very interesting infections on *canelo*, a small tree species that was now a very rarely encountered host of *misodendrum*.

So, early the next morning, *Claudia* helped Robert saddle his horse. They stopped by the house and picked up the lunch that *Claudia* had prepared. They rode their horses up a trail on the mountain in back of the house and crossed to a valley beyond another mountain. As they trotted along the mountain trail, the absence of the little dog tugged at their hearts; he had become entangled in the brush and drowned while Robert was trying to rescue *Claudia*.

As they rode up the trail to the top of the first mountain, Robert was overjoyed to see the expanse of the virgin, old-growth *Araucaria* pine forest and to be riding among many large trees, most hundreds of years old, and others thousands of years old. What treasures! But, several mountains to the south this forest was under attack by a large consortium from *Santiago* that was trying to confiscate the land and then harvest the trees. Dropping into the second valley, he found *misodendrum* plants on some of the understory shrubs that were not the usual hosts such as the *Nothofagus* trees that he had collected from before. *Rosa* said that this area was a relic from past glaciation and there were many plant species here that today only occurred much farther to the south. This was the area that *Claudia* had mentioned.

Rosa took Robert to the small grove of *canelo* trees that were considered sacred by the *Araucanian* Indians. Robert was thrilled to find several *canelo* trees infected with *misodendrum*. This was specifically *Misodendrum brachystachium*, which had linear, leather-like green leaves. He had never seen any *misodendrum* on *canelo* before. He collected a few leaves and placed them in his plant press, being careful to not disturb the *misodendrum* stem itself and the infection site. He realized that this find was a great treasure and began to consider what he might do to propagate both host and parasite and increase their geographic ranges.

Claudia had prepared a delicious basket lunch and *Rosa* was on her best behavior. She was thrilled to see Robert's reaction to the *misodendrum* parasitizing *canelo*. Robert thought that *Rosa* was actually being quite nice to him and for once she seemed to enjoy being with him. What happened next is something that Robert would recall many times during the rest of his life. Aspects of this memory would keep him alive during the next year when he was in Vietnam.

He probably had a little too much to drink and before he realized it, his eyes began to droop and he could not stop himself from falling asleep. As he fell asleep, he thought he saw *Rosa* watching him. Robert suddenly awoke, but could not move. He could open his eyes but could barely move his legs or arms. He said, "*Rosa*, what the hell is going on? Did you drug me? What is happening to me?" *Rosa* laughed and said, "So, the *gringuito* is awake, huh?"

She came over to where he was lying, very deliberately kneeled down, and taking his face between her hands, kissed him full on the lips. Now, Robert was not exactly a ladies' man but he had kissed a few girls when he was in college although he had never seriously dated anyone. This was a kiss like none he had ever experienced before! She had kissed him full on the lips and when their lips met it seemed as though she drew something from his being. She caressed his face and kissed him again.

Then she smiled at him again, unbuckled his belt and began sliding his pants down his legs. As she did so she continued to smile at him. She slid off his socks and underwear. As she removed his underwear he saw what he had realized as he awakened, that he had the largest, hardest erection that he had ever had in his life. What had she given him? Was it in the wine? And he couldn't move or do anything, except watch her. Why was she doing this? Was she crazy? She carefully folded his pants and shorts and laid them on the blanket next to their lunch basket.

She then dropped down to her hands and knees crawled toward him, all the while looking into his eyes. He would never forget those flashing brown eyes, those eyes that had a depth you could see into. She said, "*Roberto*, I love my parents more than anything in this world, I especially love my mother as only a daughter can love her mother. I almost lost her yesterday and you gave her back to me. You are a fine young man but you are very shy. Since I will probably never see you again, I want to share with you something that is precious to me."

She then slowly slipped off her riding britches and carefully folded them and placed them on the blanket next to his folded clothes. She removed her panties and lifted her shirt, holding it up around her hips. As she lifted her legs to straddle him he saw that she was as excited as he was. He thought, "What in the hell is going on here?"

She gently positioned herself over him. He detected a faint musky scent as she lowered herself onto his penis, letting him slide in all the way, and then moving gently up and down. He had an orgasm almost immediately, certainly faster than he wanted and as he passed out again he heard her say, "*Roberto*, I am giving you a part of me, and this is my gift to you for giving me back my mother. I have behaved rather badly to you, and this is the least I can do to make amends. Thank you, *Roberto*, for giving me back my mother. She is the most precious thing I have in my life."

The rest of the afternoon passed too quickly for the both of them. Robert soon regained his ability to move and they made love again twice more until finally Robert was so tired that he could hardly move. At several times he wanted to tell *Rosa* that he loved her, but then he remembered all that had happened that day and before and he forced it out of his mind.

Later, in Viet Nam, he would regret that decision. Besides, at that time he wasn't yet sure that he really loved her. Maybe he would say something later. *Rosa* seemed to be not at all tired and when Robert mentioned the fact, she laughed and said, "Someday I will be a **machi,** and they have many unusual talents."

"Speaking of unusual talents, what was that drug that you gave me?" He asked. "I have never heard of such a thing and it was so powerful."

She replied, "Dear *Roberto*, there are many things that you do not yet know about medicinal plants. **Palwe** is a rarely known and rarely used plant that greatly increases sexual desire. You know that it is not used much in Chile because it is not necessary. We Chileans don't need it." Robert thought about that for a while and made a mental note to find out more about **Palwe**. *Rosa* said no more about it but winked at him as he thought about what she had said just now.

They talked a great deal about almost everything that afternoon. Robert had already told her about the draft and that if he enlisted he might get a less dangerous assignment. For the rest of his life Robert would regret that decision. *Rosa* suggested that he stay in Chile and not enter the military service. But, he said he had to go and that he would be back as soon as he could after his year of service. At any rate, she was going to return to the university and hoped that the demonstrations supporting *Allende* had stopped so that classes could begin again. She said that her mother was afraid of what was going to happen in Chile, for *Juan*, and for her, and for *Miguel*.

CHAPTER 17
Folk Singing – 1940s to 1960s

"Levántate Huenchullán:" (Rise *Huenchullán*
– one of the *Mapuche* heros from the time of the Spanish conquest.)
– Verse from the protest song *"Arauco tiene una pena"* composed by *Violeta Parra*

During the night flight back to the States, Robert had a series of persistent dreams, about *Rosa* of course, and what had happened that day before he left, but the music that *Juan* and *Claudia* had introduced him to kept pounding in his head. It was such a rich experience that he could not stop from remembering song titles and verses, in a cacophony of musical vibrations. It was obvious that both *Claudia* and *Juan* had an instinctive love of music, especially that of their native Chile. Chileans are by nature a happy people. Although many are rather poor financially, they typically are wonderfully circumspect of their socio/financial condition and seek humor wherever they can find it, regardless of their social or economic positions, and much of that humor comes out in the form of songs.

During Robert's many visits to their home, the *González's* had shared their love of folklore music with him, explaining the history and purpose of every song. They knew all the current folk singers and sometimes one or more of these would pass by their house and much singing would result. There were many singing groups during the 1960s and 70s. The more popular ones included: *El Conjunto Cuncumén, El Conjunto Millaray, Las Cuatro Brujas, Los Cuatro Cuartos, Los de Ramón, Los Huasos Quincheros, Las Jaivas*, and *Las Conejitas* (for children's songs). And there were many more.

Juan and *Claudia* explained to Robert that there are basically three groupings of Chilean folklore music: (1) music from *Santiago*, the capital, and other cities, that has a distinctive quality and might include both wealthy and poor people; (2) music from the countryside, which mainly includes people who were born and lived in the country, most of whom are poor or, at the least, live lives filled with hardship; and (3) music of the native aborigines, the *Araucanian* (*Mapuche*) Indians, who had lived on the land which is now Chile at least 14,000 years before the arrival of Europeans. To a smaller extent, this group also includes music of Rapa-Nui, Easter Island, which was annexed by Chile in the mid-1800s. When a *Mapuche* sings, his or her voice exposes all the dark past of the past several centuries that their people have experienced. All their songs are monotonous and sad, and the topic is always about suffering.

Chilean folklore music was generally music of the common people, mostly written by and for people of the *campo*, or countryside. They celebrated the social life of families, such as in *"Mi abuela bailó sirilla"*, or a wedding, *"El casorio"*. They describe the happy time of courtship such as in *"Poema 20 de Pablo Neruda"*, *"Ojitos de agua dulce"*, *"Ende que te vi"*, or *"Niña de cara morena"*.

Romance plays a large part in Chilean folklore. A young man's first love is described in *"Ende que te vi"*. *"Qué bonita va"* describes the beauty of a young girl. With you I will go, in *"Contigo me voy"*.

More sadness was expressed in songs such as a reflection on the unmarried pregnant daughter in *"Huija"*, or just to generally suffer in *"Sufrir"*, the lonely man in *"El solitario"*, sadness of the soul in *"Qué pena siente el alma"*. Loneliness in general is covered in *"Camino de soledad"* and love and sorrow in *"Una pena y un cariño"*.

"El huaso ladino" is about an honest cowboy. *"Mocosita"* is about a young girl who abandons a man who loves her. *"Pa' mar adentro"* is about the life of fishermen. A martyr is lamented in *"El martirio"*. A couple of good buddies are celebrated in *"Los compadres paleteados"*. Revenge is described in *"El guatón Loyola"* in which a bully is trapped under a table in a bar and punched by all of his so-called friends in payment for being such a bully.

Chilean folklore also recognizes the importance that material things like tools play in the lives of country folk. Examples are: a wool cap in *"El gorro de lana"*, a red rose in *"Rosa colorada"*, large pots in *"Cantarito de Peñaflor"*, a white tablecloth in *"Mantelito blanco"*, a three-colored poncho in *"Manta de tres colores"*, silver spurs in *"Espuelas de plata"*, a foot path in *"Senderito"*, or a small adobe house surrounded by cat-tail plants in *"Ranchito de totora"*. *"Aradito de palo"* recognizes the importance of this essential tool, a wooden plow, in the life of a farmer. A tool from which to drink *mate* can be either a simple gourd or a much fancier affair. In *"Matecito de plata"*, an elaborate, silver-adorned gourd that the family used long ago is remembered, and lamented with great nostalgia by the person who wrote the words many years ago.

Chileans are extremely nationalistic and remember their history with great affection, such as songs of the War in the Pacific in 1879-1883 in *"Batallones olvidados"*, old battle flags in *Los viejos estandartes"*, or a female Chilean spy living in Peru in *"Romance de Leonora Latorre"*. The cavalry, again probably reminiscent of the War of the Pacific, is celebrated in *"Canción de la caballería"*.

There are happy times too, though, such as in *"Santiago está de fiesta"*, or the *cueca*, a popular country dance, in *"Apología de la cueca"*, or if you are going to Chile, in *"Si vas para Chile"*.

Some songs are simply silly, such as *"La rana"*, in which the adventures of a frog are elaborated upon. *"El Diablo se fue a bañar"* describes the adventures of the devil when he finally meets his match in the singer's mother-in-law.

A young man remembers, with fondness, the priest in the little village where he grew up, in *"Cura de mi pueblo"*. Another man remembers the fondness he had felt when working with wood, in *"Tallando"*. A young man recalls the thrill he felt every time a young girl showed her petticoat, in *"La enagüita"*. Another young woman admits that she is in love with the sacristan, the young man who assists the priest, in *"El sacristan"*.

Chilean folklore can also be quite sad and nostalgic, such as in *"Mi viejo"* or *"Porque tengo pena"* or love and hate, in *"Una pena y un cariño"* or sadness of the soul, in *"Qué pena siente el alma"*.

A particularly sad song is *"El corralero"* in which a worker at a ranch is told by his foreman to take the old horse out to the field and cut its throat because it is old and has outlived its usefulness. The singer laments his task and recalls that the horse worked so hard during its life and actually had been the most intelligent of all the horses on the ranch. As he goes to the shed to get the machete, the horse follows him and nuzzles him as he sharpens the knife. The man then realizes that he cannot kill the horse.

Instead, he decides that he will take care of it until the horse dies of old age.

Juan and *Claudia* began to sing to the public in 1963 at a music festival in *Viña del Mar*. They called themselves *"Los de Juan"*, perhaps not very original, but two other family groups, *Los de Ramón* and the *Conjunto Cuncumén*, had become very popular singing Chilean folklore music, and so they thought, why not. They were a family group too. When they were only small children, *Miguel* and *Rosa* danced the *cueca* while their parents played various country songs. Later the children would play instruments with their parents as a family group.

Although the family started their music career playing all popular Chilean songs, they began to focus first on old songs of the *Araucanian* Indians, and then on the songs expressing the social unrest that had begun to surge across the working class in Chile. In one important aspect the theme of both types of music was identical, a cry from an oppressed and down-trodden group of citizens. As they joined voices and hearts with other popular contemporary musicians such as *Violeta Parra* and *Víctor Jara*, their outcry began to be heard.

In 1969, they made an extensive tour of Chile, Argentina, and Peru. In 1970, they toured Brazil, and later that year, they toured Spain, France, and the Netherlands. In 1972, they returned to Paris where they gave a recital in the Olympia Theater, and then continued on a 60-day tour of Belgium, Germany, Spain, France, and the Soviet Union. In early 1973 they returned to Chile and to their home in *Lonquimay* to recuperate and to begin to make record albums of the songs they had collected.

There was always an abundance of poor people in Chile. They survived by living in an almost medieval top-down economy, doing menial work for relatively poor salaries or wages. World War Two resulted in a lot of money going into the world economy and some reached the Chilean economy. But by the early 1960s this stimulus was losing steam. The population had grown and the feeling was that wealthy people were doing well but the majority was not doing so well.

The new president, *Eduardo Frei Montalva*, embraced the Alliance for Progress championed by U. S. President John F. Kennedy. But *Frei* made some big mistakes by confiscating some productive farmlands from hard-working owners and then parceling them out to the poor, many of whom either did not know how to farm or were simply lazy. These actions began to alienate the wealthy. Perhaps this was also partially a result of widespread use of the radio and television as more people could see and hear how well other people were doing. A growing demand arose in Chile that poor people deserved a life with more quality in it, and their voices clamored louder than did those of the wealthy. A call for socialism thus arose in Chile. Vocal critics called it Communism and this triggered even more intolerance from the upper classes. Folk singers were quick to come to the aid of the poor and disenfranchised.

Although several singers began to retrieve and collect the old country songs, which became known as folklore, only one had a true passion for the poor and the misery of the lives in which they were entrapped. That person was *Violeta Parra.*

Born in 1917 as *Violeta del Carmen Parra Sandoval*, she eventually followed the legend of her father, an important folklorist in the region of *Ñuble*. *Violeta* had eight brothers and two half-brothers. When she was still young her father lost his job. Her mother had to maintain the family by doing anything she could, such as washing and mending clothes, and selling and buying what she could to help her family survive. The children also did what they could and began singing for their friends and charging admission. They sang in trains, restaurants and anyplace where people were gathered, going as far as *Chillán* and *Parral*.

At age twelve, *Violeta* composed her first songs and sang and accompanied them on the guitar. At age 20 she went to *Santiago* and continued her hard life there, singing in small bars, circuses, theaters, on the radio, and wherever she could find an audience. Although it was a difficult life, she began to take an interest in Chilean country music.

Her big chance came in 1953 when she sang a recital in the house of *Pablo Neruda*. *Radio Chilena* was impressed with her performance and commisioned her to collect Chilean folklore music. She spent the next year traveling the length of Chile seeking out local folklore music and recording it for posterity. In 1954, she was awarded the *Caupolicán* Prize as folklorist of the year.

As a consequence, she was invited to Poland and the Soviet Union and lived for two years in Paris. When she returned she lived in *Concepción* and *Santiago*, singing and recording her songs. She also began to paint and weave and traveled again to Europe and other countries to exhibit her songs and artwork.

Several other folk singers had also begun to address the challenge of poverty in Chile. But, *Violeta Parra* was a person coping with personal problems, having had two marriages and a lost love, but also bursting with compassion for the common people, especially the poor, and this probably made her music more poignant.

The earlier songs of *Violeta Parra* represent perhaps the most melancholic of all Chilean music, even those sung by native Chileans, lamenting the loss of the past and their land. Two songs which represent *Violata Parra's* sadness are "What have I gained by loving you?" in (*"Qué he sacado con quererte"*), representing her loss of a lover who apparently did her wrong, and *"Veintiuno son los dolores"* in which she claims that she feels 21 hurts from a broken love affair.

Violeta was by her nature a sad person, and probably suffering from bi-polar disorder. The songs she created represent her moments of brilliantness, inspired by interludes of deep despair. On February 5, 1967, during one of these desperate moments, she committed suicide at the age of 50.

Violeta had been quick to recognize the growing dissatisfaction in her beloved Chile during the 1960s. She produced a number of melancholy songs reflecting the state of the common people and their growing dissatisfaction with that condition. Perhaps the song which best describes this recognition is *"La carta."*

Me mandaron una carta
They sent me a letter
por el correo temprano,
by early mail,
en esa carta me dicen
in this letter I'm told,
que cayó preso mi hermano,
that my brother is in jail,
y sin compassión, con grillos,
and, shackled, without compassion,
por la calle lo arrastraron, si.
they dragged him down the street, yes.
La carta dice el motivo
The letter says that the motive

de haber cometido Roberto
for the arrest of Robert
haber apoyado el paro
was that he supported the strike
que ya se había resuelto.
that since had been resolved,
Si acaso esto es un motivo
In case that this is the motive
presa voy tambien, sargento, si.
then I will go to jail, sargent, yes.
Yo que me encuentro tan lejos
I am so far away
esperando una noticia,
waiting for news,
me viene a decir la carta
this letter arrives and tells me
que en mi patria no hay justicia,
that in my country there is no justice,
los hambrientos piden pan,
the hungry ask for bread,
plomo les da la milicia, si.
the military responds with lead, yes.
De esta manera pomposa
In this pompous manner
quieren conservar su asiento
they want to keep their position
los de abanico y de frac,
those who use fans and wear fancy coats,
sin tener merecimiento, si.
without deserving them, yes.
Habráse visto insolencia,
Have you ever seen such insolence,
barbarie y alevosía,
barbarity and treachery,
de presentar el Trabuco
to present the blunderbuss
y matar a sangre fría
and kill in cold blood
a quien defensa no tiene
people who are powerless
con las dos manos vacias, si.
with both hands empty, yes.

La carta que he recibido
The letter I received
me pide contestación,
requests an answer, *yo pido que se propale*
I ask that they divulge
por toda la población,
for all the population,
que el {León} es un sanguinario
that the {lion} is blood thirsty (nickname of the then President
Alessandri)
en toda generación, si.
in each generation, yes.
Por suerte tengo guitarra
Luckily, I have a guitar
para llorar mi dolor,
to cry away my sorrow,
también tengo nueve hermanos
I also have nine brothers
fuera del que se engrilló,
besides the one who is in jail,
los nueve son comunistas
the nine are Communists
con el favor de mi Dios, si.
by God's favor, yes.

This is a terribly sad, and even bitter, song, but it is probably not the one by which we should remember *Violeta Parra*. Perhaps one should, rather, pay tribute to one of the brightest products of her tormented life, the song, *"Gracias a la vida"*, and which seems to run counter to her sadness. It is a song of hope and extreme happiness as the singer expresses her gratefulness for the blessings she has enjoyed in her life.

"Gracias a la vida, que me ha dado tanto
Thanks to life, that has given me so much
Me dio dos luceros, que cuando los abro
It has given me two eyes, that when I open them
Perfecto distingo lo negro del blanco
I clearly distinguish black from white
Y en el alto cielo, su fondo estrellado
And I can see the high sky with its starry depths

Y en las multitudes, el hombre que yo amo
And among many people, I see the one I love
Gracias a la vida, que me ha dado tanto
Thanks for life, that has given me so much
Con él las palabras que pienso y declaro
And with it the words I think and state
Madre, amigo, hermano, y luz alumbrando
Father, friend, brother, and light shining on
La ruta del alma del que estoy amando
The road of the soul of the one I love
Gracias a la vida, que me ha dado tanto
Thanks to life, that has given me so much
Me dio el corazón, que agita su marco
Life gave me a heart that trembles within its constraints
Cuando miro el fruto del cerebro humano
When I observe the fruits of the human brain
Cuando miro el bueno tan lejos del malo
When I observe the good so far from the bad
Cuando miro el fondo de sus ojos claros
When I observe the depth of your clear eyes
Gracias a la vida, que me ha dado tanto
Thanks to life, that has given me so much
Me ha dado la risa y me ha dado el llanto
Life has given me laughter and it has given me tears
Así yo distingo dicha de quebranto
Thus I can distinguish happiness from sadness
Los dos materiales que forman mi canto
The two substances that make up my song
El canto de ustedes, que es el mismo canto
Your song, that is the same song
El canto de todos, que es mi propio canto
The song of everyone, that is my own song
Gracias a la vida
Thanks for life
Gracias a la vida"
Thanks for life

After a lifetime of sadness and many sad songs, perhaps this song of joy is the one song by which we should remember *Violeta Parra*.

A large portion of Chilean folklore songs has always reflected a brutal reality of the hardships of life for the common and, especially, poor people.

A whole new sense of grief and despair was reflected in Chilean folklore just a few years before the military coup in 1973. As President *Allende* struggled to socialize his political agenda, much resistance was stimulated by the wealthy. The United States encouraged public unrest in Chile by funding and encouraging demonstrations. This caused economic hardship for business owners and they, in turn, demanded that the police control this civil unrest, which they were unable to do.

Both sides committed violence. Critics began to be killed, or simply disappear. New songs reflected this violence, sometimes in subtle ways. An example is given in *"Arriba en la cordillera"* when a disappeared father's body is found up in the mountains with two bullets in his chest, a metaphorical reference to the thousands of people who began to disappear after the coup began in the following decade.

On September 11, 1973, another folk singer and champion of human rights, *Víctor Jara*, was informed as to what was happening in downtown *Santiago*. He rushed to the State Technical University where he worked as a teacher. He joined a group of students in a show of solidarity against the ongoing coup. They remained in demonstration all night. The next day the university was assaulted by military forces, many students were shot outright, and *Víctor Jara* was taken prisoner. He and many surviving students were taken to the National Soccer Stadium and detained as political dissidents.

Rumors had it that he was tortured and taunted by his captors, his hands were smashed, and eventually chopped off, but apparently not all of that was true. But he was taunted to play the guitar with his now-injured hands. He would not, or could not, cooperate with them and one of his captors then shot him in the head. His body was found on September 18 by his wife, one among many in a pile of cadavers. Someone counted 44 bullet holes in his body.

Víctor Jara was a genius as a writer of protest songs, and his songs subtly, and not so subtly, reflect his dissatisfaction with the worsening economic situation in Chile. It is less subtly elaborated on in a medley of songs written and sung by him, such as: *"La canción del martillo"*, *"El aparecido y el soldado"*, *"¿Quien mató a Carmencita?"*, *"Ni chichi ni limoná"* and many, many more.

A classic protest song of *Víctor Jara* was *"Movil-Oil Special"*.

Los estudiantes chilenos
The Chilean students
y latinoamericanos
and Latin American students
se tomaron de la mano
took each other by the hand
mata tire tirun dín.
A pun on *Mandan dirun dirun dán* in children's nursery songs but it actually
says Kill, shoot, shootie.

En este hermoso jardín
In this beautiful garden
a momios y dinosaurios
to extreme right wingers and reactionaries
los jóvenes revolucionarios
those young revolutionaries
han dicho BASTA – Por fin-.
have said ENOUGH – Finally.
Que viene el guanaco (Movil-oil Special)
There comes the water cannon truck
y detrás los pacos (Movil-oil Special)
and behind the police
la bomba delante (Movil-oil Special)
the tear gas in front
la paralizante (Movil-oil Special)
the paralyzing bomb
también la purgante (Movil-oil Special)
and also the laxative bomb *y la hilarante (Movil-oil Special)* and the laughing
gas bomb
ay, que son cargantes (Movil-oil Special)
oh, they are so tiresome
estos vigilantes (Movil-oil Special)
these policemen
el joven secundario (Movil-oil Special)
the secondary student
y el universitario (Movil-oil Special)
and the university student
con el proletario (Movil-oil Special)
with the proletariat
quieren revolución.
they want revolution.

En la Universidad
In the University
se lucha por la reforma
they fight for reform
para poner en la horma
to hold back
al beato y al nacional.
sanctimonious and chauvinistic people.
Somos los reformistas
We are the reformers
los revolucionarios
the revolutionaries
los anti-imperialistas
the anti-imperialists
de la Universidad.
of the University.

After hearing this song, and its message, there is little doubt as to what the military *junta* thought about *Víctor Jara.*

But, as with *Violeta Parra,* there are many other beautiful songs by which we should remember *Víctor Jara.* Said to be one of the most beautiful in Latin America is: *Te Recuerdo Amanda.*

Te recuerdo Amanda
(I remember you Amanda)
la calle mojada
(the wet street)
corriendo a la fábrica
(running to the factory)
donde trabajaba Manuel.
(where Manuel worked).
La sonrisa ancha
(The broad smile)
la lluvia en el pelo
(the rain in your hair)
no importaba nada
(with nothing else on your mind)
ibas a encontrarte con él
(you were going to be with him)
con él, con él....
(with him, with him...)

Con él
(With him)
son cinco minutos
(only five minutes)
la vida es eterna
(life is eternal)
en cinco minutos
(in five minutes)
suena la sirena
(the siren wails)
de vuelta al trabajo
(in returning to work)
y tu caminando
(and you walking)
lo iluminas todo
(you illuminate all)
los cinco minutos
(those five minutes)
te hacen florecer.
(make you bloom like a flower).
Te recuerdo Amanda
(I remember you Amanda)
la calle mojada
(the wet street)
corriendo a la fábrica
(running to the factory)
donde trabajaba Manuel.
(where Manuel workied).
Con él
(With him)
que partió a la sierra
(who took to the mountains)
que nunca hizo daño
(who never hurt anyone)
que partió a la sierra
(who took to the mountains)
y en cinco minutos
(and in five minutes)
quedó destrozado
(was wiped out)
suena la sirena
(the siren wails)

de vuelta al trabajo
(in returning to work)
muchos no volvieron
(many never returned)
tampoco… Manuel
(neither did…Manuel).
Te recuerdo Amanda
(I remember you Amanda)
corriendo a la fábrica
(running to the factory)
donde trabajaba Manuel.
(where Manuel worked).

Every time that Robert had visited *Juan* and *Claudia*, he marveled at how a country as small as Chile and with a relatively small population, could produce such a rich variety and quality of folklore music. Social injustice had, almost overnight, yielded a series of stinging political songs that the powerful in the United States and Chile could not ignore. As his plane touched down at Miami airport, he realized that tears had been running down his cheeks for quite some time. He hoped that he could get back soon to Chile. He realized that there was an ache in his heart for *Rosa*!

CHAPTER 18
A Dark Day – January, 1974

"Por la razón o la fuerza:" (By reason or by force.)
– Part of the Chilean national anthem since 1812.

osa and her mother rose early that day. *Paulina* was still asleep in her crib. *Rosa's* mother quickly packed a lunch for *Rosa* and they both went out into the barn to fill a bag with oats for the horse. They said *"Chao,"* and *Rosa* started the long ride up into the mountains to see how the sheep were doing on the new summer forage.

Quinto wanted to come along but *Rosa* sent her back as she began to canter up the trail. This was the dog that *Roberto* had given her mother on that last day as he left the valley almost a year ago, and she had to admit that she missed him, even with his strange habits and customs. She laughed to herself and wondered if *Roberto* suspected that he had a daughter in Chile. *Quinto* sat there for a while and watched her go. Then, as she returned to the house, she saw the cars coming down the valley road.

The train of three cars, two black sedans and a military vehicle, turned off the main valley road and stopped at the turnoff to the *González* farm. After a few minutes, the military vehicle turned to the side by the gate, stopped, and three men got out. The other two cars drove up the side road and right up the main road to the main entrance at the back of the house. It was barely dawn and still rather chilly for a summer day. As two men got out of each car *Quinto* began to bark, growing more agitated the closer they got. The men walked toward the house, removing small machine guns from under their coats.

Inside the house, *Juan* and *Claudia* arose, glanced out of their upstairs window, and quickly donned their robes. *Juan* then said, "*Mi amor*, I think our destiny has arrived!" *Claudia* responded, "Stall them while I hide *Paulina*. I love you." Then she kissed him and took *Paulina* out of her crib and went toward the closet.

The men arrived at the house. One man shot the barking *Quinto* and went around to the front of the house. The other men stepped up to the main entrance at the back porch as the door opened. *Juan* stepped outside and exclaimed, "*¡Por Dios!* What is happening?" Then he saw *Quinto* thrashing around on the ground and yelping. "What do you want?" he asked, fear filling his voice. One of the men said, "We are here to put an end to your subversive socialist music." With that he shot *Juan*, spraying him across his chest with a half-dozen shots. *Juan* fell backward as if a mighty tree had fallen and hit the porch floor with a loud crash.

The two men burst into the house, shouting and turning over furniture. *Claudia* came down the stairs and screamed. One man shouted, "*¡Puta desgraciada, muere subversive!*" (Disgraceful whore, die you subversive!) They shot her in several sprays of bullets. The men left the bodies where they had fallen then collected guitars and other musical instruments and some furniture and piled the pieces and a few papers and rugs in the middle of the downstairs front room. They threw a kerosene lamp onto the pile and tried to start a fire, but at first it only smoldered with few flames.

One man shouted, "I see lights at the next ranch, I think someone is coming." Then they left in a roar of squealing tires and flying dirt. By the time the two sedans arrived at the turnoff, the military vehicle had already fled and was speeding down the road toward *Curacautín*.

Only halfway up the mountain road, *Rosa* barely heard the first staccato bursts of gunfire and could not imagine what they might mean.

Then she felt a dark premonition and galloped back down the trail. As she rounded the last curve above the house, she saw three cars just leaving the turnoff to their road and turning onto the main road. She could not imagine what could have happened.

Then she saw smoke billowing up from the front side of the house. As she galloped closer, she saw *Quinto* thrashing around on the ground and yelping as if in great pain. Then she felt more than saw her father lying on the porch. She ran up to him but he was dead. "*¡Mamá!*" she cried and ran into the smoke-filled house. The pile of debris in the middle of the room was just starting to burn fiercely but she quickly pulled at the rug under the blazing mass and dragged most of the fire out into the yard.

She ran back into the house and through the smoke she could see her mother lying on the floor in a growing pool of blood. From the magnitude of the wounds and the number of bullet holes she knew that she could do nothing for her. "*¡Paulina! ¡Paulina!* Where are you?" *Rosa* stepped over her mother's body and ran upstairs into the bedroom. The baby crib was empty! *"Paulina, Paulina! ¿Dónde estás?"* Her quick scan over the room revealed nothing. She looked in the closet – nothing! Then she looked under the bed and saw *Paulina's* little hands wriggling above her blanket. *Rosa* pulled her out and could see no injury. She held the baby close to her chest, and cried, "What will we do now, *Paulinita*?"

Her parents had heard rumors that the Pinochet regime did not like the old Chilean folk music and tried to discourage people from singing or listening to it. Had they done this? What insanity! She thought as tears filled her eyes and she sat down hard on the floor. She didn't know how long she sat there but she slowly became aware of *Quinto's* yelping in the yard.

She held *Paulina* close to her and went out to see *Quinto*. Although she was in obvious pain, her tail wagged when she saw *Rosa*. She had chewed off the rest of her injured leg and was licking the stump. *Rosa* knelt beside her and saw her hind leg lying on the ground. She tied a rag bandage around the stump and that seemed to sooth *Quinto* a lot. She then limped over and sniffed *Juan's* body and later went into the house and did the same at *Claudia's* body. Then she went over to *Paulina* and lay down beside her bed. She seemed to understand that the two adults were dead and she lay there looking at *Rosa*, wagging her tail each time she spoke to her or patted her head.

Soon, neighbors streamed into the yard and ran up to the house. Many asked, "What happened?" "Why?" "What had these poor people done to deserve this?" One voice in the crowd murmured, *"Así mataron a mi hijo en Santiago, fueron los milicos."* (That's how they killed my son in *Santiago*. The military did it.)

Rosa handed *Paulina* to a neighbor and collapsed onto the ground, sobbing. "What would she do now? Her parents had been killed in a senseless act of violence. Thank goodness, *Miguel* was still safe in *Santiago*. But, *Roberto* was gone. Where was Vietnam? What would she do now?"

CHAPTER 19
Miguel – 1974

"Voy a contarles la historia, ay de la bala, ay de la bala, y si el pulso tengo bueno, voy a hacer fama, voy a hacer fama:" (I will tell you a story of the bullet, yes of the bullet, and if I have a good pulse, I will make the bullet renowned, yes I will make the bullet renowned.)

Verses from *"La Bala"* (The bullet.)

– A protest song written by *Víctor Jara*.

Miguel was a few years older than *Rosa*. He was born in 1945. As a young boy and teenager he sang folk songs with his family. His parents recognized him as an exceptionally smart young lad and, so, sent him to high school in *Temuco*. *Juan* had family members living there and they were happy to shelter *Miguel*. For his last year of high school, he transferred to a school in *Santiago* and lived with another relative, at the same 2266 *San Alfonso* address where Jean and *Luisa* had stayed many years before.

Miguel was an active young man and had a part-time job working in a supermarket. Then, after he graduated, he worked for several years in one of the French-owned mines near *Santiago*. Robert had met *Miguel* only once, when he had visited his parents in *Lonquimay* and when Robert happened to be there working in his tent preparing plant samples.

While working in the mine *Miguel* had become an active member of the local mine workers union. Soon he began work with the government agency

CORFO, which was responsible for developing policies to enhance economic development. *Miguel* was very much in favor of the *Allende* candidacy during the 1970s presidential campaign and worked hard in this new role. While working at *CORFO*, he married and soon he and his wife had two sons.

Because of his political leanings, and his former experience singing folk songs with his parents, he became a good friend of *Víctor Jara*, then a lector at the Technical University in *Santiago*. Their friendship became stronger when *Víctor* learned that *Miguel's* parents were the ones who sang folk and protest songs.

It was with great exuberance and no small amount of trepidation that the *Allende* supporters entered the new presidential term. From the beginning there was great opposition from the wealthy elite of Chile because they felt that their position of privilege in society was threatened. The end of the *Allende* presidency was assured, though, when the U. S. government became involved in promoting and funding civil and subversive activities. It started with secretly funding workers' strikes and any public demonstrations that weakened the *Allende* government. It worsened with the suspected involvement in several political assassinations, and it culminated in the not-so-secret efforts of Henry Kissinger and Richard Nixon to initiate a military coup against the Allende presidency.

After the coup on September 11, 1973, the situation rapidly spiraled downward. The military was quick to cleanse the country of any subversive individuals or organizations such as trade unions. Union members were among the first to be targeted and the military began to identify them. The spaghetti manufacturing factories of Lucchetti and Carozzi had strong unions. The factories were surrounded one day after the workers had started work. The doors were blocked shut and everyone inside was shot as they tried to escape.

Miguel was quick to see the emerging dangers and became a French citizen in early 1975, drawing on the fact that his grandfather had migrated from France in 1920. He assumed that that would give him some degree of protection. He had a good, giving heart and helped many union members to escape from Chile, the main method being to get them into a foreign embassy that would give them protection.

Initially *Miguel* thought that the coup leaders would not harass a small fish like him, but several incidents occurred that made him begin to fear not only for his safety but for his life. On New Year's Day, 1974, he, his wife and their two small children, visited some distant relatives in *Conchali*, a suburb on the north side of *Santiago*. Prior to that, the military had decreed that there could be no gatherings of more than 5 people. A distant cousin of *Miguel's* wife was visiting from the United States, with her 4-year-old daughter. Chileans are, of course, gregarious and extremely friendly, so a get-together was planned so that all the cousins, and friends and neighbors, could have a chance to visit the visiting mother and her infant daughter.

Sometime between 9:00 AM and lunch, several dozen individuals had stopped by to offer their greetings. Everyone was aware of the crowd rule so greetings were short and to the point, leaving a core of perhaps 13 or so visitors on the property in various stages of coming or going. The table was set up outside under the grape arbor and loaded with food and drink.

Suddenly the roar of a small airplane was heard above the conversation. It circled over the house at a low altitude and, on one of its over-flights, a cloudy material spewed from the plane. As the cloud drifted down to the ground, a strong odor of gasoline was noted, and it fell on the food and the plants in the patio. The food had to be discarded and several days later most of the plants were either visibly injured or had died of chemical poisoning. Of course, this broke up the festivities.

Several days later, the outraged, and fearful, victims were invited to a small get-together on the beach near the village of *El Quisco*, on the Pacific coast. Approximately 8 individuals were gathered on the beach and engaged in conversation when a small airplane flew over and then circled around above the group at extremely low altitude, as if taking photographs. Of course, this broke up the gathering and all scurried back to their automobiles and left.

These experiences, and others, had a profound effect on those affected and made them afraid, or even terrified, which was exactly the effect that the military wanted. *Miguel* returned to *Santiago* and began to realize that he must leave Chile before he was killed.

Miguel was quite ingenious, though, and while he prepared to leave Chile, continued with his schemes to get refugees past the police and into either the Italian or French embassies. Once he pushed a refugee dressed as a nun seated in a wheelchair into the Italian embassy. But, word soon got around that the police knew who he was and were actively seeking him. So, *Miguel* left Chile late in 1974. His wife drove him to the bus station and he took a bus to *Mendoza*, Argentina. He wanted his wife and two sons to go with him but she chose not to go. How he escaped is rather miraculous but the situation was still rather chaotic and he somehow slipped through the cracks.

And, for a while, the cracks were pretty large. The military tried to force the *Carabineros* to help with domestic obligations but many *Carabineros* were not sympathetic to the ideals of the coup. They could not realistically resist the well-armed military. Most of the street police were only armed with .32 caliber revolvers and carried only a few bullets.

So, many really decent and honest policemen did what they could to help the population at large. They tried to not be as zealous as the military in enforcing the new laws. The public, of course, knew this and coined the term *"Sandías"*, meaning that they were red on the inside but green on the outside, green being the color of their uniforms. This is the opposite from what one might suspect but Chileans can be very sarcastic in their humor and everyone knew what this term meant. In fact, many *Carabineros* served as a buffer between the military and the public, especially those directly affected by the military's actions. They served a very valuable function in relaying rumors and news of dead or disappeared individuals to their relatives and loved ones.

A friend of *Miguel's, Don Humberto Soto*, had friends in *Mendoza* and they helped *Miguel* get a fresh start. He had taken some savings with him with which he purchased a small bar. But, when *Miguel* heard that the Chilean secret police were looking for him, he began drinking. He sold the bar and fled to northern *Brazil* where his friends said he might find refuge. They sent him to the small city of *Boa Vista*. He spent a few days looking for a contact, an elderly man of European extraction who owned a dairy farm.

Miguel worked for him for a while and they got along very well, becoming good friends. *Miguel* told his friend that he wanted to bring his wife and sons to live with him but that his wife was not willing to leave Chile until he had a secure job and a safe future. So, they made plans to build a yogurt plant. At last it looked as though *Miguel* was going to do well and could build a prosperous future for his family.

Neither *Miguel* nor his Brazilian friend could have foreseen the extent to which the Chilean military would go to find and punish any one they considered as subversive. This is why Operation *Cóndor* came into being, in which the dictatorships of Chile, Argentina, Brazil, Paraguay, Uruguay and Bolivia cooperated with each other.

At least once a month *Miguel* would call his relatives in *Santiago* and they would relay his messages to his parents in *Lonquimay*. On one of the calls he learned that his parents had been killed. In 1976 or 1977 his calls ceased altogether. No one had any idea what might have happened. Several months later, a *Carabinero* stopped by the former house of *Juan* and *Claudia* and told *Rosa* what little he had been able to find out about the fate of *Miguel*.

The *Carabineros* in *Lonquimay* and *Curacautín* had been good friends of the *González* family for many years. When the military coup occurred in 1973, the *Carabineros* in general had not been very sympathetic to the military nor the coup. Most *Carabineros* stationed in the countryside or in small towns had come to know and respect their neighbors. They were not about to cooperate in a blood bath. So, one way in which they could still serve the community would be to milk the military authorities for whatever information they could and then pass it along to victims' families.

What they had learned was that *DINA* operatives had traced *Miguel's* whereabouts and finally discovered that he was working at the dairy farm. When *DINA* operatives had begun asking around about him in *Boa Vista*, friends had gotten word to him about their questions. *DINA* had several teams involved in tracking down and killing people. Usually, a first group would locate the person of interest, and then a second, or third, group would move in and dispatch the victim. Every step was carefully planned so as to be secretive, yet make sure that they eliminated their target.

Miguel quickly packed some clothes and what little money he had and ran out the back door, into the surrounding forest and back into town. He purchased a bus ticket to *Venezuela* and left with only what he was carrying. Apparently he was already under surveillance because when he got off the bus in *Venezuela* another group of operatives was waiting for him. As they approached, *Miguel* bolted and ran into the surrounding forest.

The operatives chased him and never even requested that he surrender. As soon as they chased him deep into the forest, they shot him point blank in the back, robbed him, and then dumped his body into the *Orinoco* River. As dozens of red-nosed *piraña* fish swarmed around *Miguel's* body, the assassins knew that the body would never be found. *Miguel* was never seen nor heard from again, leaving a widow and two small children, and he joined the ranks of *los desaparecidos.*

The tragedy of *Miguel,* and that of his parents, was experienced several thousands of times in the first few years during and after the military coup, causing immeasurable grief to their families. And for no reason except to show how bestial the human spirit can be!

But, in the midst of all this tragedy, there occurred another event to the family that, in the short run, was tragic enough, but in the long run, brought out a little of the best of the human spirit.

A distant cousin of *Miguel's,* Nanno, worked at the Veterinarian School at the *Quinta Normal* in *Santiago.* On the day after the coup on September 11, he was arrested because he was identified as a socialist and accused of being involved in transportation of arms to be used by *Allende* sympathizers. He was taken to the soccer stadium and after several weeks transferred to a jail in *Santiago* where he was questioned and then tortured.

His brother, *Enrique,* as soon as he heard that Nanno had been arrested, fled to Canada before he could be arrested. He still lives in Canada at the time of this writing.

At the jail, Nanno was subjected to various forms of torture, the most notable being what was known as the 'Russian Torture.' In this torture, he was forced to sit on a large rock and strapped to it in such a way that he could not move about. A jug of water was placed a few inches above his head and a small hole punched in it such that a drop or two of water would pass through every few seconds and land on Nanno's head. In the short term this does not seem like a severe torture, but after several hours, then days without sleep, few victims can resist and will 'break'.

But, Nanno did not 'break', even after constant questioning as to where the 'arms' were. Nanno did not reveal where the 'arms' were because he knew nothing about the 'arms.'

Then the inquisitors tried a different approach. They clamped electrodes on his nipples and testicles and applied increasing voltage of electricity. Nanno pleaded for mercy because he did not know where the 'arms' were. The military then tried one more 'trick' to get him to reveal the location of the 'arms.'

During their investigation of his possible guilt, they learned that he had a girlfriend and that she was pregnant. So, they arrested her and brought her to the interrogation room and made her stand in front of Nanno. He still would no reveal the location of the 'arms.' After several more unsuccessful attempts to get him to talk, the officer in charge walked up to her and held a pistol to her head. He looked at Nanno one more time with a questioning expression on his face, then, changing his expression to a smile calmly pulled the trigger. The girl was instantly killed. Nanno still could not reveal anything about the 'arms'. The soldiers hauled out her body and to this day, no one knows where she is buried.

After that experience, Nanno almost lost his sanity. His captors finally realized that he was innocent of any involvement in Allende's regime, and so, when the Human Rights Group demanded his release, they were only too happy to comply, and he was released to the care of his parents.

He endured many years recovering from this terrible ordeal. He developed many nervous tics, some of which he still retains. He aged prematurely and now has the appearance of an old man. Then, during *Michelle Bachelet's* first term as president, she initiated a program to help former prisoners like Nanno, to attend the university and study a profession. It took Nanno several years, but he now has a law degree. His full-time work-profession is to offer his legal expertise to Chileans with no voice and he is now at some peace with himself.

A political regime will be judged by history on any one of many merits. The *Bachelet* presidency certainly had its faults, but in this case, and for Nanno, a small, and deserved, justice was served.

CHAPTER 20
A Letter to *Rosa* – April, 1974

"Mantelito blanco de la humilde mesa, en que compartimos el pan familiar." Verses
from *"Mantelito blanco."* (The white tablecloth from our humble table where
we shared bread.)
– Song from Chilean folklore.

Several months after the death of her parents, *Rosa* was clearing out
some of their clothes and other personal belongings. In her mother's
old trunk she found her grandmother's *mantelito blanco* wrapped
around a bark-covered package, wrapped in the manner of the old *Pehuenche*
documents she had seen occasionally as a child at her grandmother's house.

The *mantelito blanco* was owned by *Rosa's* great-grandmother. It was said
to have been made from the finest linen in France during the 1700s and was
a precious family heirloom. Inside the bark-covered parcel there was a letter,
addressed to *Rosa*, from her mother! She unfolded it with shaking hands and
began to sob. After a few minutes, she was able to begin reading again.

The letter read as follows: '*Rosa*, my dear, dear *Rosa*, I have loved you
more than anything you can know and share with you the deep, deep sorrow
you are feeling now. Several months ago, about the time of the military
coup, I had a premonition that your father and I will soon leave this earth.
Within that premonition your brother *Miguel* also faces an uncertain future.'

Rosa had to sit down and she cried for a while. Then she continued
reading. '*Rosa*, as you know, I am a *Pehuenche* **machi**, just as my grandmother

and my mother were before me. We have certain powers. The powers are small at first, but they grow more powerful as we grow older and gain wisdom. We can't make the dead rise or anything like that but we are able to do certain simpler things. For one thing, we can see into some of the future. I see that someday you will also be a **machi**, and you will understand how we feel, and know what are your responsibilities, to your family, and to the community.'

'*Rosa*, you must not repel *Roberto*. I know that he will father your child. He is a good young man. Eventually he will fall in love with you and you will have a good life together. Soon he will save my life and much later he will try to save your life. I can't see the details, but I feel in my heart what the future brings. The two of you have much to give our *Pehuenche* community. Know that I will always be with you to the extent that I am able. I will try to send signs. At first you will not recognize the signs, but it is vital that *Roberto* study and analyze them. Remember also that every time you see one of these signs, you will know that I am near to you and your family. I bless you, your mother, *Claudia*.'

Rosa sat there on the floor, too stunned to move for a long time. 'Soon he will save my life!' She reread that phrase several times. "How can that be?" *Rosa* was confused. Then she remembered seeing him jump into the river to save her mother's life, only a little over a year ago, a few days before he left for Vietnam, but how could her mother have known that was going to happen? And her mother had written this letter to her even before then! Just then, a breath of wind blew a cluster of leaves against the bedroom window, and *Rosa* shuddered, cried again, and said, "*Mamá, Mamá*, why did you have to leave me, what will I do now?"

But, *Roberto* was gone, gone to Vietnam as a soldier, and during the past year she had lost contact with him. He was in the field and isolated from communications. Then she cried again as she felt the terrible loneliness in her heart. What was she going to do now? *Roberto* didn't even know that she had become pregnant with his baby. She couldn't return to the university, even if she could afford to go.

She had to take care of the little ranch and her baby and must help *Miguel* as best as she could. Her parents had a little money hidden away but it would not last long. She would have to increase the sheep and cattle herds and hire some help for the animals. The military would certainly never allow her to sing again even if they allowed her to live. She felt terribly alone, even though occasional gusts of wind blew leaves against the window, and even though she suspected that it was a sign from her mother.

CHAPTER 21
Vietnam Highlands – 1974

"El derecho de vivir, poeta Ho Chi Minh, que golpeas de Vietnam, a toda la humanidad, ningún cañón borrará el surco de tu arrozal, el derecho de vivir en paz:" Verses from *El Derecho de Vivir en Paz* (The Right to Live in Peace, poet Ho Chi Minh, who fights in Vietnam, to all of humanity, no cannon will erase the trench around your rice paddy, the right to live in peace.) – Protest song written by *Victor Jara.*

As the patrol worked its way down into the little valley, each man knew that they were walking into an extremely dangerous situation. The valley, more of a wide ravine actually, was surrounded by rice paddies, and broken into narrow, shallow ravines. This was not the more typical well-defined rice growing area in the delta where the paddies were large and separated by narrow walkways. Here the visibility was not so good as there were scattered lines of trees in the ravines and along the watercourses, but there were only a few workers in the paddies and there didn't seem to be a trace of Viet-Cong.

As the patrol moved into a small woodlot, or copse, Robert could see through it to the clearing a little further down the ravine. Several Vietnamese peasants were working in the clearing. As the last man entered the copse, shots started to ring out. Viet-Cong! As each man sought shelter, the firing quickly became so intense that the quantity of bits of leaves and twigs falling made it seem like snowflakes were falling around them.

Robert threw himself down behind a slight rise and wriggled out of his pack and then pushed it in front of him on the rise. The soldier next to him was struggling to remove his pack and Robert rolled over to help him. Just as Robert removed the pack, the man slowly rolled toward him and Robert saw the bullet hole in his forehead and a single drop of blood trickling down his face.

The patrol leader was shouting commands and there was the beginning of a little return fire. Robert could clearly hear the tweets of whistles as the Viet-Cong officers issued commands to their soldiers. As Robert began to assess the situation he looked toward the rim of the little ravine and his heart fell as he could see a line of white pith helmets moving around the ravine edge! There were dozens, if not more, and that was only in the direction that was visible to him.

Now the firing was becoming more intense as the Viet-Cong moved into their positions, and large chunks of bark and tree limbs began raining down on the patrol. The men were firing desperately but it was becoming very clear to every man that they were badly outnumbered and would likely die there before day's end. Their firing slowed a little as they tried to conserve ammunition. The radioman had been hit and the radio smashed by the same bullet. Robert pulled out half of his full ammunition clips and re-arranged them on the ground in front of him so he could reload more quickly. He knew they weren't going anywhere because there was no place to go except closer to the Viet-Cong. They must really be enjoying this! Not a good situation for us!

As he began to control his excitement and his firing, he tried to overview their situation. He noticed that further down in the ravine the little cluster of peasants was huddled together and screaming. The Viet-Cong were not firing at them, though. Every few minutes he could hear a scream from one of the men in his patrol as the withering fire from the Viet-Cong hit their target. By now, though, the ring of Viet-Cong had completely surrounded the little ravine, putting the peasants right in the center of fire from both adversaries and he knew that it was only a matter of time before they would be killed by stray bullets.

He rolled over on his back and slid down a little for more cover and to think a little more about what was happening. As he glanced behind him he noticed a figure standing off about 30 meters in front of the ravine edge. It seemed to be a woman dressed in some kind of strange dress he had not seen since he had left Chile and her feet were not touching the ground.

Fascinated, he forgot about the firing and as he stared at the figure he thought he could hear the figure speak to him, *"Roberto,* you must help them as you helped me." Robert thought to himself, "What kind of crap is this? Am I finally losing my mind?" The figure then repeated the request, this time in Spanish, *"Roberto, ayúdales como tú me ayudaste."* "Help them like you helped me!"

Robert thought he was going into shock! It looked like *Claudia, Rosa's* mother whom he had pulled from the river in Chile a year earlier! This was impossible! As he heard more screams from his men, he thought, "This can't be! I must be cracking up from the situation." Now she was pleading with her arms and repeating her request. Almost without thinking, he wriggled out of his belts and other paraphernalia and threw them down along side his pack on the low ridge in front of him. As he stood up he heard some of his mates say, "Robert, get down, are you fucking crazy?"

As he ran down the slope toward the peasants, he thought he must indeed be crazy. Bullets clipped off bits of his uniform but none touched him. He thought to himself, "Boy, I am so dead!" When he neared the group of peasants he saw that the only ones still alive were a skinny old man, a skinny young woman, and a baby. Without hesitating a second, he grabbed the old man and woman together and threw them over his shoulder. He then picked up the baby and cradled it in his arms. He turned around and began to run as fast as he could, staggering all the way with a mass of legs and arms sticking out in all directions. When he got back to his patrol, he jumped in headfirst and fell into a clump of arms, legs, and the woman's long black hair. In a flashback he remembered *Rosa's* long, black hair.

As his men pulled the Vietnamese peasants off him, he looked over to the figure and heard her say, *"Bien hecho, m' ijito.* Now you must save *Rosa's* sanity, and yours. Well done my son." Then her image disappeared and Robert wondered what he had just seen, or imagined he had seen. One of the men stepped up beside him, slapped him on the back and said, "Robert, we thought your ass was grass. Why did you do that? You must be fucking crazy!"

All Robert could realize was that he was still alive and hadn't even been hit! And, the silence – the firing had stopped! He heard a faint tweeting and someone said that the Viet-Cong were leaving. Were they leaving out of respect for what he had done? They certainly weren't afraid of his small patrol. He was grateful for having survived the ordeal! But, what had just happened?

Robert was nearing the end of his one-year tour of duty in Vietnam, and the war was gearing down, when he was wounded. It happened several weeks after he was given new orders. After his patrol returned to the base and word got around about what he had done, his base commander was afraid that he might be going mentally unstable and decided to change his assignment to something perhaps a little safer.

Because of Robert's past experience as a smokejumper he thought he would feel comfortable serving as an aerial artillery spotter. So, Robert was reassigned to the Da Nang airbase and spent several weeks as an artillery spotter flying in a small two-place airplane. He and the pilot would fly around possible Vietnam troop concentrations and call in artillery fire to the best effect.

Sometimes they would fly around a crash site and direct artillery fire around the site as Vietnam soldiers surrounded the site looking for the pilot and/or his crew. He knew they knew they were there because the forest would literally twinkle as rifle fire from the ground was aimed at their plane. Usually they were too high to be hit but frequently after they returned to the base the many bullet holes in the plane had to be repaired before it could be flown again.

On his last mission, the plane was hit by ground fire and the pilot lost control. As the plane dropped lower and lower the pilot tried to land in a river. But the plane crashed into the river and flipped over. As the plane struck the water, Robert saw the pilot's head snap back and forth. Robert struck the side of the plane and was momentarily knocked out. When he came to, the plane was filling with water and Robert knew he had to get out, fast.

He cut himself out of the seat harness and pushed out the hinged window. He somehow forced himself out and into the water. He swam to shore and climbed up the bank and hid in the thick undergrowth while he caught his breath. He saw a few bubbles surface where the plane had rapidly sunk. The pilot did not surface, and Robert knew that he was dead.

Robert pulled out his revolver and checked to see that it was loaded. Then he scrunched down into the undergrowth as he heard the noise of a motorboat coming up the river. He strained to see through the brush as the boat moved past and was disappointed to see that it was a Viet-Cong boat. It slowed opposite his hiding place and then trolled back and forth as the crew searched for any evidence of the wreck or survivors. He could see the crew gesture with their arms as they were apparently discussing whether they should go ashore. Finally, the boat turned back into the current and speeded up as it moved away.

It was now near dusk. Robert hid in the same dense thicket all night, holding his revolver in front of him in case the Viet-Cong returned and he needed to defend himself. With first daylight, he inventoried his belongings and began to ponder what he might do next. He had no supplies, other than 12 extra bullets for his revolver. His water and emergency food rations had sunk with the plane. He decided to not drink from the river yet, as he decided to head east, to where his last look at the map had indicated approximately where the U. S. lines were.

Robert stayed hidden during that day and traveled toward the east at night. On the morning of the third day after the crash, he heard several Huey helicopters flying toward his general direction. For the last several hours he had sensed that some Viet-Cong were tracking him. He was afraid that they would soon catch him. So, when he saw that the choppers were going to fly almost directly over his location, he decided to take a chance and jumped up, waving his shirt, trying to get the pilot's attention. The Viet-Cong were now close behind and when they saw the first chopper turn and begin to circle Robert, they quickly set up a mortar and began to lob rounds at him. The Viet-Cong were very good with mortar fire.

As the chopper circled again in preparation to land, its gunner sprayed the Viet-Cong with machine gun fire. But, even as the gunner fired, a mortar round was already in the air. As the chopper circled again, the last mortar round exploded a meter from where Robert was standing. The explosion lifted him several meters in the air and threw him about four meters or so off to one side.

From the first moment, Robert felt no pain. His only thought, as he flew through the air and saw a leg slowly rotating away from him, was that some poor dumb schnock had just lost a leg. He fell hard to the ground, but still felt no pain. His last memory as he passed out was of an American medic crouching over him and beginning to administer first aid. Then, he entered into a coma that would last a long time. A few months later, the war in Vietnam was over.

CHAPTER 22
The World Turned Upside Down – 1974

"Contemplando en mi memoria, hacia aquel lugar, En el horizonte de mi mente, se ha escondido el sol, como un recuerdo que me llega, de su corazón. Como un recuerdo que me llega, de su corazón." (Contemplating in my memory, toward that place. In the horizon of my memory, the sun has hidden itself, like a memory I arrive, from your heart. Like a memory I arrive, from your heart.) Verses from *La Conquistada* (The Conquered One)
— Song from Chilean folklore.
St. Patrick Hospital, Missoula, Montana – July, 1980.

Robert's mother came to the hospital that morning, just as she or her husband had each day for the past 6 years. Robert had been in a coma since the day when a mortar blast had blown off his left leg just below the knee. The shock of the explosion had traumatized his brain in such a way that he had gone into a deep coma and no treatment had yet brought him back into consciousness.

He was first treated at the VA hospital in Great Falls but since his coma had remained and it appeared that he might never again regain consciousness, he was sent to St. Patrick Hospital in Missoula. They had started a large and aggressive physical therapy program there and since he would be closer to his parents, it was felt that it would be less of a strain on them if he was closer to where they lived, and the aggressive program would help him retain some of his muscle tone.

Year after year went by, with little sign of improvement. Robert remained in a deep coma. One day a group of student nurses visiting from Chile stopped at St. Patrick Hospital to study the hospital's physical therapy techniques. They were told about Robert, that he had worked in Chile, and how long he had been in a coma. When they were shown the physical therapy techniques being used on him, they spontaneously burst into song, in Spanish! After singing a short medley of Chilean folk songs, they moved on to the next patient. As they were leaving, one of the therapists glanced at Robert as she passed by his bed, and thought she noticed a tear in his eye.

After that day, Robert's parents brought in a portable record player and twice a week when Robert's mother brought fresh flowers for his room she, or her husband, would remain at Robert's side for several hours, either reading aloud to him, or sitting there with him listening to Chilean music, with long-dried tears on their grieving faces.

Today, Robert's mother was especially jubilant as she had brought a small vase of branchlets of **Chilco** (*fuchsia*) plants with her to place on the table next to his bed. She knew that he would especially appreciate them if he could see them. He had sent her seeds of this plant years ago when he was collecting medicinal plants in Chile and she knew that he would be particularly pleased as he had loved his work in Chile. Not only were *fuchsia* plants valuable as medicinals, they also produced unique and beautiful flowers.

As she approached his room she thought she heard voices from within. Not wanting to interrupt in case the nurses were discussing something of a private nature, she hesitated outside the partially open door and listened. She heard what seemed to be a young lady imploring something to someone in the room.

Drawing upon her high school Spanish, she thought the voice said something like, '*Por favor, Roberto, tú tienes que ayudar a Rosa. Ella necesita tu ayuda. Por favor, anda donde ella.*' (Please, Robert, you must help *Rosa*. She needs your help. Please go to her.) Then she heard a weak voice that she recognized as Robert's, "*Claudia*, you look so young, what has happened to you? What has happened to *Rosa?*"

Robert's mother dropped the vase and it smashed on the floor. She ran back to the nurse's station screaming, "Robert is awake and he is speaking!" The nurses and an on-duty doctor ran to Robert's room, burst through the door, and immediately began taking readings from the various instruments attached to Robert. Robert's mother followed them and said to Robert, "Thank God you are awake. Robert, do you feel alright?" Robert weakly raised a hand toward her and said, "Mom, I think I'm going to be okay."

She phoned her husband and told him what had happened, and while waiting for him to come to the hospital, she returned to Robert's room and asked, "Robert what happened to the young lady with whom you were speaking before I entered the room? Where had she gone so quickly before the nurses came and how had she left the room without my seeing her? She was speaking to you in Spanish with so much vigor and passion."

Robert waited for a long moment before answering, "Mom, I honestly don't know. But, I think that was *Claudia*, a middle-aged lady I met in Chile. Yet, now she appeared to me as if she was only barely in her early twenties. She told me that her daughter, *Rosa*, was in some kind of trouble and needed my help. As I recall, I think she also appeared to me when I was in the coma but I couldn't answer her, I could only hear her. When I was in Vietnam, she also appeared to me, but as the middle-aged lady that I knew in Chile and asked me to help some Vietnamese peasants who were in danger of being killed."

They continued talking for quite some time. By this time Robert's father had arrived and the three of them hugged each other and mingled many tears of joy for the fact that Robert had finally emerged from his coma. After much conversation to catch up on what had happened during the last six years, Robert announced that he was going to work hard on his physical therapy as he had to go back to Chile to see what he could do to help *Rosa*.

He told his parents who she was and when they saw the firmness in his eyes and voice, and they sensed the love that he felt for her, they looked at each other and even though they didn't want him to go, agreed that this would be the best thing that he could do to help with his rehabilitation.

When the nurses finally came in that evening and began to shoo out Robert's parents, Robert's mother noticed that the vase of *fuchsia* flowers that had fallen to the floor when she dropped it, was now standing on the nightstand, and that the vase, which she had seen shatter, was holding the flowers and was not broken. She never told anyone what she had seen, but for the rest of her life she pondered what it meant.

CHAPTER 23
Back in Chile – November, 1980

¡Pucha que es linda mi tierra!
(Gosh, my country is beautiful!)
– Verse of song from Chilean folklore

Robert and *Rosa* just lay there on the bare ground, hugging each other, not believing what had just happened and that they were finally together again! Their eyes were filled with tears and both were sobbing. After a while *Paulina* came up to them and started to both laugh and cry at the same time.

Then she began to kick Robert and scolded him, *"¿Tú, huevón desgrasiado, por qué dejaste a mi mamá sola? ¿Por qué me dejaste sola?"* (You mean, awful man, why did you abandon my mother? Why did you abandon me?)

Then, she, too, began to sob and crawled into Robert's lap and hugged him. *Rosa* said, *"M' ijita."* Then both she and Robert held *Paulina* tightly in their arms.

Mother and daughter gazed into Robert's eyes as he asked, "Where are your parents? This place looks as if it hasn't had much care for quite a while."

Rosa answered, "They are both dead, *Roberto*, killed by the military for singing their so-called subversive music. We think *Miguel* is dead too, because we haven't heard from him or seen his body. We only have the word of a business partner in Brazil who said that the *DINA* police were asking about him, and then he just disappeared! Another rumor placed him in Venezuela, where he is said to have been killed. We just don't know. He has never contacted his wife or me. He has simply disappeared!"

After a while *Rosa* invited Robert into the house to have tea. As she prepared it she told him about the charcoal spot on the ceiling and how the house had almost burned down the day her parents were killed. She said she had tried to clean up everything as best she could. She told him about the terror, which soon turned to grief, that she felt when she saw her dead parents. She told him how *Quinto* had been shot in the leg, how she had to trim the stump and then bandage her, and that she had recovered quite well, what a good companion she was for her and *Paulina.* Then she suddenly became silent. She brought in the tea and cookies and invited *Roberto* and *Paulina* to sit. She poured tea for herself and then sat down.

Robert then said, "You know, when I was in that dark place during the coma, one of the things I remember distinctly was Chilean folklore music. I swear that I heard song after song that you and your parents played for me during my visits here. *Rosa* looked at him with her large eyes and then left her place at the table and disappeared upstairs. When she came back down she was carrying a guitar and said to Robert, "This is the only musical instrument the *milicos* didn't destroy. I have so missed playing it. I simply didn't feel like playing music any more after my parents were killed and you were gone. But, my dear *Roberto*, this song I play gladly for you."

Then she played the guitar and sang to him this song from Chilean folklore:

Si vas para Chile
(If you go to *Chile*) *te ruego que pases*
(I beg that you go)
por donde vive mi amada.
(to where my love lives.)
Es una casita
(It is a tiny house)
muy linda y chiquita,
(very pretty and tiny,)
que esta en la falda
(it's in the shadow)
de un cerro enclavada.
(of a nearby mountain.)
La adornan las parras,

(Grapevines decorate it,)
la cruza un estero:
(a brook crosses it,)
y al frente hay un sauce
(and in front there is a willow tree)
que llora, que llora,
(that weeps and weeps,)
porque yo la quiero.
(because I love her.)
Si vas para Chile
(If you go to Chile)
te ruego, viajero,
(I beg you, traveler,)
le digas a ella que
(to tell her that)
de amor me muero.
(I'm dying of love for her.)

During the next few hours, *Rosa* and Robert talked constantly. She shared with him more details of the brutal killing of her family, he told her about his experiences in Vietnam, of having seen and heard *Claudia* urging him to save the lives of the Vietnamese family, and then seeing a much younger *Claudia* when in the coma, urging him to help *Rosa*.

Robert teased *Paulina* and played with her and *Quinto*, often just doing silly things that they could share with each other.

They became accustomed to each other and fell in love and Robert began to get to know the daughter he never knew he had. *Rosa* showed Robert the letter that her mother had left for her. They discussed what it might mean, but they had to admit that *Claudia* had correctly predicted her own and *Juan's* demise and that *Miguel* faced an uncertain future. *Miguel* had disappeared in 1974, shortly after their parents were killed by the *Pinochet* regime, and rumors speculated that he had fled Chile and spent several months, and perhaps years, fleeing from the DINA, the Chilean Secret Police.

Rosa also told him about the murder of mother's cousin. *Jaime Guzmán de Aldunate* was a lawyer who lived in *Santiago*. From one of *Santiago's* leading families, he had vigorously defended copper miners during several of their strikes during the *Allende* regime. He disappeared. Several weeks later, one of the neighborhood *Carabineros* stopped by the house and told his widow that he had been killed and his body was in the general cemetery in *Viña del Mar*. So, she hired a cab to take her from *Santiago* to *Viña*, which is a distance of over 80 kilometers, to the general cemetery there.

Upon her arrival, the soldier guarding the cemetery would not let her in. Finally, after much crying and pleading he let her in and led her to a pile of perhaps several dozen naked bodies. The soldier helped her examine the bodies until finally she found her husband. His throat had been slit from ear to ear and, from the numerous bruises on his body, it was evident that he had been tortured as well. By this time the soldier was also crying. He helped her load the body into the cab and she returned to *Santiago*. He had left a widow and two children. After that episode, his wife was never really normal again and she slipped deeper and deeper into insanity as she grew older.

That evening, when the three of them were seated at the supper table and having a rather sparse bite to eat, Robert asked *Rosa*, "How were you able to get by? You obviously don't have much money. How did you and *Paulina* survive all these years? Why didn't you marry?"

Rosa replied, "*Roberto*, we almost starved to death. My parents left some money hidden but it has been stretched very thin. Jean and *Luisa*, who had moved to *Santiago*, also sent a little money. We also sell a few sheep and cattle and have kept a small garden. *Gracias a Dios* for the people of *Lonquimay*! They supported us to a large extent all this time. They loved my parents and my grandparents as well, and have tried to repay all that my ancestors have done for them over the years. But, they are poor too and could not give much."

"But, *Roberto*, my mother appeared to me in my dreams and said you would come, but that you were badly hurt. That is what kept *Paulina* and me going. I loved you *Roberto* and I somehow knew that you would come someday, if you could."

Robert arose and went over to the chair where *Paulina* was seated. He bent down on one knee in front of her and said, "*Paulina*, you are a beautiful young lady. Today I found out that you are my daughter." After a long pause, he continued, "I left your mother long ago. I don't know how I could have been so stupid as to abandon such a beautiful young daughter, and her beautiful mother, both of whom I have come to love very much."

"*Paulina*, if you and your mother will let me come back into your life, I promise that I will never leave you alone again, as long as I live." He turned toward *Rosa*, "*Rosa*, if you will be my wife I will try to be a good husband to you and a good father to this little urchin."

"When I was in the coma," he continued, "your mother came and spoke to me and said that you were in terrible straits and needed my help. The day I awoke from the coma, my mother also heard your mother speaking to me in my hospital room. *Rosa*, your mother had the face, body, and voice of a young woman! And I swear that I will never leave you again. I will try to make up for my absence. If you and *Paulina* will have me, I have found a great treasure here in Chile and I will stay with you, and take care of you, as long as I live." Then he stood up.

Paulina also stood up, looked him square in the eyes, kicked him once hard in the shin of his good leg, and then jumped into his arms and began crying. *Rosa* came over to the two of them, hugged them both tightly and replied, "*Roberto*, oh, yes, yes, yes! I have loved you since that first day I saw you camped down by the river. Such a bashful, humble, young man! When you were a little tipsy you accidently touched me and turned beet red of embarrassment."

She continued, "What a nerdy young man! *Mamá* was afraid that you were never going to follow your heart and pursue me. Maybe that is why she encouraged me to take you to that *canelo* grove on the mountain on the day before you were to have left Chile, and that's why she gave me the **Palwe** to give you. Maybe she also knew in her heart how both of us felt toward each other and that was why she appeared to you first in Vietnam and then later in the hospital. She must have been watching over you just as she was watching over me and *Paulina*."

At any rate, Robert had a new home, and a new family. He settled in pretty quickly, helping make repairs to the house while *Rosa* worked with the sheep and cattle herds. They discussed what their future might be and decided to sell the livestock but maintain a large garden. *Rosa* wanted to pursue her apprenticeship as a **machi** so she could better serve the communities of *Lonquimay* and *Curacautín*.

Robert had an idea that perhaps they could also work to form a cooperative to help market and sell native handicrafts as well as prepared medicinal plants. Robert's partners at Pharmtec offered financial assistance that had been postponed when *Claudia* and *Juan* were murdered. With that income they built a small office/museum in *Lonquimay* to serve as headquarters for the cooperative.

At about that time in Chile, tourism began to become quite popular, especially from neighboring Argentina but increasingly from the United States and Europe and their business began to do quite well. It was an increasing asset for the community. Ever since the Chilean government nationalized the valley in the late 1800s, the living standards of the natives, by modern criteria, had not been good.

Since the *Pehuenches* had historically always been pretty much self-sufficient, they usually had enough to eat and clothe themselves, but the increased availability of material goods such as automobiles, televisions, *etc.* were luxuries that most could not afford. Certainly, as the economy improved, life got a little better and by the late 1980s various government programs and better roads resulted in a much better standard of living for all.

CHAPTER 24
Santa Teresa Church, *Lonquimay* –December, 1980

"Entre el mañio y los hualles, el avellano y el pitrán, entre el aroma de las chilcas, vive Angelita Huenumán:" (Amongst the *mañio* trees and the young *robles*, the *avellano* and the *pitrán*, among the scent of the fuchsias, there lives *Angelita Huenumán*)

– Verses from *Angelita Huenumán*
– Song written by *Victor Jara.*

The little church was filled with people, and many more were standing outside in the beautiful early summer day. There was a feeling of great festivity in the air! A bride and groom, both simply dressed, were standing before the priest, both with radiant smiles on their faces. In fact, all the parishioners were smiling and the festivity of the occasion would have been highly contagious to any visitor on that day.

Robert's parents were there, escorted to the front row by *Paulina*. They had flown to Chile a week earlier from Missoula and had since been special guests of Robert and *Rosa*. They loved *Rosa* and *Paulina*, and the *Araucaria* pine forests surrounding the *Lonquimay* Valley. Robert, *Rosa*, and *Paulina* had met them at the airport in *Santiago* and his parents were quick to understand why Robert had been so anxious to return to Chile after he awoke from his coma.

After the service got underway, the priest began his homily, "Dearly beloved. We are gathered here today to join together this man and this woman in holy matrimony. Normally the Sacrament of Holy Matrimony is a rather short service. But I am going to depart slightly from this tradition by saying a few words, so that we may all share in the joy of this day."

"We all know this woman, *Rosa González*. I dare say that there is not a person in *Lonquimay* who does not know *Rosa González*. Her grandparents were stalwart citizens in this valley. We all knew her wonderful parents, and we have suffered with her during these last years as she raised her daughter alone in the world after her parents were murdered."

"With help from all the *Lonquimay* community, she survived and raised a beautiful daughter. During this time, she had many suitors, some undoubtedly only trying to be of help, but certainly others who had developed a real affection for her and her daughter. But *Rosa* had a great faith and she knew that one day her only true love would come back, returning from a far-off country, and from a far-off war where he was severely wounded."

"We all urged her to move on, to leave the pains of the past, to forget the man she thought she loved and hoped would return. But, if anything, *Rosa* is stubborn. And she struggled to survive, managing her parents' farm as best she could, and raising a few sheep."

"All of us here today know that her faith has been fulfilled, her *Roberto* has returned! Most of us didn't know *Roberto* very well. We knew him mostly as a shy young man, interested only in learning about medicinal plants. We have been told that he did not initially have any affection for *Rosa*."

"However, we learned a great deal about *Roberto* on that day in 1973 when *Claudia*, *Rosa's* mother, fell into the river and was drowning. We learned a great deal about *Roberto's* character when the rescue party finally arrived at the river and found him in the chillingly cold water. We saw him hanging onto a submerged branch with one hand, holding *Claudia's* face out of the water with the other so that she wouldn't drown."

"He had hung on like this for over an hour while *Rosa* went frantically seeking assistance! When his rescuers dragged him out of the water, still holding onto *Claudia*, the only remark he made was, 'Take your time but hurry up.'"

"Then he collapsed and spent the next several days with a fever and severe chills. We know that only a few days later he left for the United States and went into military service and spent some time in Vietnam, was wounded, and then spent several years in a coma, suffering from his wounds."

"We welcome the parents of *Roberto* with open hearts and we know that they are impressed with their new daughter, and a beautiful granddaughter that they didn't know they had."

"And so, *Roberto* and *Rosa*, it is with great pride and joy that today I pronounce you husband and wife. *Roberto*, you may kiss your bride, and *Paulina*, don't watch your parents as they kiss."

After the wedding, Robert, *Rosa* and *Paulina* entertained Robert's parents. His parents fell in love with *Rosa* and especially *Paulina*. She was such an adult young lady. They all took a tour of southern Chile, from *Temuco* down south to *Puerto Montt* and even to the island of *Chiloé*. Robert showed them where he had collected medicinal plants and told them something about the history of the area. *Rosa* took along her guitar and sang many folklore songs. Robert's parents even picked up a little Spanish during their visit.

About a month after Robert's parents had returned to the States, Robert, *Rosa* and *Paulina* were eating lunch in their house when there was a knock on the door. Robert went to answer the knock and there stood the mailman with a special delivery letter that needed a signature. Robert said he could sign it but the mailman said, "No, it must be signed by the recipient, a *Señorita Paulina*."

After signing for the envelope, *Paulina* opened it and began to read the short message, "*Nuestra querida Paulina*" but then she stopped and said, "*Mamá, Papá*, the rest is in English." So, Robert took the letter and read, "*Nuestra querida Paulina* - you know what that means don't you *Paulina*?" "Of course, *Papá*, but what does the rest say?"

Robert continued to read the letter, "During our all too short a visit with our son and his lovely wife, and especially their beautiful daughter, we have come to realize that we have a treasure in all of you. We shall plan to visit you often and hope you come to visit us often as well. *Paulina*, you are an intelligent young lady, so, we have placed a small amount of money in a bank account for you and your education. We love you and want only the best for you. Love, *los abuelitos*."

As *Paulina* examined the letter, something fell out of the envelope. It looked a little like a Chilean *carnet*, or identity card. But it was a bank passbook from the First National Bank of Missoula, Montana. Inside was a deposit made out to *Paulina* for the amount of $100,000. Robert and *Rosa* were stunned! Then they smiled as they realized that the expenses for *Paulina's* undergraduate education were covered.

CHAPTER 25
Santiago, Chile – 1981 – *Paulina's* notebook

"Batallones Olvidados" (Forgotten Battalions)
– Title of song by *Los Cuatro Cuartos.*

Prior to 1970, Jean and *Luisa* had sold the house they built near *Lonquimay* to *Juan* and *Claudia*. The house was a fair distance from the village and they wanted to be nearer to their friends. They moved to the village of *Lonquimay* and lived there for several years. After the murder of *Juan* and *Claudia* they moved to *Santiago* to live in the house at 2266 *San Alfonso* they had inherited years earlier from *Luisa's* cousin *Juana*.

After Robert returned to Chile, he, *Rosa,* and *Paulina* made frequent trips to *Santiago* to visit them. Robert would drop off his medicinal plant materials at a shipping company and they would stay with Jean and *Luisa* for several days, each family group enjoying the other's company.

After supper, Jean related stories of how he had come to Chile and how he met *Luisa*. *Luisa* would recount stories she had heard as a little girl from now long-dead ancestors. At first *Luisa* was somewhat hesitant to say much but as she grew to respect Robert more and more, and to love *Paulina* more and more, she began to recount stories that even Robert thought were almost unbelievable. Robert and *Rosa* were, of course, interested in the historical aspects of the stories, but little *Paulina* was especially fascinated by the stories.

And, soon she began to record the stories in a notebook that she carried with her whenever the family went to *Santiago*. Robert and *Rosa* encouraged her to record the stories in both English and Spanish as she was becoming bilingual in both languages and it was good practice for her and she was continually learning new words. As she grew a little older, she also began to draw sketches of what her great grandparents described in the settings of the stories.

Jean related to them as to why he had come to Chile and included the part where he had saved *Luisa* from abuse by the drunken sawmill laborers, leaving out no details. *Rosa* laughed because she had heard the story many times. After *Luisa's* embarrassment and the redness in her face subsided she was inspired to tell them why she had come to possess bright red, curly hair, a rarity among *Pehuenches* like herself.

She leaned back in her chair and began to muse in a dreamy way, "Back in the 1600s, when our ancestors on my father's side of the family lived in villages around the city of *Buenos Ayres*, both the natives and the Spanish initially got along very well. Each group developed a dependency on the other. The natives provided animals and produce for food and the Spanish paid them with textiles and other material things that enriched their lives."

"My great-great-grand mother had served as a maid for a noble Spanish family there in *Buenos Ayres*. She was just a young girl and she became enamored with the son of the family. He was a good boy and it was hoped by her parents that they would marry and she would live a good life. But, as you might suspect, she became pregnant!"

"At about that same time, the good relations between our peoples deteriorated. Certain evil people, on both sides, began to agitate for a separation of the two groups. *Buenos Ayres* was growing rapidly and more land was required for the expansion. Fights between the two groups became more and more frequent and eventually several people were killed. The natives were looked down upon as inferior people, much as were the Negroes in the United States, "she said as she glanced at Robert.

"My ancestors were forced to move further west to avoid increasingly violent confrontations and the young girl gave birth to her baby out on the *pampa* with only her parents to support her. They never saw her suitor again, nor any of the family they had worked for. All they had were memories and a red-haired child to nurture. There were no more red-haired children in our family until I was born in 1900. My parents, though, did not think of the curly red hair as a curse but rather as a blessing. As my father used to say somewhat as a joke, 'All of our ancestors had straight, black hair. Here comes *Luisa* to break the monotony.'"

Of course, everyone laughed, especially *Paulina* as she said, "Oh, thank you *bis-abuelita* for that story. I have been born into an extremely strange family and I want to learn as much as I can about it."

After *Paulina* said that, *Luisa* seemed deep in thought. She finally arose from her chair and went into her bedroom for several minutes. They could hear her rummaging around in one of her blanket chests. She was carrying something in her hands when she returned and as she sat down, held it up in front of them and said, "*Paulina*, this is the only record we have of a distant cousin named *Rafael*. I never knew much about him and many years passed before we finally learned anything more about him."

She continued, "He was orphaned as a young boy during the pacification wars of the 1860s and was then raised by a neighboring family who had become very close to one of the Catholic priests who were missionaries in our country. He was baptized and the priest changed his *Pehuenche* name to *Rafael*, apparently because he had a talent for drawing. That was, indeed, a strange name for a *Pehuenche* boy born in our homeland in the *Lonquimay* territory and before the Chilean government completed their campaign of pacification of the *Araucanian* people."

"*Rafael* was an intelligent young boy and was fascinated by stories that the priest told him. When 19 years old he left the *Lonquimay* Valley, headed north to *Santiago*, and volunteered to fight in the War of the Pacific. He was never heard from again. He never sent back word from Peru, nor did any of the soldiers who returned from there after the war know anything about him. I guess that is not so surprising as he was an orphan and I barely knew of him only as a cousin on my mother's side of the family. I had completely forgotten about him until one day in 1966, two Chilean army officers came to our door and said they had something to give us that was found on *Rafael's* body!"

She related what little the officers knew about *Rafael* and what had happened to him, "There was a particularly vicious battle in June of 1881, in which 35 *Buin* regiment soldiers had fought for 13 hours against nearly 3,000 Peruvians, and won, but only 10 Chilean soldiers survived the battle. That unit had been so badly wiped out that they were taken off the battlefield and they and survivors of other battles were ordered to return to *Santiago*. To march back to *Santiago* didn't seem unusual because, after all, they had marched all the way to Peru from *Santiago* on their way to the war.

Somehow his group became lost in the *Atacama* Desert, early in their march. Mining personnel found their mummified bodies in 1966. All the party had apparently died of thirst and/or exposure. *Rafael's* diary was found on his mummified body and has been in my possession ever since. Here it is, child, for you to read and to keep for future generations. I have tried to decipher what it says but my eyesight is not what it used to be. Now, *Paulina*, it is your responsibility."

The diary was a small notebook consisting of perhaps several dozen tattered pages loosely bound by hand threading that had replaced the original binding. The pages were wrinkled and the faded writing was barely legible. *Paulina* was delighted with the challenge of reading it and told her *bis-abuelita* that she would tell her all she could the next time they came to *Santiago*.

By the next time her family had returned to *Santiago*, *Paulina* had studied the diary and gleaned a narrative of what *Rafael* had experienced in the war. One evening the family sat down after supper and *Paulina* began to read her narrative, "*Rafael's* diary starts after his unit arrives in *Callao*."

"I bless Father *Jaime*, for he took me under his wing when I was an orphan and taught me how to read and to write, for otherwise what I have seen will be lost. I thank God that I am able to leave these writings as a testament to what has happened to me in these troubled times. The day before yesterday we drank the last of our water. Most of those in my group are already dead, those few of us remaining will soon also depart this life. I took out my little notebook which I carried throughout the war, and never recorded a single experience. I guess I became so used to the war that I did not think it to be of any interest to anyone else. Then, last night as I was becoming delirious and lay there on the sand, wrapped in blankets but still very cold, I reflected on what I should have written and prepared to die."

"As I had these thoughts, I thought I heard my name softly called, and then heard it again, but I tried to ignore the voice as I feared I was nearing death. '*Rafael, Rafael, Rafael*, it is I, your mother.'"

"There, a few meters away I saw a young woman standing, holding out her arms toward me, repeating my name, '*Rafael*.' 'You never knew me except when you were only a baby. I was killed during the War of

Pacification, as was your father. We hid you under an overturned cart just before we were killed. So, you survived! Because of my gift as a *Pehuenche* **machi**, I was able to watch over you as you grew into a young man. I guided Father *Jaime* to you and encouraged him to help you. We are proud as to how you responded to his teachings.'"

"As she spoke and moved about, her necklace of silver squares jingled slightly. 'Your father and I love you *Rafael*, and soon we will be together again. Do not be afraid.'"

Rafael continued his narrative, "The next day I wrote these words as soon as light allowed me to see the pages and before I died. I felt a strong compulsion to leave a record of some of my experiences of the war. Maybe it was a wish of my mother, I don't know."

"I traveled from *Temuco* to *Santiago* shortly after we heard that the Bolivian city of *Antofagasta* had fallen to the Chilean army. That was on Feb. 14, 1879 but we did not hear about it until several weeks later. By then I was in *Santiago* and cheered with everyone on April 5 when it was announced that Chile had declared war on both Peru and Bolivia. Oh, the joy and enthusiasm amongst the Chilean people when they heard the news! Even I, as a *Pehuenche* lad standing in the plaza was hugged by upper class women of *Santiago* as they celebrated the news, even by some of the *engreido* representatives of the *Aldunates* and the *Supercasseaux.*"

"However, I could not enter the military. Officials were adamant that a *Pehuenche* boy could not serve in the military. That honor was reserved for Chileans. So, I lived in *Santiago* for the next year, getting work where I could find it and learning more about my adopted country. I was the object of much prejudice because of my *Mapuche* heritage, but with some people I was respected because I worked hard, didn't steal, and could read and write, both in Spanish and in **Mapudungún**."

"My luck changed, however, in late 1880. The major sea battles had been fought and won by the Chilean navy and the army was moving across Peru in a pacification program. It was a long, slow campaign and cost the Chilean government a lot in blood and money. In 1881, President *Aníbal Pinto* organized a new expedition against *Lima*, and ordered an army of 42,000 men to be sent there. Because there was a scarcity of potential soldiers, I was finally accepted into the army."

"This war was very inconvenient for the Chileans. They were already expending many resources in the pacification of *Araucanía* in 1880. The pressure of the war in Peru diverted attention from the war in *Araucanía* and the natives took advantage to renew their insurrection and were able to recover all their former lands up north to the *Biobío* River. This caused great consternation in the Chilean government and they wanted to quickly finish the war in Peru and return to the southern war of pacification."

"After we arrived in Peru, *Patricio Lynch* proved himself to be a superior administrator. He organized campaigns against the remaining Peruvian troops and stopped looting and pillaging by Chilean troops. He then took the war to the mountains where the Peruvian troops had retreated. Most of the Peruvian professional troops were gone by this time and were replaced by natives, descendants of the Incas, who were brutal in their fighting methods. Thus, much of the fighting now became focused as guerrilla warfare."

"By this time I had received several minor wounds, from gunshot and bayonet and knife, but was able to recuperate and fight on. Maybe because of my *Mapuche* background and blood, I was able to be a formidable soldier, certainly equal to what my Inca relatives could offer. My experiences were too many to recount here as I now realize that my time on this earth is limited. We are lost in the *Atacama* and our water has been depleted. Soon we shall die. I leave this record so that any of my cousins who read this account may know that I died with dignity and honor."

"My group was part of the *Letelier* expedition. The troops were dispersed in small garrisons in each village in the Peruvian mountains. These villages were surrounded by thousands of natives who were invited by Peruvian officials to rise in rebellion against the Chilean invaders. As this knowledge became known to our officers, it was felt essential to reunite our forces and retreat as soon as possible from the mountains and go toward the north in order to avoid a possible rout."

"In these, my last moments, I will describe my last battle while I am still lucid. It was the worst one I was ever in and should be remembered by all Chileans forever. The location selected to cross the mountains in retreat was the mountain pass known as *Las Cuevas*. This pass had to be protected in order to facilitate the passing of the Chilean division to *Casapalca*. The pass was located at more than 3,500 meters between the villages of *Quillacancha* and *Quillacocha*."

"The force chosen for this difficult task was a company of the *Buin* regiment led by Capt. *José Luis Araneda*, part of the *Buin* delegation. We were to guard the pass and resist until the *Letelier* division could safely pass. In the *Buin* delegation, we were one captain, 3 lieutenants, 78 soldiers, and a 10-yr-old boy who was the bugler."

"After an exhausting march through countless mountain valleys, we finally arrived at the pass. Nearby was a *hacienda* called "*Sangrar*", which we occupied in order to gain some protection from the wind, snow, and cold. The *hacienda* was owned by a man named *Norberto Vento*. His son, *Colonel Manuel Encarnación Vento*, was ordered to lead a group of 440 well-armed regular soldiers and about 1,000 native soldiers to our location and wipe us out."

"Our captain decided to leave 14 soldiers at the *Las Cuevas* pass, as sentinels, and 2 on the crest. *Sargente Zacarías Bisivinger* and 5 soldiers were sent to a neighboring *hacienda* for provisions, and corporal *Oyarse* with 4 soldiers went to the west as a lookout. The rest of us (53 soldiers) were quartered in the *hacienda*."

"Later we were to learn that the *Letelier* division, because of bad weather, had been forced to return to the *Oroya* road. We were, thus, isolated and waiting for reinforcements that could not arrive. Our captain, though, was confident that we would not be attacked, or surprised at least, because the sentinels could signal by screaming a warning that they needed to return to the *hacienda*."

"When the Peruvians arrived, they were very tired from a long and difficult forced march over very rough terrain. They were tired, thirsty, and hungry. They surrounded Sargent *Bisivinger's* patrol and after a brief fight, killed them all. We in the *hacienda*, however, heard the gunfire and assumed the worst. All the other soldiers were ordered to return to *Sangrar* except for the sentinels who were to remain at their posts."

"That afternoon, of June 26, 1881, the mountain guerrillas began their attack. There were 15 soldiers at *Las Cuevas* pass under Sergeant *Blonco*, and 4 officers and 50 soldiers distributed between the chapel and the main house of the *hacienda* and we made preparations to resist."

"Hundreds of guerillas scaled the cliffs to assault Sergeant *Blonco's* position at *Las Cuevas*. Thankfully they were repelled. But, the more Peruvians that were killed, that many more were replaced. The same scene occurred at the *hacienda*, although we were better sheltered by the rock walls of the main house and could fire in a more secure and deliberate manner. We inflicted great losses amongst the guerrillas."

"After hours of intense combat, Lieutenant *Guzmán's* group had to retreat back toward the chapel, with 4 deaths and 7 wounded. The combat was without quarter. Finally, we heard the Peruvian bugler order a cessation of fighting. The Peruvian officers offered a dignified surrender, promising to save their lives. However, Capt. *Araneda* knew that the Peruvian officers would not be able to control their soldiers and we would be killed anyway. The Captain also knew that we had a large quantity of ammunition which he did not want to fall into enemy hands, so he ordered the bugler to signal 'No!'"

"The guerrillas attacked with renewed fury as *Vento* decided to eliminate the Chileans as soon as possible so that his men could finally eat, drink, and rest. However, each attack was met with a furious resistance. *Vento* ordered the chapel to be set on fire, and while the Chileans stationed there ran toward the main house, they ran into a solid wall of Peruvians.

Lieutenant *Guzmán* saw as his only escape to run toward *Las Cuevas* and join Sergeant *Blonco's* detail. Then the shooting stopped. For long minutes, the only sound we could hear was that of falling snow!"

"Our Captain then decided to trick the Peruvians into believing that there were many more of us than in reality. He ordered all of us to scream and shout and run back and forth behind the *hacienda* walls as we shot. Wounded soldiers reloaded and handed the arms to us so that we could fire more rapidly. Then the firing stopped again! Later we learned that the Captain had written a note and forged *Letelier's* name advising us that they were very close and would arrive momentarily with 600 well-equipped reinforcements. He had tied the note around a rock and threw it into the plaza.

The Peruvians, thinking it had dropped from our Captain's pocket before the battle, took it to General *Vento*. *Vento* was fearful that the Chilean reinforcements would arrive soon but he was so enraged that the Chileans had desecrated his father's *hacienda* that he was determined to make one final advance to try to kill all the Chileans. But, as this final, brutal assault began, 38 Peruvians were killed in the first moments and this caused a great panic among their troops and they ran from the field."

"In the silence that followed, we did not know what had happened, so we anxiously awaited the Peruvians' next move. Unbeknownst to us, Lieutenant *Guzmán* had successfully arrived at *Casapalca* where he was given two regiments to help us at the *hacienda*. They arrived at 6:30 the next morning and were amazed at what they saw at the battle scene. Corpses were strewn about and the chapel and *bodega* destroyed by fire. But, as they entered the *hacienda* grounds they saw the tricolor Chilean flag and knew there were some survivors."

"This was the end of my involvement in the War of the Pacific. I was only slightly wounded at *Sangrar* but General *Letelier* said that we had done enough for Chile and our company was disbanded and sent back to *Santiago* with many wagons full of wounded. We, the walking wounded were to serve as escort for this train. I was very grateful to have survived this war. I fear I shall not survive here much longer. Most of my compatriots have fallen asleep, from exposure to the dry air and no water, and I fear I shall soon follow."

"I write these last words by the light of a candle. I hope they are legible and will be found someday. *Rafael.*"

After *Paulina* finished her narration, the family sat in silence, *Luisa* and *Rosa* in tears! Finally, *Luisa* stood up and walked over to *Paulina* and hugged her, saying, "Bless you my child, you have done a great deed today, not only for our family but for Chile as well."

"And, *bis-abuelita*, I learned a lot about Chilean history," she replied. "With your permission, I am going to donate *Rafael's* notebook to the Military Museum in *Santiago*, along with some sketches I made during my research."

Luisa replied, "*Paulina*, that is an excellent idea. And I will tell you something else about *Rafael*. The army officers who told me about the discovery of his body also told me that his remains would be placed in a temporary grave in the military mausoleum in *Santiago* and if we so chose some time in the future, his body could be moved to a family gravesite. I have thought a lot about it and believe it would be a good idea to inter him in the family mausoleum in *Talca*. It is where the relatives of aunt *Juana* are buried and technically he was a relative on his father's side of the family. At least he would have a final resting place and we could pay our respects to him from time to time."

Postscript - What *Luisa* did not know previous to *Paulina's* reading of the diary, nor had anyone in the family ever known, was that *Rafael's* mother was a **machi** and she had been given another small gift of humanity just before she and her husband were slaughtered by the Chilean military during one of the Pacification battles. What *Rafael* experienced as he lay dying, and did not record, was the manifestation of that gift.

As he breathed his last, he sensed that to his side were standing several figures, two to be exact. Although his parents had been killed when he was only a baby, he somehow knew that the figures standing there were his parents. So, the words he had heard the day before were not due to his imagination! His mother was dressed in a splendid robe and around her neck was a necklace of small shining silver squares and triangles. As he lost consciousness he saw the couple motion toward him to rise and come to them.

CHAPTER 26
Conguillío National Park – The Sloths – 1981

It was very obvious to all of the family that *Paulina* was an extremely intelligent young lady. One day during a visit of Jean and *Luisa* to Robert and *Rosa's* house in *Lonquimay*, they inquired if *Paulina* had any interest in attending college, and what she might like to study. They knew, of course, that she had been planning for a long time to attend college, but she was interested in so many things that she could not make up her mind about what to concentrate on. At the moment of their visit, she was reading the journal of Charles Darwin. Jean noticed that and asked why she was so interested in Charles Darwin.

Paulina replied, "*Mira bis-abuelito*, Charles Darwin came to southern Argentina and Chile while we were still savages. He marveled at a beautiful land at that time almost untouched and dis-spoiled by human hands. In southern Argentina he discovered skeletons of many animals that had apparently died only a few years before his visit. Maybe our ancestors were responsible for their demise."

"What animals were that?" inquired *Luisa*.

"Why, *bis-abuelita*, there were many, but I am thinking specifically of the giant ground sloths," replied *Paulina*. "Some people think that they were still alive only a few years ago."

Luisa and Jean glanced at each other, nodded with slight smiles on their faces, and then Jean said to *Paulina*, "Young lady, I think it is time that we make a visit to the *Conguillío* National Park. The land within it was declared as a national park in 1950. The land used to belong to our ancestors and there is something there that you should see."

Paulina was quick to ask, "*Conguillío* is a strange word, what does it mean?" Jean answered, "It is a *mapuche* word that means 'water with *araucaria* seeds'. When we get there you will see thousands of the majestic *araucaria* pine trees, many more than what we have around *Lonquimay* because they were not cut down and sawed for lumber. It is indeed a magical place."

Rosa had been there once when she was a little girl but had almost forgotten about it. Now she remembered and, with a smile, said, "I think that is a very good idea. I will start to pack some things to take."

So, early the next morning, the five of them loaded themselves into Robert's Land Rover and headed south into the *Conguillío* National Forest. They drove up the valley of the *Río Lonquimay* to just outside the eastern border of the park, a little past the *Estero El Azul*. Robert parked the car. Jean decided to stay in the car and wait for them. He was getting pretty old and did not feel he could climb very far over the rough ground. The remaining four walked and climbed a little way up on the southern side of the valley floor.

Paulina was confused by all that was passing but suspected that it must be something important. *Luisa* soon stopped at the base of a cliff. *Paulina* had no idea why she had stopped there as there was only a sheer cliff face punctuated by a narrow strip of twisted and deformed bushes of *Ciprés de la Cordillera* forming a narrow green line up from the base of the cliff where they were standing. *Luisa* and *Rosa* walked up to this dense line of green shrubbery and began to pull apart some of the branches.

Rosa said, "*Paulina*, come here and see what we have found." *Paulina* looked at where they were holding apart the foliage. There was a narrow slit in the cliff face! *Luisa* said, "Come on, let's go in and see what we might find."

After the four of them had squeezed in through the crack in the rocks, they came into a small valley. The valley floor was covered with a dense carpet of grass punctuated with a scattering of shrubs and trees. "Now," said *Luisa*, "let us sit here on this fallen tree trunk and wait."

Paulina thought to herself, "Boy, what is going on here, are these people crazy or what?"

After a few minutes of silence, *Paulina* thought that she heard crunching noises and occasional grunting sounds. *Luisa* motioned for them to follow her toward the noise. They carefully crept through the bushes and just beyond the brush line was a small clearing. There in the clearing were several large creatures, nuzzling and cuddling with several other much smaller creatures.

Luisa turned toward *Paulina* and quiered, "*Paulina*, do you know what those creatures are?"

Paulina gasped and responded, "Those are giant ground sloths! There are adults and young ones! I thought they were all extinct!"

The four of them remained there for perhaps an hour, watching the small group of giant sloths feeding and caring for their young. Finally, *Luisa* backed away and they all walked back to the slit in the rock cliff and returned through the slit to the outside world. They were careful to replace the branches exactly as they had found them.

Paulina was ecstatic! She was full of questions, such as, "Why are those creatures still alive? Why are they still living in that valley?"

They soon arrived back at the car, Robert drove them farther into the park and they stopped at a picnic area along the south shore of Lake *Conguillío*. *Rosa* brought out the picnic lunch and they ate, Jean and *Luisa* related to *Paulina* what they knew about the sloths. "We don't know too much about these marvelous creatures. We know that there were other large animals but that they were all killed long ago by our ancestors, probably for food. But, at some point, our ancestors realized just how unique were these creatures and they decided to maintain this small group in this hidden valley."

"*Paulina*, you are a descendant of *Pehuenche* **machis.** As such you have a powerful force in your hands. But, you also have a great responsibility. Now you know about the giant sloths. You are one of a handful of *Pehuenches* with that knowledge. As a future **machi**, you are also learning about the beneficial attributes of medicinal plants. You are a smart young lady and I sense that you realize the enormity of that knowledge. We trust that you will use it wisely."

As they drove back to *Lonquimay* later that day, *Paulina* continued to ask many questions, questions that Jean and *Luisa* were delighted to try to answer. Occasionally Robert and *Rosa* exchanged glances and each could see the pride in the other's face as they listened to *Paulina's* questions, and discussion of their answers. At several times, Robert had to choke down tears of joy and pride as he thought about his wonderful family and life.

CHAPTER 27
Her name was *Leonora Latorre* – 1982

"Tus ojos dos verdes lagos, llenos de melancholia, tus labios suaves y sabios,
fueron tus armas de espía:"
Song verses from *Romance de Leonora Latorre*

(Your eyes like two pools of green jade, full of melancholy,
your lips soft and all-knowing, your weapons of spy.)
– (The Ballad of *Leonora Latorre*)
– Song verses of the *"Cuatro Cuartos."*

Shortly after their visit to *Conguillío* National Park, Jean had suddenly fallen ill and died. After the shock of Jean's death, *Paulina* and *Luisa* became even closer. After their mutual experience when *Paulina* had read from her notebook about the history of *Rafael*, *Paulina* and her great-grandmother became very attached to each other and during breaks from school, *Paulina* would travel on her own to *Santiago* to visit *Luisa*. She would take the train from *Temuco* to *Santiago* and spend a few weeks at *Luisa's* home in *Santiago*. *Luisa* would recall stories from her childhood that *Paulina* would record in her notebook. They would wander all over *Santiago*, visiting shops, museums, churches, and any other place of interest. *Paulina* always had lots of questions.

On one of her trips to *Santiago*, *Paulina* told *Luisa* about a book she had just read. It was called *"Adiós al Séptimo de Línea"*. It was a massive book, consisting of five volumes in all, written in 1955 by *Jorge Inostrosa Cuevas*, a native of *Iquique*. It was an extensive history of the War of the Pacific and contained a mixture of adventures involving real personages and some fictitious ones. It had immediately inspired the musical group, *Los Cuatro Cuartos*, to compose a stereo record entitled "*¡Al 7° de Linea!*" on which were recorded, in the form of music, some of the major campaigns, battles and personages of the war. Both the book and the music revived Chilean memories about the war and stirred the national pride.

Paulina was fascinated with the book and read all five volumes with great interest. After all, her cousin *Rafael* was a soldier in that war. *Paulina* said she admired *Leonora Latorre*, one of the fictitious members of the Chilean Secret Service, who heroically did her part for Chile in the war. There was much speculation by many Chileans that she really existed but no one knew for sure, and none of her possible relatives had come forward with any information. The *Cuatro Cuartos* album contained a stirring ballad called, "*Romance de Leonora Latorre*" that supposedly paid tribute to her exploits as a spy. It is a stirring ballad about her imaginary exploits as a spy for the Chilean secret service.

Paulina somewhat wistfully remarked to *Luisa* that it was a shame that most people believed that *Leonora* did not really exist. So many years had passed that Chileans would probably never know for sure. *Luisa* chuckled a little and said to *Paulina*, "Let's take a bus ride to the *San Bernardo* suburb of *Santiago*." *Paulina* was always ready to accompany her *bis-abuelita* so she said, "Let's go", but wondered what *Luisa* had in mind.

They had to take several buses as the *San Bernardo* suburb was near the southern edge of *Santiago*. After they got off the bus along the *Avenida Colón*, *Luisa* led her several blocks farther north along the *Avenida* to a short street. That street was only a block or so long but *Luisa* stopped and pointed up at a street sign and there, lo and behold, was the name of *L. Latorre*. "So," *Paulina* said, "*Leonora Latorre* must have been a real person or she wouldn't have a street named after her, right?"

It was obvious to *Luisa* that *Paulina* was very interested in this observation and she said to *Paulina*, "On the way home, let's stop by a distant cousin of ours whom I have not seen for many years. I think he is still alive. He is a descendant of *Hernán González*, who lived during the time of the War of the Pacific, and he has some information that you might be interested in learning."

So, they took a bus north on the *Avenida Vicuña McKenna* and got off a few blocks before the *Plaza Italia*. *Luisa* said that *Hernán* lived in a *cul de sac* of a very short street named *Rebeca Matte*. As they walked there they passed another short street and *cul de sac* named *Periodista Jose Carraico Tapia*. *Luisa* said, "This street used to be named *Belgrado*. The three houses in this *cul de sac* have an interesting history. They were constructed very long ago, just after the turn of the last century. They were the headquarters of a United Nations project during the 1960s aimed at promoting the use of wood in the Chilean economy."

"At that time, concrete was the major construction material but it was very expensive to use in low-cost housing for lower income people. Many experts from foreign countries worked here on various aspects of wood technology and forest management. Approximately a dozen Peace Corps volunteers also were detailed here to fill in for the scarcity of Chileans trained in forest management. In the late 1960s, these headquarters were moved to larger new facilities in *La Reina*, a suburb east of here."

"During the coup in 1973, these buildings, and the new buildings at *La Reina*, were confiscated by the military and used to hold and torture people resistant to the military regime. Some very bad things happened here during the decade after the coup. Now, in 1982, you can see that the military has recently abandoned these three buildings and placed a chain across the street entrance and entry to that street is prohibited. The street name has also been changed, I presume to somehow deny its past history. While the military occupied these buildings, neighbors would often hear terrible screaming and sounds of torture. The man who we are going to visit now lived on the *Calle Matte* for many years and heard these screams. He is quite old now and very invalided so I am sure he will be home. His daughter takes care of him."

Paulina knocked on the door, and after a long moment passed, they heard someone walking toward the door. When the door opened, there stood an elderly woman. *Luisa* introduced herself and asked about *Hernán* and if they could pay their respects to him. The woman said, "Of course, I know who you are, you are *Luisa Piñon*. You probably don't remember me but we met many years ago at a family reunion in *Lonquimay* shortly after the deaths of *Juan* and *Claudia*. Please come in, I will tell *Hernán* that he has some very special visitors."

After a minute or so, an elderly man came shuffling into the living room. As he looked at them his face brightened and he reached out his hand to *Luisa* and then hugged her. Then he looked down at *Paulina* and said, "So, you must be the little *Paulina*, my how you have grown! The last time I saw you was in 1974 when we traveled to *Lonquimay* to visit your mother and several others in the family who had survived the coup. You were just a baby then and we helped you and your mother as best as we could. We tried to get her to move to *Santiago* but she would have none of that. She had faith that her *Roberto* would return some day and all would be well."

As he spoke, *Paulina* could not help but notice the horrible burn scar on the left side of his face. She tried not to stare at it but her gaze lingered on it for longer that she knew was polite. As they settled in the sofa, *Hernán* said to her, "I see that you have noticed the scar on my face. Most of my body is covered by scars as ugly as that one. What happened to me to cause those scars was a burden that I have carried with me for my entire life, not for me but for what the family lost. Such sorrow!"

He continued, "When I was a little boy, about 9 years old, we lived in *San Antonio*. My sister, *María Inéz*, was 18 years old, and was preparing to go to *Santiago* to study obstetrics. It was a Sunday morning and she had to leave the next morning to take the bus to *Santiago*. On this Sunday she rose early in order to prepare breakfast for our mother, as a surprise, and for the rest of us. So, in order to prepare breakfast early, a neighbor had given her a small can of gasoline to help with starting a fire in the stove. She didn't know how flammable gasoline was and the open can exploded, showering the both of us with the flaming gasoline! I was burned on the side of my face and the burning gasoline splashed the side of my body. Even though I could not see through the flaming gasoline, I managed to run outside and jump into the irrigation ditch next to the road at the front of our house to extinguish the flames."

"As I emerged from the water, and not in too much pain as the cold water had momentarily soothed the burn, I could hear *María Inéz* screaming and I ran back into the house to help her. She was engulfed in flames! I grabbed the rug and wrapped it around her to smother the flames. She was in terrible pain. We were both taken to the hospital. I was bandaged and released. The next day, my mother, sister and brother went to the hospital to visit *María*. She was bandaged over her entire body except for her eyes. I could see the fear and pain in them and felt so sorry for her. The nurses would not let us stay long, and as we were leaving, the doctor came in and determined that she had just died."

Hernán continued, "But enough of that, let's talk about what your grandmother mentioned to my daughter when she answered your knock on the door. You have an interest in a lady named *Leonora Latorre*. I imagine you have read the novel about her. You realize, of course, that the novel, while containing many true historical events, actually contains no known facts about *Leonora Latorre*. It is simply fiction. And, you would be hard pressed to find anyone in Chile who knew of her or what she did. She was said to be a spy for the Chilean government. Well, after we have *once*, I will tell you what I know about *Leonora Latorre*."

As they waited for *Hernán's* daughter to set the table for *once*, *Paulina* walked around the parlor and viewed the many photos and relicts on the walls. *Hernan* said, "Most of those relicts were collected by my grandfather *Raúl* before and during the War of the Pacific. He certainly led an interesting life."

"His home was in the village that would later be called *San Antonio* and today one would say that his family was of the upper class. They were descendants of some of the earliest settlers in Chile. By the time *Raúl* was born the family was not quite as well off financially but they had enough money to live well and educate all of the children as they grew up. *Raúl* was educated as an engineer. As a young boy, he was fascinated by the sea. When he graduated from the technical school, he worked hard and saved a little money. He had little interest in the opposite sex, at that time. With the small amount of capital he had saved, he was able to purchase a small steam-powered boat, and with that boat, he began to ferry supplies to the other commercial fishermen around *San Antonio*. He specialized in ship's chandelery such as rope, sails, and nets. As his business grew, he spread his interests as far north as *Callao*, Peru."

"In order to support his work in that area, he purchased most of his supplies from the W. R. Grace Company in *Callao*. They were a New York-based company and had come to Peru in 1854. They initially sold all kinds of supplies for ships such as rope and related items, but soon concentrated on supplying the merchantmen harvesting *guano*. The *guano*, or bird droppings, had accumulated in the coastal desert for millenia and were easily extracted in large quantities. It was extremely valuable due to its high phosphorus and nitrogen contents and, thus, had high commercial demand for the manufacture of fertilizer and gunpowder."

Hernán continued, "He continued his chandlery operation even after the initiation of the War of the Pacific in 1879. Most of the Chilean and Peruvian authorities knew him, and since he only dealt with small, private fishermen, he was allowed by both sides to continue his chandlery business along the Peruvian coast, at least at the beginning of the war. By 1880 the naval war was still active and, although the Chilean army was beginning to successfully gain footholds on the coast, the occupiers had their hands full with their attempts at vanquishing the Peruvian troops as they retreated toward the mountains."

"It was on one particular day during this time that *Raúl* came into the port of *Callao* to re-supply his commercial stockpile. After overseeing the loading of his boat, he walked back into town to spend the evening very near the dock in a small tavern called *El Totino*. It typically served seamen and was a pretty rough place, but *Raúl* knew his way around and was not afraid. On this particular occasion, as he was leaving the tavern very late in the evening to return to his boat, he thought he heard loud voices, and some screaming, coming down one of the side streets along his route. The screaming stopped but the cries of several men grew louder. There was a full moon, and soon he could see a single figure, apparently a woman, running along and being pursued by 2 Peruvian soldiers and a man in civilian clothes."

"As the woman ran down the steep side street, he could see that she was running directly toward where he was standing in the shadows and watching. As she passed the spot where he was standing, he grabbed her arm and pulled her into the shadows of a nearby doorway. He placed his finger on his lips, urging her to be quiet, and pulled her deeper into the shadows as the 3 men ran past. The two of them stood there in the shadows for a few minutes and when they could no longer hear voices or footsteps of the pursuers, he urged her to walk with him as he chose another route to the dock where his boat was tied up. He was a little surprised that she would do as he requested, he being a stranger, especially a sailor. As they scurried along he cast side-glances toward her and saw that she was dressed in very fine clothes, typical of that worn by women of the Peruvian aristocratic class. But, he also noticed that the clothes were dirty and ripped in many places. She was also wearing a shawl that covered all of her face except for her eyes. In the center of the shawl was a large blood-soaked stain!"

"When they arrived at his boat he urged her to quickly go below and wait while he stoked the boiler and prepared the boat to leave. He pointed the wheel toward the open sea, and once the boat was underway, he locked the wheel and went below to see how she was doing. He lit a small lantern and looked at her. She was lying on her side on the bunk and had apparently passed out. Her shawl had come loose and her face was covered with blood. He began to wipe away some of the blood with a whisky-soaked rag and was astounded to see that her nose had been cut off! He bandaged her as best as he could and then went back on deck to check his course."

"Early the next day, as *Raúl's* little steamboat was chugging along several kilometers out to sea and in a southerly direction along the coast, the lady he had rescued the night before came up on deck. She sat down on the railing and sobbed uncontrollably. *Raúl* knew he could not console her. He asked her where she wanted to go."

She replied, "There is no place I can go. I am a secret agent for the Chilean government. I have been very ill for the last several weeks, and the day before yesterday when I was suffering from a terrible headache, I made a mistake in judgement, and I was caught by the Peruvian secret police. They tortured me and because I would not tell them what I had been doing, they beat me and then to spite me, cut off my nose. Yesterday evening I escaped and have been running ever since, going from one safe house to another to find safety. But, all had been compromised and I had nowhere to go. In desperation I was running down to the harbor, hoping to find someone who would help me. Then, the secret police nearly caught me again as I was fleeing. If I could not find help, I was going to jump off the cliff and kill myself. I have nowhere to go now, I have been identified, my face has been horribly disfigured, I am shamed, and I cannot return to my home in *Santiago*. I don't know what to do."

Raúl then told her, "Well, with the war gaining momentum, I probably cannot continue to ply my trade in *Callao*, so I think I will return to *San Antonio* and work along the Chilean coast for a while hauling supplies to fishing boats. I will have to obtain my supplies from suppliers in *Valparaíso*."

He continued, "Since I will be returning to *San Antonio*, why not come with me. It will take several days of travel and you can begin to recover from your wounds. When we arrive there, you can decide where you might go and what you might do. Perhaps you will be willing to go back to your family in *Santiago*."

She replied, "When I left I had no one except for my father and sister. My mother died shortly before I left for the north to be a spy. My sister is in high society and will have nothing to do with a sister who has no nose and who failed as a spy. My fiancé was killed in the war so I have no further reason to live."

Raúl replied, "Well, it will take us several days to get back to my home port in *San Antonio*. I invite you to come with me and spend some time at the *fundo* of my parents. You can consider all that you might do, and more importantly, recover from your injuries and give your wound a chance to heal. By the way, what is your name? Since we will be together for several days, I at least need to know what to call you."

She hesitated and then said, "Thank you for your kind offer, also it was very brave of you to help me escape from *Callao*. The Peruvians would have killed you outright if they had caught us together and suspected that you were helping me to escape. My spy name is *Anita*. I will not tell you my real name in case we are captured."

So, after an uneventful passage away from the combat zone along the Peruvian coast, *Raúl* took her to meet his parents at their *fundo* just outside of *San Antonio*. She remained there several weeks while *Raúl* made another trip to the north to pick up some more equipment, this time from *Iquique*.

When he returned to *San Antonio*, he discussed with *Anita* what she had planned to do now. He said that he was willing to accompany her to *Santiago* so that she could reunite with her father and sister. It would be a grueling trip but they could use his parents' carriage and that would make it as comfortable as possible.

She agreed but made a single condition, that he would take her to the convent at the *San Francisco* church in *Santiago* and leave her there. He was not to inform her father of what had happened. She decided that the only alternative for her was to become a novice nun and spend the rest of her life in seclusion so that she could repent for her failure as a spy. Besides, her disfigured face would have made her a social outcast in Chilean society and she could not stand to be laughed at, or even worse, stared at like she was some kind of monster.

So, *Raúl* did as she wished and dropped her off at the convent next to the church of *San Francisco* in downtown *Santiago*. After he helped her down from the carriage, she turned to him and thanked him for his kindness and courage. She stood on her tiptoes, pulled up the bottom portion of the bandana covering her face and gave him a kiss on the cheek. Then she turned toward the convent door. As she knocked on the door, he called out, "*Anita*, I don't know your real name."

As she entered the now open doorway, she hesitated, then turned toward him and said, "My real name is *Latorre, Leonora Latorre*. Bless you *Raúl*."

Raúl never saw her again. His business did very well, especially after the war ended. He spent several more years with his chandlery business and eventually sold the business and retired to his parents' *fundo* near *San Antonio*. During that time he was haunted by the memory of *Leonora Latorre* and wished he had done more to help her. After 10 years passed from the time he had left *Leonora* at the entrance to the convent, he made a trip to *Santiago* and after some searching, found the name and address of her father, *Antonio Latorre*.

He did not know if her father was still alive but felt that he should relate to him what he knew of her history during the short time he had known his daughter. He felt a moral obligation to do this even though he had promised *Leonora* that he would never contact her family. The maid answered the door and led him to a spacious parlor furnished richly in fine carpets and furniture. Finally, a very elderly man entered the room, shook *Raúl's* hand and asked him would he could do for him.

As *Raúl* related his tale, the old man stared in disbelief and then broke down and convulsively cried. After some time he stopped, and asked *Raúl* to forgive him for his discourteous demeanor. He said he had missed his daughter so much, especially after her sister died of cholera. He then said, "*Raúl*, would you accompany me to the convent? Let us find out if she is still alive!"

They took the trolley to the convent at the church of *San Francisco* and, after arriving there, were admitted in and asked to wait after *Antonio* inquired about the status of his daughter. After a long wait, a nun finally came out and told them that *Leonora* had died 2 years earlier. She could tell them few details but only that Sister *Ana* (her convent name) had been very ill during her time in the convent but that she was a very spiritual woman and had spent several years reflecting on her sins. After an apparent rebirth, she gave of herself to support her sister nuns whenever they were engaged in any kind of community or faith service. Because of her facial disfigurement, she always chose to remain out of public sight.

Before they left, the nun took them down into the catacombs and showed them where *Leonora* was interred. *Antonio* fell to his knees and prayed for several minutes. Then, before they left, *Antonio* bent to the ground and kissed the ground covering her grave. Later that day, as *Raúl* was departing, *Antonio* told him of his gratitude for having come to *Santiago* and recounting of his experience with his daughter. Now he could die in peace. All he wanted to do now was to honor her memory.

"So," concluded *Hernán*, "That concludes most of what I know about *Leonora Latorre*. *Antonio* had some authority with the *alcalde* and the street that you and *Luísa* visited was named shortly thereafter."

"What a tragic story," remarked *Paulina*. "But one that I am happy to know about. So many of my ancestors gave so much for life and for Chile that I am humbled and honored to be a member of this amazing and wonderful family. Goodby *tio Hernán* and thank you so much for sharing with me this history today."

Postscript - *Leonora's* body was buried in the catacomb beneath the convent. Several years after the visit by *Raúl* and *Antonio*, her bones were disinterred and reburied in a wall niche in the Catholic Cemetery in *Santiago*. The exact location of her burial was subsequently lost.

What neither *Raúl*, nor *Antonio*, nor anyone else knew at that time was that *Leonora* had symptoms of *Chagas* disease, and along with the misery that she felt for her facial disfigurement and life of isolation, it likely contributed to her shortened life. *Chagas* disease was rather common in northern Chile and Bolivia, especially at that time. It was caused by the protist *Trypanosoma cruzi* and spread by the *vinchuca*, or "kissing bug", but no one then knew anything about the disease or the organism that caused it. The disease was first described in 1909, by the Brazilian physician *Carlos Chagas*. The symptoms can be quite variable and may vary from person to person. Some infected persons develop fever, swollen lymph nodes, and headaches. In about a third of these individuals, further symptoms develop several years later, including enlargement of heart ventricles, leading to early heart failure.

As of this writing in 2019, a vaccine has not been developed. *Chagas* disease was first described by the naturalist, Charles Darwin, when he visited southern Argentina in 1833. He had heard of the "kissing bug" and its habit of feeding on blood of its victims and actually allowed an insect to feed on him. He was likely infected during this encounter as during the remainder of his life he would periodically become ill with symptoms that we now suspect as being caused by *Chagas* disease.

CHAPTER 28
The Fire of 1983

"It was a skin bubbler."
– Smokejumper jargon to describe an extremely hot and fast burning fire.

This chapter is about a forest fire, a particular forest fire in the *Lonquimay* Valley that occurred in the year 1983. The danger of a potentially devastating forest fire in the area was always present but no major one had ever occurred during the memory of even the oldest residents. This is partially because the *Pehuenche* residents of the region were particularly careful with the use of fire in the wild. And, most of the *Araucaria* pine stands were nearly pure in species composition, all trees were of the same relative age (very old), and with trunks of large diameter and dense crowns that limited light penetration to the forest floor. This resulted in a rather sparse growth of understory shrubs and other plants.

In order for a forest fire to start and then spread, several factors must be present. Firstly, there must be a sufficient quantity of fuels, these are the organic materials that combust, or burn, if the temperature is sufficiently elevated. Fuels include the stems, branches, and bark of standing trees, and also grass, forbs, and accumulated dead branches and leaves on the forest floor.

In the case of old-growth *Araucaria* pine, the trunks of the old trees were large and, under normal circumstances, difficult to ignite. Unfortunately, however, the most plentiful understory plant in this region is a species of bamboo called *Quila* (*Chusquea* sp.) and it can be very abundant wherever some sunlight breaks through the not overly dense crown system of the pines. Its plentiful and intrusive woody stems can make walking through the understory very difficult, and painful, as the broken stems have sharp ends.

Secondly, the fuels must be dry enough to ignite and once ignited, then remain ignited. *Quila* stems are small in diameter, about one cm, and dry stems ignite easily. Thirdly, environmental factors such as relative humidity, moisture content of the fuels, and wind, must be favorable for the fire to continue to burn. Lastly, there must be a source of ignition, in other words, something to start the fire. In forests near population areas, ignition is often in the form of careless human activity such as a discarded cigarette. In more remote areas, fires often start from so-called dry lightning strikes, in which there is lightning but no associated rain to quell the resulting flames. Occasionally, fires are deliberately started by arsonists.

The spring of 1983 started out dry. The preceding winter had not produced much snow and the spring flora in general was sparse indeed. Many people planted gardens but soon realized that the effort might have been in vain. The *Quila* plants normally flower rather lightly. but every ten years or so, they produce extremely abundant flower crops and then, when the stems die back, the amount of understory fuels is much heavier than normal. This happened to be a year when the *Quila* plants had a heavy flower crop, and then the stems died back, producing a much heavier quantity of dry fuels.

By early December 1983, the dreaded *"Sur Negro"* winds (black southerlys) out of the south had begun. These steady winds originate at the South Pole and as they move north, carry extremely dry, cold winds from the south. The winds blow northward along the length of southern Chile, drying the already parched land and dry vegetation. *Sur Negro* winds only occur once every decade or so but their arrival usually means a much higher danger of forest fires, and to a lesser extent, agricultural fires.

Unless a parcel of forest land is bordered by a river or agricultural crop land, or a highway, all of which serve as natural fire breaks, forest fires during a *"Sur Negro"* event have the potential to burn intensively during most of the summer until early fall rains reduce the moisture content of the fuels. This year was particularly grave as a heavy flower production of the *Quila* plants coincided with the arrival of the *Sur Negro* winds. Maturation, and subsequent death, of the delicate flowers produced a lot of flash fuels making it easy for any possible fire to ignite. Concurrent death of the stems resulted in even more fuels, which were heavier and able to sustain and produce a hotter fire and perhaps ignite large *Araucaria* pine trees. The *Araucaria* tree is a conifer that produces a large amount of resin in the foliage and in the wood and bark. Once a large tree is ignited, these resins produce flash evaporation and can create explosive conditions.

Robert and *Rosa* were awakened early one morning by a frantic pounding on the door. As Robert arose and threw on his robe, he noticed that there appeared to be a faint yellow-reddish glow in the south, but when he looked at his watch he noted that it was too early for the sunrise. Before he arrived at the door, he already had formulated a plan of attack for what he knew was going to be a fire of gigantic proportions and a great danger to the village of *Lonquimay*, and their house! As he opened the door he recognized the mayor of *Lonquimay*. *"Buenos días, Don Gustavo. Qué placer de verlo tan temprano!"* greeted Robert. ("Good morning, *Gustavo*. What a pleasure to see you so early in the morning!")

"Perdóneme, Don Roberto, pero hay un problema que viene en nuestra dirección," replied *Gustavo*. ("Please forgive the early intrusion, but there is a problem that is coming in our direction.")

"Adelante Gustavo, qué pasa?" asked Robert. ("Come in *Gustavo*, what is happening?") *Rosa* came into the entry room as *Gustavo* and Robert closed the door and entered. *"Hola Gustavo,"* she said with a smile and offered her hand. *"Buenos días, señora,"* he replied.

"Roberto y Rosa, perdónenme, pero traigo malas noticias. Ustedes recuerdan que los inversionistas de Santiago pusieron el aserradero a unos kilómetros al sur de aquí en nuestros terrenos. Anteayer, un grupo de indios hizo una manifestación cerca del aserradero. Ustedes saben cómo es,- - - intercambiaron gritos, insultos, etcétera," explained *Gustavo*. ("Excuse me *Roberto* and *Rosa*, I'm afraid I have some bad news to convey. Do you remember the investors from *Santiago* who put the sawmill on tribal lands several kilometers south of here? Day before yesterday several tribal members went there and demonstrated against them. You know how it is, - - - words and insults were exchanged.)

"Bueno, parece que en represalia, unos obreros prendieron fuego a nuestros terrenos al lado. Fue una tontera quizás, para asustar al grupo. Pero los estúpidos del norte no sabían del peligro de la sequía. El fuego ya está aumentando y el viento está trayéndolo

para acá, a Lonquimay y a su casa," dijo Gustavo. ("In retaliation, several workers at the sawmill started a small fire on adjacent tribal lands and taunted the Indians to put it out. But these stupid northerners didn't realize the danger of what they were doing, and the fire immediately got out of control. The wind is carrying it towards us, here to *Lonquimay,* and to your house I might add.")

"Por favor, Roberto, ¿nos puede ayudar, o recomendar lo que se pudría hacer para salvar nuestro pueblo?" asked *Gustavo.* ("Please, *Roberto,* can you help us, or at least recommend what we might do? We know you have experience with fighting forest fires and we need help to save our town.")

Such a conflagration had never occurred in recent history in the hills surrounding the valley upstream from *Curacautín* to the Argentine border. In most of southern Chile, during normal summer weather in which the *"Sur Negro"* winds were absent, forest or plantation fires were relatively uncommon as a shallow water table allowed active plant growth during the summer. When the occasional fire did occur, the Chilean police force, the *Carabineros,* had a crack forest fire suppression team that had a sterling record of professionalism of quickly suppressing such fires. In most cases of plantation or forest fires in the Central Valley, the *Carabineros* fought these fires mostly with water by digging a shallow pit and placing a suction tube from a portable gasoline powered water pump.

The military government in *Santiago* provided little assistance to combat fires in this region at the time. Ownership of the ancient tribal lands had been in dispute during the past century. Some previous governments were sympathetic to the Indian's cause but the military government was not and it wanted to end the Indian land ownership problem.

It was felt that it would be a good lesson to the *Pehuenches* living in the valley and help convince them to not fight the takeover of their lands by special interests. So, as the fire danger increased, little effort to assist the *Pehuenches* appeared to be forthcoming.

The mountains surrounding *Lonquimay* were covered with dense forests of *Araucaria* pines. The forest cover continued from the lands bordering the *Naranjo* River Valley and then west across the *Biobío* River valley and as far to the east as the Argentine border. This forest type covered thousands of hectares and represented a rich resource for the *Pehuenche* people.

From his past experience as a smokejumper, Robert knew that decisive actions needed to be taken and taken now rather than later. Robert immediately dressed and set out with *Gustavo* to the mayor's office. *Rosa* would come a little later after *Paulina* was awake and the livestock were taken care of. The first thing Robert did when he arrived at the mayor's office was to request a map of the area between the sawmill and *Lonquimay*. He had hiked in that area but needed to be refreshed as to the exact geography. What was available was not a topographic map but rather a simple line drawing with the water courses drawn in, but better than nothing, thought Robert.

Gustavo penciled in the estimated height of the mountains between each of the water courses and noted that there were three mountain ranges between the sawmill and the *Naranjo* River. Robert sat down and began to think about possible strategies. He began to feel an increasing sense of dread.

At eight a.m., others began to come into the mayor's office and the mayor explained what they were considering. After a dozen or so were assembled, Robert outlined what he thought should be done, or what could be done with their limited resources. Just after he started, two *Carabineros* also arrived. They were normally stationed in *Curacautín*, but *Lonquimay* was a part of their extended responsibility.

Robert instinctively knew that a ground assault on the fire and the construction of fire-limiting control lines would be too dangerous, especially with the quantity and dryness of the fuels, in addition to the continued blowing of the wind. Plus, there were too few potential fire fighters and no equipment except for some farm implements. Robert recalled the famous series of fires in 1910 in Idaho and considered that a series of back-fires might be effective and that really was the only recourse realistically available to them. During the Idaho fire, many individual fires had grown in intensity and combined to form a super conflagration that seemed to have a mind of its own and even jumped across wide barriers such as rivers and lakes.

He recalled working in the Tally Lake Ranger District before the year he started smokejumping and remembered marveling how the 1910 Idaho fire had jumped across the several kilometer-wide Tally Lake. A witness said that the fire arrived at the lake's edge, hesitated a long second, and then simply jumped across the lake. In that second, the heat of the fire had volatilized the pine oils and terpenes and ignited them and then the slope across the lake had simply exploded in flames.

Robert knew that backfires would be the only realistic tool they had that could be effective in this situation, but they also could be dangerous to start and manage. The steep mountains might allow a fire to jump across the intervening valley and ignite the slope on the other side and trap the fighters between the two fires. He recalled the Mann Gulch fire in Montana in 1949 in which 12 smokejumpers had perished when a seemingly innocuous fire had jumped across a ravine below them and then quickly burned upslope to trap them before they could escape.

In order to facilitate an effective control of the fire, Robert and *Gustavo* set up the first command post in the mayor's office in the village of *Lonquimay*. Robert knew from past experience that a quick response was necessary, even though he wasn't sure what that response might end up being. He asked *Gustavo* to appoint a dozen trusted individuals as foremen, people he could trust to do as they were told. Each foreman was to be in charge of a dozen equally trustworthy men. These crews would need to move rapidly to wherever they were needed, whether it was to set backfires or put out spot fires that were certain to appear. They had no radios. The *Carabineros* also had no radios, only a telephone link to the regional headquarters in *Temuco*.

Gustavo, along with the *Carabineros*, needed to commandeer several pickup trucks and drivers to patrol the highway alongside the *Naranjo* River. Each truck would carry half a crew. Their job was to simply drive back and forth between pre-established points along the road. When a spot fire occurred, they were to drop off the half-crew to remain and control the spot fire and go to the staging point to pick up the other half-crew and continue with their patrol. Robert suspected, and hoped, that none of them might ever see a spot fire but someone had to be there in case they did occur.

The biggest communication problem was between the valleys. There were no roads that could support vehicular traffic. So, Robert set up a field command post just across the *Naranjo* River from town. His plan was to send in a small crew to set a series of control burns on the east side of the creek closest to the sawmill. The biggest problem was that of quick communication. The crew had to be able to communicate with him and he had to be able to send messages to them.

As the crew prepared to carry out their mission, Robert told them that they must walk quickly the length of the creek up to its source and then as fast as they could, move back downstream, setting fires in a steady line as they walked back. They had no flares or other fire ignition equipment so Robert had an idea. Each crew would carry several jugs of kerosene with them. When they were to start the backfires, several men would move along quickly, sloshing a little kerosene onto suitable vegetation and then move along.

Two men following fast behind them would only be striking stick matches and throwing the ignited matches onto the kerosene-soaked vegetation. They would not stop to make sure each site ignited and lose time. Instead, they would move swiftly along and keep striking and throwing lighted matches. If only a portion of the fires ignited, they would quickly merge with nearby fires in the now very flammable kerosene-soaked vegetation. If they were lucky, those fires would coalesce and quickly form one big front as it moved up the hill. Hopefully it would reach the top of the mountain before the fire near the sawmill arrived at the top and then the two would merge and die down for lack of fuels.

Robert wasn't very happy about it but *Rosa* volunteered to ride on horseback and relay communications back and forth. She was excellent with horses and was probably the best person available for the job. She would go with this first crew to the base of the stream and wait for them to set the backfires, and then ride back to inform Robert what they had done while the crew walked back to the field command post.

But, as luck would have it, when *Rosa* and the first crew arrived at the base of the creek, they could see that the fire had already topped the hill by the sawmill and was just beginning to move downslope at a fast pace. So, *Rosa* galloped back to Robert as the crew began their walk back. Before *Rosa* arrived, Robert had already guessed as to what was happening. He saw a tremendous column of smoke building up as the fire moved up the first mountain slope. When the fire arrived at the top of the mountain, it seemed to stop for several long seconds. Then there was a mighty roar, as if a thousand freight trains were rolling past at the same time.

The ground shook and this was accompanied by a mighty flash of flame and a roar as the fire jumped across the first valley and in one long second ignited the vegetation on the opposite mountain-side. This is what had happened during the Idaho fire in the United States in 1910. The heat of the fire was so intense that it volatilized the organic materials in the vegetation and then ignited everything in one mighty flash and roar. The flash of light and roar elicited shouts and screams in *Lonquimay*. Some people began praying.

When Robert saw and realized what was happening, he knew that to attempt a second backfire along the next stream would be too risky, because as fast as the fire had moved, they would have to depend on only one more backfire and that was at the bottom of the hill along the *Naranjo* River. Thank goodness *Rosa* was back and he asked her to ride over to all the ground crews along the river and tell them that he was planning to set a series of backfires at the bottom of the mountain next to the river and that they would need to start the fires as soon as *Rosa* rode up with the order. The first backfires should be in the back of their house. He would be there to extinguish any spot fires that developed near their house or outbuildings. *Gustavo* would remain with him to relay any last-minute instructions to the other fire fighters.

The fire fighters would then need to be especially vigilant to seek and quickly suppress spot fires that would certainly start from such a close series of backfires. During the next few minutes, *Rosa* played a vital role as she galloped back and forth on horseback relaying commands to the fire fighters and their responses to Robert who was now on the line, issuing commands as the need arose.

The spot fires coalesced quickly and the collective backfire swept up the slope. The combined backfires actually created a strong wind that roared up the slope. Embers flew into the air and were blown back toward town by higher winds. Some embers landed in town and started small fires that were suppressed by the town's fire department crew and residents. Everyone worked through the night as the fire eventually died down due to the slight moisture uptake by the fuels as the relative humidity rose. When daylight returned, the steadily increasing glow from the other side indicated that their backfire method might prove to have worked. By noon the other fire arrived at the top of the mountain and spit angry showers of embers onto the town of *Lonquimay*. By now, though, not much could scare these people as they worked wearily to extinguish the last of the small spot fires scattered here and there.

They had done it! With the cooperation of virtually all the adults in the town, and with their faith in Robert's wildfire fighting experience, a miracle had been performed! Just before noon on that day, several bus-loads of fire-fighting *Carabineros* arrived in town to patrol the burned over areas and extinguish small fires. Thousands of hectares of prime *Araucaria* pine forest had been lost, but the "*Sur Negro*" had done its worst and the town of *Lonquimay* had survived! And the rest of the *Araucaria* pine forest north of the river had survived! And, their house had survived!

Early the next morning, as townspeople assembled in the town plaza to greet the dozens of fire fighters coming in, Robert met *Rosa* and said, "Well, honey, we did it, you did it!" They embraced and hugged for a long time, just standing there in each other's arms. As they just stood there, hugging each other, they became aware of people standing around them. As they parted, dozens of people came up, shook their hands and said, *"Gracias Roberto y Rosa por un trabajo bien hecho."* ("Thank you, Robert and *Rosa,* for a job well done.") After awhile Robert and *Rosa* looked at each other and Robert said, "Come on. Let's go home. Our beautiful house is filled with smoke but at least it's still standing and not just a pile of ashes."

As they walked home Robert suddenly recalled that moment a decade earlier when *Rosa* had given herself to him and that the fire today had incinerated that area as well as the *canelo* grove with its unique single *misodendrum* infestation.

CHAPTER 29
A Last Challenge – 1983

"Tengo una petaquita, para ir guardando, las penas y pesares, que voy pasando; Pero algún día, pero algún día, abro la petaquita, y la encuentro vacía:" (I have a little secret place, where I hide my pains; But one day, but one day, I opened the little place, and found it to be empty.)
– Song verses from *La Petaquita* (The Little Secret Place)
– Song by *Violeta Parra.*

In January of the previous year, two plant pathologists from the Department of Plant Pathology at the University of Minnesota had returned from a plant-collecting trip in southern Chile. They had come on a foray specifically to collect forest pathology specimens. One of the pathologists was a specialist in parasitic plants and he had collected quite a number of pressed and whole specimens of various species of *misodendrum*. The pressed specimens were packed in a bundle and some not pressed larger specimens were packaged in cardboard boxes.

Although they had a USDA certificate to collect these specimens, when they returned to the United States at the Miami airport, the overly zealous USDA inspector there insisted on sending the specimens to their Washington, D. C. facility for further inspection and fumigation. While the specimens were *en route* back from Washington, the truck carrying them crashed and one of the boxes was ripped apart. Most, but not all, of the specimens were eventually recovered and forwarded to the scientists at the University in St. Paul.

A week or so after the excitement of the fire in *Lonquimay* dissipated and there was a return to normalcy, *Rosa* began to complain of occasional pains in her abdomen. They had begun several days after the fire had been brought under control. She thought that perhaps the nearly constant bouncing up and down on a galloping horse had stretched or broken something loose in her abdomen, causing the pain.

But, the pains persisted. After several weeks had passed and the pains got worse, Robert insisted that she have a medical examination. A visit to the doctor in *Temuco* quickly resulted in another visit, this time in *Santiago*. The specialist there said she thought that *Rosa* had stage-2 ovarian cancer and that it needed to be removed immediately.

Ovarian cancer is a terrible disease for a woman to experience. The cancer starts when cells in the ovary begin to grow out of control. In healthy ovaries, normal cells replace cells that wear out and die or to repair injuries. However, abnormal cancerous cells are sometimes formed and, instead of dying, continue to grow and divide and create new abnormal cells to soon form a tumor. These cells can eventually move into the bloodstream or lymph vessels of the body.

Many types of tumors can start in the ovaries. Some tumors are benign, and these can be surgically eliminated by removing that ovary or that part of the ovary containing the tumor. Other tumors are malignant or cancerous. In these cases, the treatment options become much more involved, complex, and sometimes much more problematic.

The three main treatment options include: surgery, chemotherapy, and radiation therapy. Surgery is the most common treatment to simply remove the cancerous cells. But, chemotherapy uses chemical medications that travel through the bloodstream to destroy cancerous cells growing both inside and outside the ovaries. Radiation treatment, using high-energy X-rays to kill cancer cells, was seldom used at that time.

Robert and *Rosa* discussed the diagnosis and, after little hesitancy, decided to go to the United States for another diagnosis. Robert made arrangements for them to fly that week to see another specialist, this time in the Mayo Clinic in Rochester, Minnesota.

Robert had placed most of his plant-collecting income, and his military pay while in the hospital, in savings and they could easily afford the trip, and although they had no health insurance, decided to go regardless of the expense. The visit to Mayo confirmed what the doctor in *Santiago* had told them, but now the tumor had advanced to a stage-4 and surgical removal of the tumor was not now recommended by the several specialists with whom they had consulted. It was too late! *Rosa* was feeling so much pain now that she was afraid to fly and so she and Robert decided to go to his parents' home in Missoula. She was afraid that she would die there rather than in Chile, but at least she would be with Robert and *Paulina*, and Robert's wonderful parents.

As *Rosa* and Robert left the hospital they continued to discuss their options, which they realized were virtually non-existent. Normally, if detected early enough, ovarian cancer was removed by surgery and then the patient was given a series of radiation treatments and perhaps chemical therapy. But, in *Rosa's* case, the cancer had progressed too rapidly! The prognosis was not good and all that could be done was for *Rosa* to be kept as comfortable as possible.

Robert and *Rosa* were in shock and *Rosa* and *Paulina* were in tears, but they began to discuss what they might do. Their discussion continued as they entered the parking lot to their rental car and, as they arrived at the car, a small sagebrush-like growth of plant material blew against *Rosa's* leg, startling her. Robert glanced at it and instantly recognized it as being a witches' broom of *misodendrum*. He remarked, "How strange that it should be here in Minnesota."

Rosa, though, gasped and grabbed Robert's hand! She had instantly suspected that it was some kind of message from her mother! She then recalled conversations with her grandmother *Luisa* several months before she died. *Luisa* had told her that the *misodendrum* plant had some powerful attributes but it was extremely dangerous to use without great care. *Luisa* told her that a *misodendrum* plant parasitizing a sacred *canelo* tree was especially powerful. Unfortunately, historically this combination had such powerful attributes that, although once fairly common in southern Chile, it had been collected so heavily that *canelo* trees infected with *misodendrum* were basically extinct. It had an almost prehistoric history of medicinal powers that none of the modern-day *Pehuenches* now understood. That knowledge had been lost! And the only relic-infected *canelo* had been incinerated in the forest fire earlier that year. Robert kicked himself for not having done anything more about it before the fire. They both recalled the letter that

Claudia had left for *Rosa* and discussed what it might mean. And then, Robert had an idea!

Most medicinal plants gained their efficacy from certain extractives such as essential oils, alkaloids, and other metabolic by-products. In fact, success of the entire medicinal plant industry was based on this premise. Previously, scientists at Pharmtec had extracted some essential oils and other metabolic components from *misodendrum* plants. They were actually quite rich in certain essential oils. But, Robert's boss had told him that the *misodendrum* leaves from the *canelo* infection were especially rich in a variety of essential oils and other components that they had not identified because of the small amount of tissue that Robert had sent.

Robert wondered if some of these components could help *Rosa*. Were there any *canelo* extracts left? His boss said, "Yes, they had been freeze-dried but the amount was very small." The problem was that even if they had a larger amount, they did not know which portions might be effective. Robert did not know if they should be injected, taken orally, or what. At the worst, *Rosa* could perhaps be poisoned if he guessed wrong. At best, she would probably die of the cancer.

As they discussed the dangers, *Rosa's* response was that she was going to die a horrible death anyway and she wanted to take a chance with whatever strategy Robert could devise. Robert conjectured that they should use the extract in as natural a state as possible. Ancestors of the *Pehuenches* had apparently used the *misodendrum/canelo* combination in the distant past and they did not have fancy equipment with which to make sophisticated extracts, so Robert felt that a ground-up concoction of plant material steeped in hot water was likely to be their best chance. And, since the ancients did not have sophisticated injection equipment either, the best chance seemed to be for *Rosa* to either drink the steeped liquid or rub it into the skin on her abdomen. They did both with the tiny amount of available material.

Robert performed the treatments once because there was only enough material for one treatment. He had no idea if it would work or not and he had used up valuable time. Two months had passed since *Rosa* first noticed the pains. And she seemed to be noticeably failing each day. Would the treatment work? *Rosa* would lose her life if it didn't and there wasn't even the slightest hint that it might work.

Finally, *Rosa's* health failed to the point where she could no longer ingest food, or even drink the very small amount of steeped liquid remaining of the *misodendrum/canelo* concoction. She grew weaker and weaker and finally slipped into a coma. They made her as comfortable as they could and waited for the end. Robert and *Paulina* were with her constantly. Robert sensed that the spirit of *Claudia* was there as well although he saw no vision of her.

Misodendrum brachystachium
(redrawn from *Muñoz*, 1959)

CHAPTER 30
The new cemetery, *Lonquimay* Valley – 1990

It was a day of festivity! Robert and *Paulina* loaded the car at the house and departed for the new cemetery. By now, *Paulina* was a beautiful 17-year-old young lady and Robert was very proud of her. They followed a few other cars up the mountain road as first dozens, and then, several hundred, of other *Pehuenche* tribe members joined the caravan. Robert parked the car at the foot of the mountain where the new cemetery was to be located.

Shortly after the coup in 1973, false claimants had appealed to the sympathetic military dictatorship to claim that the *Pehuenche* ownership of much of the tribal land was false and obtained the legal right to do whatever they wished with the land. This included harvesting the *Araucaria* pine forests that were prevalent there. Tribal elders had lost title to the land where the old cemetery was located and, and after continued desecrations by military sympathizers, decided to relocate it to a more secure site, deep in now-secure tribal lands.

Robert unlocked the trunk and removed the funerary box containing the bones of *Claudia* while *Paulina* removed the box containing the bones of her grandfather *Juan*. Even though she was only a baby when he was killed, she felt a great affection for him, as she did for her grandmother *Claudia*. She wished that they had the remains of her uncle *Miguel* but nobody knew where he was buried, if in fact he ever had been buried. At any rate, today they would erect a **goji totum** in his memory so his spirit would have a place to rest at this now holy place.

Robert had been raised as a Catholic but he had seen enough mysteries since he came to Chile and lived among the *Pehuenches* and so he had a healthy respect for their religion. At the new site, they placed the boxes on the ground and turned to retrieve another set. Their hearts, and especially Robert's, were heavy as he remembered *Claudia* and *Juan* and how they had come to such untimely, and needless, deaths.

As Robert and *Paulina* paced back down the trail, Robert's thoughts shifted to reflect on the incredibly satisfying life he had experienced so far here in Chile. It was all due to *Rosa* and her wonderful family. Now he had his and *Rosa's* daughter, *Paulina*, and the love and respect of the residents of *Lonquimay*. As *Rosa* and her entourage approached in another car, through tears he could see that many other cars had arrived and people were unloading more funerary boxes of relatives. Others were unloading packages of picnic materials and laying out picnic blankets.

He said to *Paulina*, "Honey, do you remember that day 10 years ago when we thought we were losing your mother? How exhausted we all were after sitting by her bedside for almost two weeks. And then I went to the extra bedroom and fell asleep. As in a dream I thought I heard someone speaking in Spanish and then as I awoke realized that it was your grandmother *Claudia* speaking with your mother. You heard them as well and ran into my room shouting, "*Papá, Papá*, come, come, *Mamá* is better and is sitting up in bed," and how we both ran in and there she was, alive! Do you remember, *Paulina*, of the joy we felt?" *Paulina* answered with an expression of joy on her face, "Yes, *Papá*, I remember!"

Almost every one of the *Pehuenches* living in the valley appeared to be at the site of the new cemetery today and all were dressed in their finest traditional costumes. Most were laughing, some were singing, children were running from side to side, screaming with happiness and joy. How lucky he felt to be a part of this remarkable group of people! Then, his eyes misted over as he saw *Rosa* stepping out of the car, dressed in the shining silver-trimmed regalia of a tribal **machi**. She smiled when he gave a little wave and she waved back.

Robert was so grateful that *Rosa's* grandmother had known of a possible remedy to use in attacking the ovarian tumor. The remedy apparently proved to be very effective but the secret of its efficacy was the essential oil in the lipid material from the *misodendrum/canelo* combination that the lab at

Pharmtec had extracted, purified, and concentrated. One of the most serious obstacles in the cancer treatment had been how to get the chemical into the tumor. And, no one in 1990 yet knew how it worked!

CHAPTER 31
Return to *Juan Fernández* – 1990

In 1981, when Jean was a very old man, and not long before he died, he and Robert developed a plan to collect medicinal plants on the *Juan Fernández* Islands. The two of them got passage on a lobster boat that periodically sailed out of *Valparaíso* and went to the island to buy lobsters that the islanders had trapped. They spent several days at the *chonta* grove and the surrounding area, but the palms were all severely diseased. Robert collected a few samples, fixed them in FAA preservative and sent them back to the United States. They were all infected with the palm-yellowing virus that caused a fatal disease.

In late 1990 Robert returned to the site, now with his young daughter *Paulina*, to find that all the *chonta* palms were gone and not a single root or stump sprout remained. Thusly, a potential extremely valuable medicinal plant was lost to humanity. Robert, though, had brought *Paulina* with him and took advantage of the trip to explore more of the island with his wonderful daughter. *Rosa* remained at home, managing their medicinal plant business.

Robert and *Paulina* decided to remain on the island for several days and explore several remote parts of it. They visited the cave where Alexander Selkirk allegedly lived for the four years when he was marooned on the island. Jean had mentioned that on the far side of the island he had found several solitary *chonta* palms and there was a series of caves in the cliffs overlooking the beach that served as home for hundreds of sea lions.

So, in spite of his artificial leg, he and *Paulina* clambered up the trail to

El Yunque where the memorial to Alexander was attached to a cliff face alongside the trail and then back down the other side on the eroded trail that remained. They spent several hours exploring the caves. Although several dozen to several hundred persons lived at any one time in the little village above the harbor where the Dresden had been scuttled, almost no one ever climbed the trail to *El Yunque* and then back down the backside of the mountain. It was a very remote place.

So, Robert felt especially blessed to explore this place with his daughter. They had become very close as she grew to be quite a young woman and both he and *Rosa* were very proud of her. The island had been declared a national park and both felt that it deserved the long-needed protection.

After climbing down the backside of the mountain, Robert became tired and sat in the entrance of one of the upper caves and admired the scenery below him. *Paulina* continued to clamber around the boulders below him, disappearing from view now and then as she entered this or that cave.

All the caves they had entered were relatively shallow and usually only a few meters deep. In the cave where Robert sat, though, the cave appeared to extend farther back and from where he sat, he couldn't see how far it went. When *Paulina* returned to see how he was doing, he suggested that they make a torch and explore the cave. It was only mid-day so they felt they had plenty of time to do so.

After making torches out of dried leaves and twigs, they lit the first torch and entered the cave. A few meters in, they encountered a large pile of rocks that had apparently fallen from the roof at some time in the distant past. They squeezed through the space on top and found they were in a somewhat larger room than the one where they had come from. They encountered several more of the rock piles and decided to climb over just one more and then return to the entrance.

As they were crawling down on the other side of the last rock pile, Robert noticed a piece of rusty iron sticking out from under a rock. He took hold of it and with some effort pulled out a broken strip of metal, badly pitted with rust but identifiable as a sword, an antique Spanish sword judging from the ironwork around the handle. He thought, how interesting, as he handed it to *Paulina*, who had just slid down from the tight opening at the top of the rock pile.

As they stood in the little chamber and looked around, they noticed several more pieces of rusty metal, some appearing to be portions of old Spanish armor. As *Paulina* lifted some pieces of arm armor, she observed pieces of badly rotted wood under some bones from the soil where she had removed the armor. She and Robert scraped away some soil and saw a yellow glint in the soil, glittering as it reflected light from their torches. They pulled out several old Spanish coins and small bars of metal, obviously all were of gold!

As they discussed what must have happened here - apparently some Spanish soldiers, or pirates, were planning to hide some plunder here for temporary safekeeping but had been crushed and killed when the roof of the cave had collapsed. Why had their compatriots not tried to save them or recover their gold? Perhaps an earthquake had caused the collapse, and its aftershocks had so terrified them that they sailed away. There was another possible explanation, perhaps the earthquake had produced a tsunami that had destroyed the ship and killed the survivors.

At any rate, as they lit their last torch, they discussed what they might do about the gold and relics. Then *Paulina* made an observation and suggestion for which Robert was extremely grateful and remembered with great satisfaction for the rest of his life. It also greatly increased the respect he felt for his daughter.

She said, "*Papá*, you know that this island is now under the protection of the Chilean National Park System. It is a treasure that should be enjoyed by all future generations of people. We aren't wealthy, but we don't need the money. I think we should leave everything as we found it and not tell anyone, except perhaps *Mamá*."

Robert then picked up scattered stones and laid them on the armor, bones, and gold coins and rotten wood and replied, "I agree 100 percent, this will be our little secret and will someday be preserved for future generations to discover and we will have shared with them the joy of our discovery." Then they smiled at each other and began their return to the surface. Just as they were leaving the entrance, they felt several tremors and thought they could see more rocks falling from the cave ceiling they had just left.

As Robert and *Paulina* worked their way back down the trail from *El Yunque*, he followed *Paulina*, his beautiful and intelligent daughter. He watched as she worked her way over the rocks in the path and then as she skipped along in places that were more level. He compared her physical build with that of her mother. Her mother had black hair, *Paulina* had black hair and the same slender build and long legs of her mother, also a slightly more delicate aqualine nose than that of her mother. Robert reflected on his incredible life in Chile and the wonderful people he had known. He didn't let *Paulina* see his misty eyes as they left the mountain trail, but his heart almost burst in his chest and the tremendous sense of pride he felt for her as he remembered what had happened the day before when *Paulina* said that they had to leave the Spanish gold where they had found it.

By late afternoon they were back in the little village in the harbor. They met with their pilot and the next morning trekked up the spur mountain to the little airstrip and flew back to the mainland. They never told the park naturalist what they had seen. *Paulina* was now a 17-yr-old young lady and Robert couldn't have been prouder of her! He knew that *Claudia's* spirit was guiding her. He wondered where his life, and her life, would go from here. All he could realize was that a great sense of peace came over him as he reflected on all of these things. What a beautiful wife and daughter he had!

When they arrived back in *Lonquimay*, they related to *Rosa* what they had seen and done. They were all very disappointed with loss of the *chonta* palm but Robert and *Rosa* were very proud that *Paulina* had suggested that they leave the Spanish gold where they had found it. *Rosa* beamed with pride in her daughter and said, "Yes, she is our daughter and I knew she would be like that and that is why I waited so many years for you, *mi amor*. She carries the spirit of my mother. She has been given much character and she has much to give to her people and to humanity." *Rosa* then told them, "My grandmother *Luisa* told me of stories of several accounts of similar situations in the southern Central Valley of Chile in which *Mapuche*, and also Spanish, treasure had been stashed and now no-one remembered where it was."

Several weeks after they returned, *Rosa* and Robert suggested that she should go to college but where she might go was up to her. She did not want to leave home, but I think even she realized that she owed it to her grandparents in Montana to spend some time with them. After all, they had deposited a large amount of money in the bank for her college expenses. And so she requested that they send some literature from the University of Montana so that she might see what they offered. Science was advancing rapidly, though, and neither she nor her parents could have foreseen where it might go. She was pretty much bilingual, actually trilingual if you included the **Mapudungún** language of her ancestors, she was intelligent, and she would have no trouble with her studies.

CHAPTER 32
Higgins Avenue, Missoula, MT – autumn – 1993

"Let it be, Let it be, Whisper words of wisdom, Let it be."
(Verses from song by John Lennon.)

Nanno Mulder left his home in Holland at about the age of 26. He had a Bachelor's degree in Biology but did not yet know what he wanted to do with his life. As a teenager, he spent a lot of time with his hobby of photography. As the second son of parents who were both medical doctors, he seemed to be destined to a life of not only plenty but also of responsibility. His problem was that he did not have a passion for anything that might eventually earn him a living.

As the war clouds of the First Gulf War began to grow, a friend of his told him that one could make a good living as a war correspondent/photographer. There was a firm in Holland seeking potential correspondents to cover the war that appeared to be coming soon in Kuwait. So, with a sense of adventure he traveled to Kuwait and was there before the war began. He photographed the looting incurred by the invading Iraqis as well as some of the vandalism as the occupation was consolidated. He never felt that he was in much danger as the invading Iraqis appeared to enjoy being photographed during their destructive activities. Even after the American/coalition forces began to push them out, he felt relatively little danger until he arrived to photograph the Iraqi's chaotic retreat from Kuwait. He preceded the movement of American/coalition forces as they chased the retreating Iraqi forces out of Kuwait and then into Iraq.

In both countries, Kuwait and Iraq, he wrote about and photographed many of the horrors he observed and experienced. He became a changed person in several aspects and although he was very good at it, he realized that he did not want to spend the rest of his life as a war correspondent/photographer. Although he had never felt to have been in any real danger, he also knew that he had been very lucky. The American/ coalition invasion of Kuwait had been carefully planned and a large armed force had been put together to execute it. It was a quick campaign and produced little of the animosity that would result later immediately after the Second Gulf War when the Americans led by President George W. Bush fumbled the invasion of Iraq and its occupation. Later, as the unrest in the Middle East continued to erupt, he was grateful for having taken the next step in his life.

As a result of his work he had earned some considerable international recognition and was invited to join a group of war photographers who were going to exhibit their work at several sites in the United States as part of a low-key war-protest tour. While not particularly opposed to the war, he became more and more concerned about the horrors he had seen and photographed. Since he was never under the direct control of the American military his photographs were particularly graphic and were especially stark representations of the war situation.

As he continued on the tour, starting on the East Coast and continuing toward California, he was becoming more at odds with himself about what he wanted to do with the rest of his life. He felt more and more disenfranchised about his lack of life goals. He was interested in many things but did not have a passion for anything that might serve him in a professional career. On this trip he met many students who did have a passion for their life's work and expectation of encountering fulfilling professional employment. He also began to feel a yearning for a female companion with whom he might share his life. As a young man in Holland, he had known a number of girls but all seemed emotionally rather shallow and he never developed a lasting relationship with any of them.

While on the bus tour toward their last major stop in San Francisco, his tour manager suggested that they make a side trip to Missoula, Montana. The student body of the university there had made particularly strong protests against the war in Vietnam and there was still some lingering protest against the recent First Gulf War.

So, it was that he found himself in a café on Higgins Avenue in downtown Missoula that crisp October evening, a day before the exhibition was to open. He sat there, eating his supper, watching the crowd of student protestors whooping and hollering as a series of protestors sang. He rather absentmindedly looked up from time to time as one protestor after another strode up to the stage and sang.

The next protestor was a young lady – with her long, black hair she appeared to resemble the popular folk singer of a generation past, Joan Baez. He watched as she climbed the stairs to the stage, and he glanced up from time to time somewhat disinterestedly as she prepared to sing. She was quite attractive. She had straight-flowing, jet black hair, a some-what hooked nose suggestive of Arab ancestry, was tall, slender, and was wearing blue slacks and a white short-sleeved pullover. She was carrying an acoustic guitar and strummed a few times as the crowd quieted down. Nanno turned his attention to his supper and listened halfheartedly as she sang through a medley of protest songs: a couple by Peter, Paul and Mary, a couple by Bob Dylan, and a last one by Pete Seegar.

He glanced up after she finished that medley and noticed that she had placed her guitar on the stand. She then stepped close to the micro-phone and said to a hushed audience, "There is someone in this audience who has never seen me before, like-wise I have never seen him before. But, destiny has brought us together to be soul mates. He will know who he is when he hears this song." A few students hooted, "Atta way to go, Pauley," and they clapped and cheered.

Nanno thought to himself, "Ah, great! I wonder what she has been smoking." She then stepped very close to the microphone and standing very erect and with her mouth almost touching the microphone she began to sing, without musical accompaniment. He returned to his supper as she began – and he could just barely hear the lyrics as she began – it was a song by John Lennon – "When I find myself in times of trouble, Mother Mary comes to me, Speaking words of wisdom, let it be." Then he began to listen a little more intently, "And in my hour of darkness, She is standing right in front of me, Speaking words of wisdom, let it be."

Her song was in English but she sang with a very slight accent that he could not identify. Then she continued to sing, and sing she did! She sang the next verse in a way that Nanno had never heard before. She sang with such clarity of voice and passion that he forgot about his supper and stood up.

"Let it be, let it be, let it be, let it be, Whisper words of wisdom, let it be."

He left some money on the table and went outside to listen to her clear, piercing voice. She sang with such clarity of voice! It seemed as though she was singing directly to him! Yes, she was singing directly to him!

As he worked his way through the crowd toward the stage, he saw that she wore a necklace consisting of many small squares of polished silver strung together. As he neared the stage, he thought he saw her glancing at him from time to time, especially toward the end of the song. He thought he saw a slight smile on her face as she sang. It seemed almost like a smile of recognition. She continued with all the verses until the last, - and as she sang it she was looking directly at him, "There will be an answer, let it be; Let it be, let it be, let it be, let it be; Whisper words of wisdom, let it be".

He finally stopped in front of the stage where she was singing and stared up at her as she finished her song. After the cheers of the crowd quieted down, she glanced down at him again, then looked him squarely in the eyes, and said into the microphone, "I have been waiting a long time for you, *gringo*, why did you take so long to find me?"

Nanno was astounded! Had they met some time before that he did not remember? How could he not remember her? All he could think about were those piercing words ringing in his ears and he felt greatly at peace with himself.

Postscript - *Paulina's* song was the last in the program, and so, after she and Nanno had stood there for a few moments, he feeling a little more awkward with each passing moment. Finally, he said, "Let's go into the restaurant and have something to drink. I already ate supper but would just like to sit with you and learn more about this stroke of destiny that we have apparently shared, or experienced, or whatever you prefer to call it."

They went into the restaurant and found a table way in the back, sat down and ordered a light meal. Then *Paulina* sat back and said, "My mother is a Chilean **machi**, a kind of medicine woman. In our family, a young woman in each generation becomes a practitioner of medicine using plants as a source of natural remedies. According to a legend that has been passed down in our family for many generations, some of us also have the ability to foretell certain things that may happen in the future. I know you don't believe this, but several things have happened in my life, and that of my father and mother, to suspect that such premonitions may, in fact, actually occur, sometimes."

"At any rate, when I was a young lady, just preparing to come to the United States to study in college, my mother told me and *Papá* the night before I left that I was going to meet a young man, you, in my last year of college, during a protest concert, and that I would sing, 'Let it be' by John Lennon. She pretty much described your physical appearance and that you had been a war photographer, that you were disillusioned, and that you were a lost soul as regards your future. She didn't say where you were from, only that we would meet and that we would fall in love, study together, work well together, and have two children."

As *Paulina* related her parents' life story, and that of her grandparents, Nanno became more and more fascinated with this young lady sitting with him and began to feel a certain attraction for her. She seemed so full of life and confidence in what she was involved, not only at the protest concert, but also what she was studying to prepare for her life's work. He felt a little envious of her confidence and determination. He wanted to know more about her.

After several hours of conversation, she slid her chair back and stood.

She said, "I have heard that life in Holland is rather risqué, and you are probably hoping that we will now go to bed together. However, my little *gringuito*, even though we will fall in love it will have to be at a more relaxed pace. I have my studies - you have your exposition. I will be here at the University of Montana until next spring when I will graduate with a Bachelor's degree. Think about what you have seen and heard here tonight and come back next fall and we can enter graduate school together and we will see what the future will bring to us."

CHAPTER 33
New Orleans, LA – 2000 – Annual Meeting of the American Phytopathological Society

A year after Robert and *Paulina* had returned from the *Juan Fernández* Islands, *Paulina*, along with her parents, decided that she would study for her Bachelor's degree in the United States. At that time she was 18 years old. She was accepted at the now University of Montana, from where Robert had graduated several decades earlier when it was known as Montana State University. She, like her father, also studied botany. Her intention at that time was to learn as much as she could about medicinal plants and then study for a Master's degree in chemistry.

By the time *Paulina* began her studies, the general physiology of plants was pretty well understood and a great shift in research was underway to understand the ecology of plant/environment interactions. She did well at the university. By 1999, when she was 26 years old and married, she and her husband, another doctoral student, Nanno Mulder from Holland whom she met during her graduate studies, were finishing their doctorates at the University of Minnesota. For her doctorate she had enrolled in the Department of Genetics and Cell Biology and he had enrolled in the Department of Plant Pathology. They made a complementary, and eventually formidable, team.

During the time of her graduate studies, *Paulina's* life took an unexpected turn. The field of molecular genetics was exploding. Gene sequencing was becoming very popular, and useful in many different areas of biology. So, when *Paulina* took a course in special problems to learn the technique of gene sequencing and needed a project, she decided to focus on some aspect of medicinal plants, but with an unusual twist. All her life she had been committed to learning as much as she could about her *Pehuenche* ancestors and their close relationship with medicinal plants. So, for this problem, which then soon led to the main theme of her doctoral dissertation, she chose to do genetic sequencing of the native *Araucánian* Indians in southern Chile.

As she started her sequencing research, she did the first trials with her own blood. To her surprise, much of her DNA had areas with high rates of methylation. She did not know what this might mean. An important finding when she explored this aspect further was that virtually all of the *Pehuenches* whose blood that she had sampled and sequenced also had an unusually high percentage of methylated DNA. At the time no one knew what had caused the high rates of methylation of DNA, or what it might mean.

As she became drawn into the excitement of this work, she wondered if her mother's DNA also had a high rate of methylation. So, she asked her mother to send a mouth swab from which she could obtain a genetic sequence. Surprisingly, her mother had a relatively low percentage of methylated DNA. The next time she called her parents in Chile she mentioned this to her father. He recalled that his business partners in Hamilton, Montana probably still had blood samples of *Rosa* from before she had been diagnosed and treated for ovarian cancer. *Paulina* got those samples and ran another series of sequencing and methylation tests. DNA from those samples was heavily methylated!

She gave a seminar on her research to the department and afterward a colleague in another department mentioned that in her laboratory they had identified one of the DNA sequences that initiated the immune response in humans. When they tested and compared *Rosa's* early and later DNA samples, their work revealed that the major gene regulating the immune response was methylated in the early blood samples and not methylated in the later samples.

What did all this mean? Her frantic research activity, and then that of her husband, came to a sudden focus when fellow scientists on the planning board of the American Phytopathological Society suggested that the two of them were to be selected as keynote speakers for the proposed "Symposium on the Interaction of Plant Pathogens on the Success of Medicinal Plants" at the next annual meeting which was to be held in New Orleans, LA.

Each year the planning committee faced the rather daunting task of identifying a new or emerging area of research focus that had not yet acquired much national attention but was backed by enough solid research to indicate that it represented a new and innovative research thrust, something that might be of value to prospective attendees and useful for their research planning. The use of medicinal plants was becoming very popular at this time and one focus of this presentation, to be presented by Nanno Mulder, was to summarize some of the major plant pathogenic diseases of these medicinal plants.

Plant pathologists, and especially extension specialists, had to be familiar with these new diseases if they were to be useful to a concerned public. And, research planners had to know what diseases were increasing in incidence or importance so they could plan useful research for their control. The second focus of the symposium, to be presented by *Paulina*, was not as well understood by the planning committee but her graduate advisor assured the committee that her presentation would be provocative.

So, exactly one year later, in a crowded auditorium of several hundred eager plant pathology students, technicians, professors, and members of the press, *Paulina* and Nanno sat at the left end of the front row waiting to be introduced. *Paulina* sat between her parents, *Rosa* and Robert, and her two children, *Sebastian* and *Alexandra*.

Nanno introduced his talk by presenting several slides showing lists, and some drawings and photographs, of medicinal plants, not only those known in Chile, but from around the world. After a brief description of the plants and the remedies they were responsible for, he opened the main theme of his presentation by remarking, "The amazing fact about most of these medicinal plants is that they have very few diseases! Why is this?"

His next slide showed a summary of all medicinal plants known in Europe, Asia, North America, and South America to emphasize the major point of his presentation. This slide was of a graph showing two more or less horizontal lines, but one ascending and one descending.

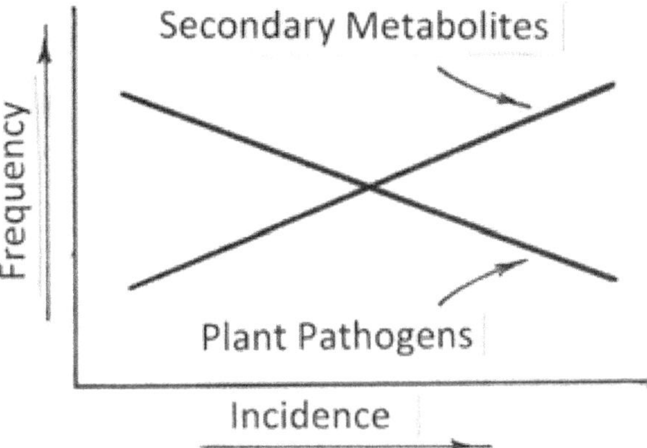

The relationship between the frequency of secondary metabolites and the incidence of plant diseases in green plants.

He continued, "The ascending linear regression line represents all the medicinal plants from around the world that have been studied in many laboratories and that are known to synthesize various secondary metabolites that have known positive medicinal effects on humans. The declining regression line represents the known number of diseases affecting each particular plant, regardless as to whether they are caused by fungi, bacteria, viruses, or mycoplasmas. Notice the sharp decline in that line toward the right side of the graph. So, what this graph is saying is that the more secondary metabolites a plant has, the fewer diseases it also has. It is a statistically significant relationship."

He continued, "I will briefly explain why that is. To begin, we must have an understanding of the important metabolic pathways present in plants. A simplified outline of primary and secondary metabolism is shown in this diagram:"

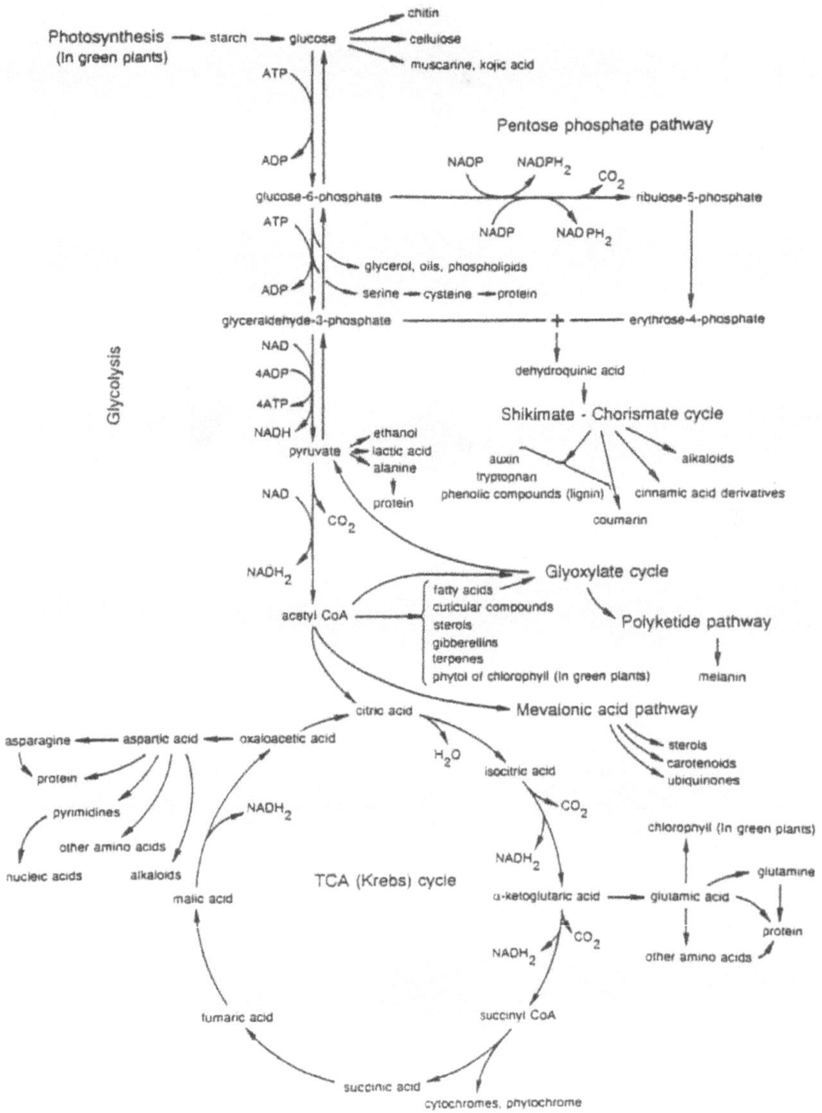

The major metabolic pathways in green plants.
(redrawn from Tainter and Baker, 1996)

As he continued his presentation, he pointed his laser light at the various parts of the diagram as he described each of them. "The major physiologic pathway in green plants is that of photosynthesis. Photosynthesis utilizes the sun's energy to make glucose, which is the energy-containing carbon skeleton starting point for all the subsequent major metabolic pathways in plants. Glucose is quickly produced and stored as starch until needed and then it is eventually transformed, as needed, into cell walls and many other carbon-containing components."

"Plants are able to use this energy via a process called metabolism. There are two major forms of metabolism, primary and secondary, that are active in green plants. Primary metabolism is responsible for the degradation of organic molecules, such as glucose, and for the production of energy and synthesis of lipids, carbohydrates, nucleic acids, and proteins. So, primary metabolism involves two basic aspects that are opposite in their actions but complementary in their effects."

"The pathways of secondary metabolism usually are only synthetic and produce metabolites that have no obvious cellular function but do tend to be specific for a particular group of plants." Nanno then made a general circular gesture toward the drawing on the screen and continued. "Pathways of secondary metabolism are particularly important for students seeking possible medicinal properties. Secondary metabolism is usually more prevalent after the active growth resulting from primary metabolism has ceased. Many secondary metabolites have no known physiologic function to the plant that produces them. They are usually produced through the Mevalonic acid pathway, the Polyketide pathway, or the Shikimate pathway."

He continued and pointed at each of these pathways on the diagram as he spoke, "The production of secondary metabolites may be a way in which plants remove and compartmentalize excess intermediates before they become toxic to that plant. They may coincidentally serve the function of preventing invasion by pathogenic fungi or insects and their production has the major secondary benefit of allowing them to survive in a dog-eat-dog world."

"A well-known example of toxic secondary metabolites is the large amount of polyphenolics produced by the Shikimate-Chorismate cycle following wounding of plant tissues. These metabolites are toxic to many potentially invading fungal pathogens, and even insects, and prevent subsequent infection or infestation. The brown color of a partially eaten apple, and some other fruits, is due to the oxidation of these phenolic materials and is a naturally evolved plant defense mechanism. So, now we can speculate as to why medicinal plants have few pathogenic diseases."

"In essence, medicinal plants have high concentrations of certain toxic metabolic byproducts, which for humans coincidently may have some medicinal properties, but for plants, these toxic materials help to protect them from infection by disease-causing organisms, or even infestation by insects. A good example for us today is the Chilean shrub, *boldo*. If one had to choose the most famous Chilean medicinal plant it would probably be this one. *Boldo* contains the alkaloid boldine and the chemical ascaridole that gives *boldo* its assertive flavor. Ascaridole is highly toxic and produces abortifacient and teratogenic effects in rats and has abortive qualities if used during pregnancy in people. In some people it may be toxic in large amounts and has antifungal, antibacterial, and antiviral qualities."

Nanno closed his presentation with this summary: "I happen to be familiar with many medicinal plants native to Chile, the country of birth of my beautiful wife who is sitting in the front row and who will continue this presentation. Her father worked as a medicinal plant explorer in Chile and his business partners studied many of the Chilean medicinal plants. Their hypothesis, which led to the formation of a successful business, was that medicinal plant remedies in Chile had undergone thousands of years of practical experimentation by native peoples to determine their efficacy."

"Their company collected many of these plants and extracted major secondary metabolites, and then began to correlate the different extractives with whatever sickness or disease the native peoples had employed them for. With the Chilean medicinal plant remedies they knew that they had a long tradition of effectiveness and it was just a matter of identifying those plants that were the most effective."

He introduced his conclusion with a list which he pointed to as he spoke, "Some of the secondary metabolites tested in their laboratory included: alkaloids, cinnamic acid derivatives, coumarin, and phenolic compounds from the Shikimate-Chorismate cycle; melanin from the Polyketide pathway; sterols, carotenoids and ubiquinones from the Mevalonic acid pathway. All the plant pathologists here already know that many of these compounds are toxic to plant pathogens. My current research is focused on exactly how these metabolites operate as medicinal remedies."

Nanno finished his presentation by introducing his wife, "*Paulina*, my better half, has worked on an off-shoot of this work and will share with us her interesting findings in the next presentation. I think you will see that serendipity is real and sometimes you can't predict where your research will lead you, even with the best of planning."

CHAPTER 34
Paulina's presentation

After the applause for Nanno had died down, *Paulina* came to the podium and spread out her notes. "Hi, my name is *Paulina* Mulder. My presentation will begin by sharing with you a little of my family history. In 1983 my mother was diagnosed with ovarian cancer. In the few weeks between the initial diagnosis and her arrival at the Mayo Clinic in Minnesota the cancer had progressed from a stage-2 to a stage-4. The future did not look good for my mother. The specialists at Mayo said that there was no hope and that surgery or other treatment would be futile. My mother prepared to die. But, my father did not lose hope. He had learned many years earlier, as a forest fire fighter, that when you are fighting a really big fire, any action is better than doing nothing."

"When he was collecting medicinal plants years earlier in Chile he was extremely interested in a parasitic plant that was, and still is, fairly common on many species of *Nothofagus* in the southern part of Chile. My grandmother had told my mother of some mysterious powers of that parasitic plant when it was parasitizing another Chilean tree called *canelo*. *Canelo* is a medicinal plant and was considered sacred by the native peoples. Many native people had also known about its strange and unusual powers and over the years had, unfortunately, harvested virtually all *canelo* trees infected with the *misodendrum* parasite, so much so that infected *canelo* became virtually extinct."

"My grandmother knew of only a single small grove of *canelo* trees infected with the *misodendrum* parasite. That grove was on her family's property in the mountains south of the village of *Lonquimay*. During my father's last week in Chile, in 1973, just before he was to go to Vietnam as a soldier, she instructed my mother to take him to a small grove of *canelo* trees that had only some of those trees with a few *misodendrum* parasites growing on their branches. It was the only remaining such grove that she was aware of. My father collected several small samples that he placed in his plant press to dry and then brought them back to the States. As we now know, that sacred grove was a magical place."

She continued with a smile, "For me it was especially magical, because my parents tell me that I was conceived on that very day in that very grove of *canelo* trees." Robert and *Rosa's* faces turned red and they smiled at each other. The audience loved her remark, though, and gave *Paulina* a standing round of applause. She said, "Unfortunately, a decade later, that grove, with those few infected *canelo* trees, was completely destroyed by a forest fire."

Then she returned to her presentation, "But, to digress, after my mother was diagnosed with ovarian cancer, and all hope was lost for her recovery, we desperately pondered what we thought was a message left by my grandmother before she was murdered by the military regime. In that message, she implied that only my father had the knowledge to save my mother. So, my father administered to mother a ground-up bit of dry *misodendrum* tissue from the *canelo* tree, all that was left of his original samples. But, we were dismayed! There was initially no change in my mother's condition and we prepared for her to die. Then, after about a week's time, she slowly improved and within several weeks she had recovered! Subsequent examinations have shown her to be free of ovarian cancer."

"Surely now, everyone here is thinking, we are scientists and know that this was probably only a chance event and there was no real cause and effect supported with credible scientific experimentation. But there persisted in our minds the intriguing possibility that something in the *misodendrum* extract had helped her body fight off the cancer."

She continued, "So, this is my story. We had no idea what might have been in the *misodendrum* extract that saved my mother. But, nearly 20 years after my father had originally sent the *misodendrum* sample to Pharmtec, the company that had employed him to collect medicinal plant samples, he received a package of recent scientific articles from his friends at Pharmtec that began to unravel the puzzle of what might have happened. He immediately called me at the university and relayed what the articles contained."

"With help from my advisor, I restructured my research to take advantage of this new information. Since the discovery in 1953 by Watson and Crick of the double-helix nature of DNA, scientists had produced thousands of research experiments and reams of scientific articles on every imaginable trait and characteristic of DNA and RNA. One of the interesting things discovered at Pharmtec was that extracts of *misodendrum* had a strong ability to demethylate DNA. At the time of that discovery, no one knew what benefit this might provide for the DNA, or for anything else for that matter, and so it was forgotten. What did this fact mean, if anything?"

"When mother was diagnosed with ovarian cancer, father sent samples of her blood to his friends at Pharmtec. They had not known what to do with them so they were placed in storage. After the methylation process of DNA was discovered, Pharmtec scientists, working with me in my early graduate studies, inspected those blood samples and were quite surprised and puzzled to discover that in mother's early blood samples, much DNA was methylated. Several years later, other scientists discovered the significant fact that methylation of the gene controlling the immune response could, in fact, stop activity of the immune system."

She continued, "Now I must give you a brief review of how the body fights infections. In many ways, cancer is an infection by a foreign organism. The first lines of defense against foreign invaders are the white blood cells. Certain specialized white blood cells, called macrophages, destroy any foreign proteins or germs encountered in the body. During an immune response, white blood cells called T cells produce a protein known as interleukin-2 (IL-2). High production of IL-2 sends T cells into overdrive to recognize and attack cancer cells. T cells are killers that use receptors to recognize and then attach these receptors to surface structures called antigens found on the invading protein. However, if the gene that programs production of T cells is kept from being activated, then no T cells, hence, no resistance response is possible."

"What my research revealed was that mother's strange recovery from ovarian cancer was suggested by a series of experimental observations I subsequently made. These early works were extremely crude then because it wasn't until nearly a decade later that gene technology had advanced far enough to prove my hypothesis, just as the roles of individual genes were beginning to be determined. I postulated that perhaps mother's DNA that encoded for the production of IL-2 was methylated and could not recognize the invading cancer protein."

"I did not figure this out from the blue. When I was a graduate student I experimented with my own blood and tried every new analytic technique as it became available. My IL-2 gene was methylated and this methylation was certainly inherited from my mother. Treatment with the essential oil from *misodendrum* removed this methylation from mother's DNA and allowed the affected gene to signal active production of IL-2, thus saving her from certain death from ovarian cancer."

"And, more had been learned of how cancer behaves in the human body. In theory at least, cancer had been thought to act as a foreign body that has invaded the body. The human immune system will normally attack and destroy any such foreign bodies, including tumors. The T cells can discriminate between foreign and host molecules. They act much like military police to watch over the immune system's defense (and act as soldier cells) to make sure they kill only foreign invaders and not damage the body's own healthy cells."

"Some cancers can actively interfere with the immune response, and in recent years, have been the object of considerable research effort. That work is not the object of this treatise. There was another reaction, however, which has come to be recognized as perhaps being very important in some instances with certain people."

"In mother's case, methylation of the DNA had stopped activity of the immune system. Something in the dried *misodendrum* extracts had removed the CH3, or methyl, groups from some of the DNA that was responsible for initiating the immune response in her body. Ovarian cancers, as well as many other cancers, are able to suppress the body's immune system which then allows the cancer to grow unchecked. Methylation of the gene controlling the immune response is one major reason for this suppression."

"A key question is 'What causes this methylation?'" "Soon-to-be-published scientific research reveals that methylation is often caused by exposure to chemical pollutants, or severe trauma. In mother's body, many DNA sites were methylated, and this was probably not a result of the spreading ovarian cancer, rather it was the result of some previous significant DNA methylation-causing event, either in her body or in the bodies of one or more of her ancestors. As early as the 1970s it was noted that in many people, many DNA genes had a methyl group on the end of the gene, which effectively prevented expression of that gene. No one then knew why, but it is now known that, incredibly, these methylated areas can survive several, or even many, generations. In other words, methylated DNA may survive gene desegregation, generation, and translocation to a new individual!"

"In mother's case, something in past generations may have caused this methylation. Perhaps it resulted from the trauma suffered by her grandfather Jean during World War I. Maybe it was produced in her maternal ancestors during the great extermination of *Pehuenches* in Argentina during the late 1800s. Or perhaps the trauma was even earlier, when a distant ancestor was seriously injured by a saber-toothed tiger or bear after the crossing of the Beringian land bridge."

"Maybe the mother whose son was killed in some tragic accident was so grief stricken that some of her DNA was methylated, or maybe the sister or mother of a girl killed in an avalanche was so traumatized by her loss that their DNA was methylated as a result."

"In closing, though, I am inclined to believe that it was the trauma my mother suffered when she returned to the house on that terrible day in 1973 and saw her mother and father lying dead in pools of blood, and perhaps some additional trauma until she knew that I, her baby, was safe."

"To this day we do not know what was in the extract that caused DNA demethylation in my mother, and coincidentally saved her life. We have tried many extracts of *misodendrum*, and many from *canelo*, but to no avail. There must have been something in the extract of that particular *misodendrum* plant parasitizing that particular *canelo* tree. Some super-purified essential oil, perhaps, that had the ability to demethylate DNA. We just don't know yet. My father has spent quite some time searching for another natural infection of *misodendrum* on *canelo*, but has found none, yet. He has also tried to artificially inoculate *canelo* trees with *misodendrum*, but so far with no lasting success. The *misodendrum* rootlets are initially able to invade the *canelo* tissue but are soon walled off by wound periderm tissue and the infection dies. You can bet, though, that we have not given up on this quest."

As *Paulina* finished her presentation and answered the last question, another round of applause went forth. Her presentation being over, *Paulina* shuffled and stacked her notes and placed them in her briefcase. The microphone was still on. As the applause began to die down, she paused, and then turned toward her left side of the room, waved, and said, *"Gracias abuelita."*

Rosa and Robert heard what she said – they were stunned! What did that mean? *Rosa* gasped and with one hand covered her mouth and with the other grabbed Robert's arm! Robert looked at her as she pointed to the side of the stage toward where *Paulina* had spoken. There were two visible figures standing there! He recognized the male figure as *Juan*! The female figure was resplendent in silver and *lapis lazuli* jewelry and the trappings of a *Pehuenche* **machi**. It was a youthful *Claudia*! She and an equally youthful *Juan* were smiling. And, as they faded from view, both gave a little wave as *Claudia* said, *"Bien hecho, nieta mía"* (Well done, my granddaughter.).

CHAPTER 35
Paulina's Notebook of Medicinal Plants

In the weeks that passed after Robert's return, he, *Rosa*, and *Paulina* spent considerable time and energy becoming acquainted. Robert was becoming more and more amazed by his young daughter. Even though she was now eight years old, Robert realized that *Rosa* and her grandparents, and her neighbors in *Lonquimay*, had done an amazing job of helping her to grow up, in spite of his absence. It wasn't long before she and Robert got along so well that a stranger would not have realized that they had been separated for so many years.

Paulina was extremely interested in learning about the medicinal plants that her father had worked with. She had gone with her mother many times to assist at the medicinal plant cooperative in *Lonquimay* that her father's company had started when she was still a little baby. Two years before her father returned, she had learned to read, and began to read, with great interest, all the literature that her mother and great-grandmother had shared with her about medicinal plants.

In the months after Robert had returned, they spent many happy hours discussing the medicinal plants that grew in Chile and the beneficial properties they possessed. Her great-grandmother told her of many of those benefits and *Paulina* recorded them in her little notebook. Not long before she was to leave to study in the United States, she announced that she had put together a booklet that contained all the information she had learned about medicinal plants. She had also drawn sketches of most of the plants that she had included in the booklet. Her parents were so impressed that they said that they would help her publish it for sale at the cooperative in *Lonquimay*.

That booklet is included here in the final portion of this novel. It was *Paulina's* intent to make a record of all the medicinal plants that her mother's ancestors had employed to improve their health and quality of life. Most of the medicinal plants listed here are native to Chile. However, when one recognizes that Spanish conquest of Chile had started 400 years previously, some plants from Europe that had medicinal properties were quickly imported and either planted or had escaped from gardens to occupy large areas in the new land. The *mapuches* were quick to recognize the beneficial properties of these newly imported plants. So, for this reason, most of these plants are also included in this booklet of medicinal plants used by the *mapuches* and focus on the specific beneficial properties that they made of these plants.

Some of the medicinal plants listed have truly amazing properties and recent research has identified many of the essential oils and other components that have medicinal qualities. If you Google the scientific name of any of these plants, you will encounter a wealth of information about their beneficial properties. Much of this information is being generated by Chilean scientific researchers as well as by other scientists from around the world. Be aware, though, that some of these plants have toxic properties and should be used only under the supervision of qualified medical personnel. These plants are presented here under an alphabetical listing of their parent family name:

Adoxaceae
Saúco, **Treyke**, Elderberry – *Sambucus australis*

Flowers are placed in boiling water and the cooled infusion is applied to eye and skin infections. Reduces inflammation, also used as a diuretic, for treatment of sinusitis and as an immune booster.

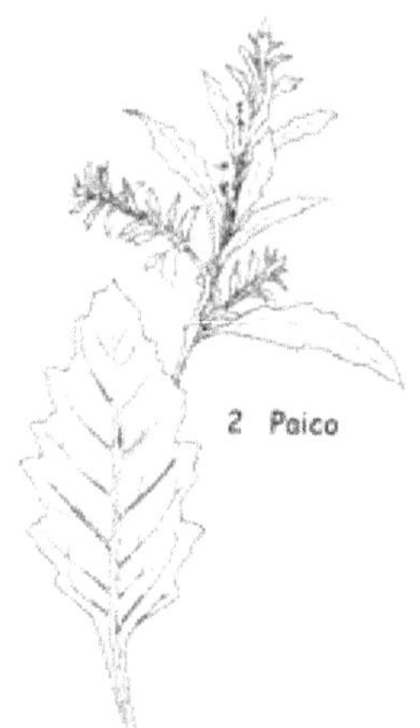

Amaranthaceae
Paico, Wormseed – *Dysphania ambrosioides*

Leaves and roots are boiled in water and taken to assist digestion, reduce intestinal worms, headache, injuries, and initiate the menstrual cycle.

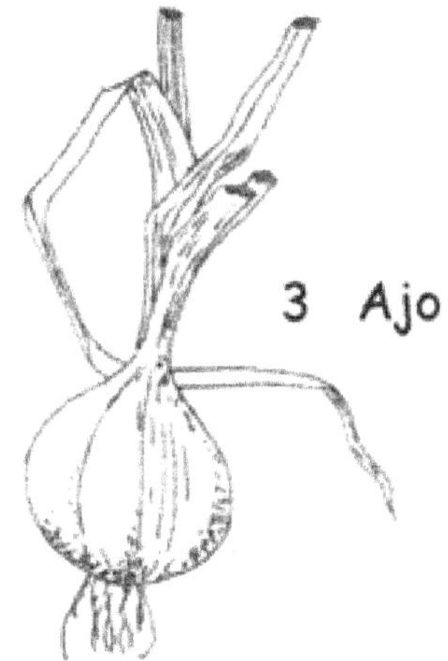

Amaryllidaceae
Ajo, **Aku**, Garlic – *Allium sativum*

The cloves are taken for flu or fever, for intestinal worms, prevention of heart attack, and to reduce weight.

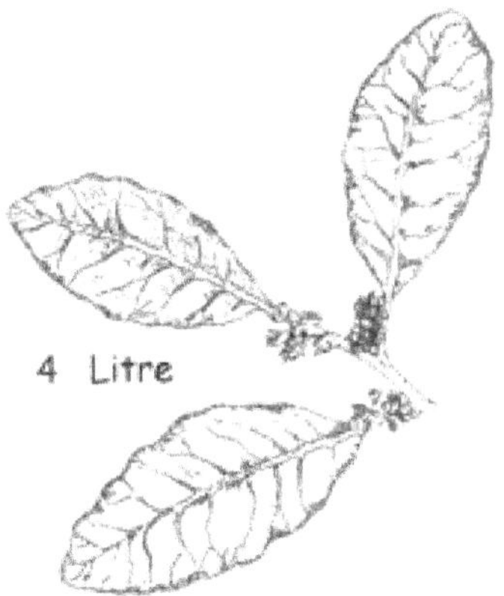

Anacardiaceae
Litre, **Lithi**, Soapberry – *Lithraea caustica*

Submerge rheumatic body parts in hot water in which leaves or branches have been steeped. But, use with care because it is also allergenic and can cause skin rash.

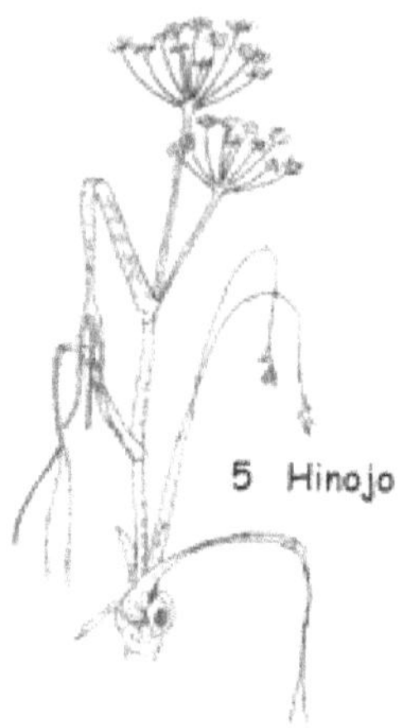

Apiaceae
Hinojo, **Hinoko**, Fennel – *Foeniculum vulgare*

Leaves and roots are boiled in water, and are taken to reduce intestinal gas and spasms, also to reduce pain in liver and stomach, also for bronchitis and coughing. Recent research suggests it has antifungal, antibacterial, antioxidant, antithrombotic, and hepatoprotective activities.

Araucariaceae
Pino araucaria, **Pehuén**, Monkey-puzzle tree – *Araucaria araucana*

Trunk resin is used to treat skin ulcers or injuries.

Asteraceae
Alcachofa, Artichoke – *Cynara scolymus*

Leaves and fruit are boiled in water and the hot water is taken for kidney, stomach, and liver health. The raw fruit is eaten with lemon juice to control diabetes.

Asteraceae
Artemisa, *Ajenjo*, **Akenko**, **Eter**, Sweet wormseed – *Artemisia* sp.

Leaves, shoots, and buds are infused in hot water, cooled, and taken for stomachache and flu and respiratory problems. It has potent antimalarial and antimicrobial activities. It also has strong diuretic properties, regulates menstrual cycle, can kill and expel intestinal worms, and repel moths and other insects.

Asteraceae
Chinita, Marigold – *Calendula officinales*

Flowers may be applied to open wounds to stop bleeding, prevent infection, and speed healing. Leaves and flowers can be infused in hot water and the cooled water taken to detoxify the liver and gall bladder. A paste made of ground tissues and mixed with vasoline can be applied to the skin to treat minor cuts, burns, and irritations.

Asteraceae
Manzanilla, **Poqui**, Chamomile – *Matricana chamomilla*

Hot water infusion of flowers is used to treat spasms, sore throat, and bronchitis, as a mild laxative, for irritable bowel syndrome, and for external use as an anti-inflammatory.

Asteraceae
Mil en Rama, Yarrow – *Achillea millefolium*

An infusion of leaves is taken for injuries, back aches, and hemorrages.

Asteraceae
Trevo, **Trevu** *– Dasphyllum diacanthoides*

Bark and spines are boiled in water tú taken or applied as a compress for fever, wrinkles, and skin problems.

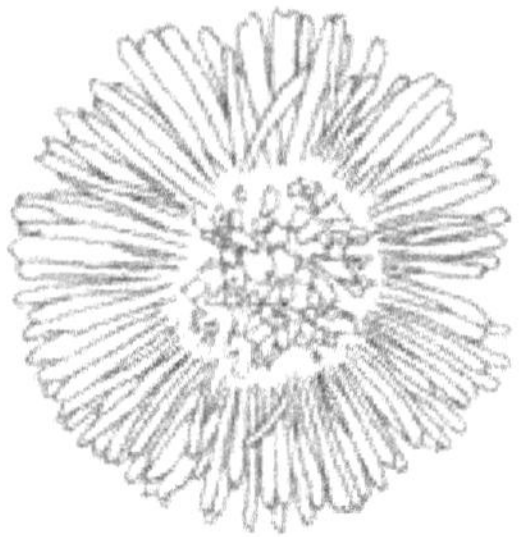

13 Tusilago

Asteraceae
Tusilago, Coltsfoot – *Tusilago farfara*

The leaves are used to make tea that is used for treatment of internal problems such as viral infections, flu, cold, fever, rheumatism, and gout, or externally for treatment of skin disorders. But, recent research indicates it contains toxic pyrrdizidine alkaloids that if used in the human diet may cause liver concerns.

14 Borraja

Boraginaceae
Borraja, Borage – *Borago officiales*

Aerial parts, including flowers and seeds, are steeped in hot water and the water is taken several times daily. It is also used for control of fever, to increase kidney health, and to treat sore and inflamed skin. It also has a high mucilage content and is good for respiratory problems.

Buddlejaceae

Matico, **Pañil**, Orange-ball-tree – *Buddleja globosa*

Leaves are steeped in hot water that is then used to wash injuries. The filtrate may be used as a dressing on skin ulcers and contusions. Extracts have antifungal activity.

Celastraceae

Maitén, **Magthun** or **Malten**, The maiten tree – *Maytenus boaria*

Leaves and seeds are steeped in hot water and the water then taken to reduce fever, for injuries, to reduce intestinal gas, constipation, and as a purgative.

Cunoniaceae
Tineo, *Palo Santo*, **Teniu** or **Maden** – *Weinmannia trichosperma*

The bark is boiled in water and the water is taken to increase health of lungs and kidneys.

Cunoniaceae
Tiaca – Caldcluvia paniculata

Leaves are steeped in hot water and the cooled water is taken for catarrh, intestinal infections, colds, and stomach disorders.

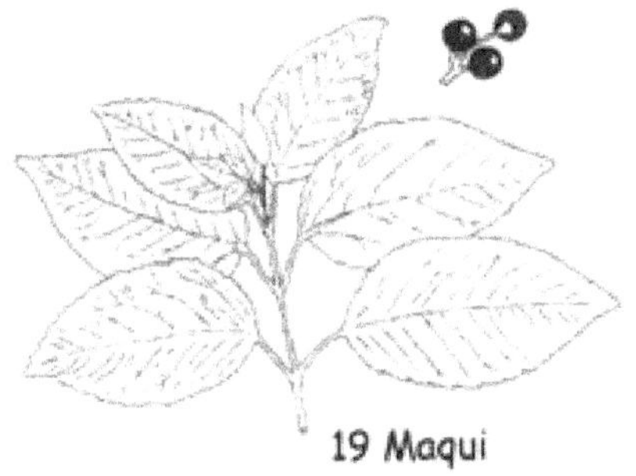

19 Maqui

Elaeocarpaceae
Maqui, **Quilon**, Chilean wineberry – *Aristotelia chilensis*

Leaves steeped in hot water are used to treat for catarrh, colds, stomach disorders, for intestinal infections, and externally as an astringent.

20 Siete camisas

Escalloniaceae
Siete Camisas, **Lun** – *Escallonia revoluta*

Branches with leaves are boiled in water and the cooled water is taken to reduce liver problems, muscular pains, and rheumatism.

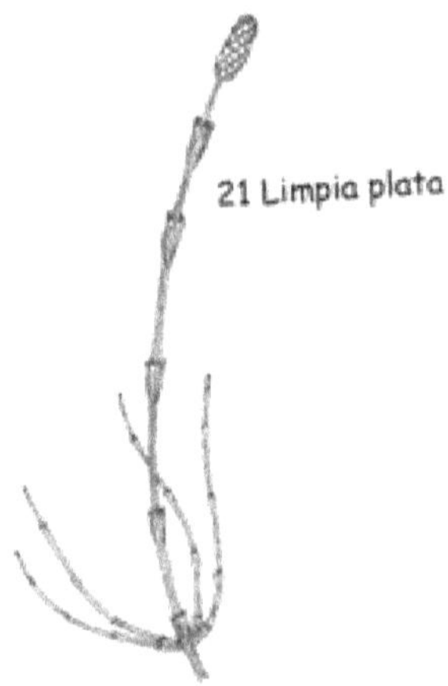

Equisetaceae
Limpia-plata, **Keltri lawen**, Andean horsetail – *Equisetum bogotense*

Entire plant is steeped in hot water and the water taken internally to reduce bladder and kidney stones, to wash injuries, and for nosebleed.

Fabiaceae
Culén - Otholobium glandulosum (Psoralea glandulosa)

The entire plant is infused in hot water and the cooled water is taken to induce vomiting. When used with *Llantén* and *Pila pila*, it is also useful for control of stomach ulcers, diabetes, and intestinal worms. Recent research shows that it also has anticancer (melanoma) properties.

23 Corre-corre

Geraniaceae
Corre-corre – Geranium core-core

Leaves and roots are mashed into a pulp and applied to reduce baby rashes and foot fungus. If steeped in hot water, the cooled infusion is taken for hemorrhages and to reduce inflammation.

24 Orégano

Lamiaceae
Orégano – Origanum vulgare

Branches with leaves are steeped in hot water and the cooled water taken to reduce coughing, earache, indigestion, and ovarial pain.

Lamiaceae
Poleo, **Koleu**, Pennyroyal – *Mentha pulegium*

Leaves are steeped in hot water and the cooled water taken to stimulate digestion, to heal skin injuries, to control asthma, to treat bronchitis and head cold. It has abortive effects, and is also used for gastrointestinal ailments, such as constipation, hemorrhoids and toothache.

Lamiaceae
Romero, **Sasin**, Rosemary – *Rosmarinus officinalis*

Leaves are boiled in water and the cooled water taken to treat bronchitis, coughing, excessive nervousness, improve liver and gall bladder function, reduce intestinal gas, control of rheumatic diseases, circulatory disorders, and because it is a mild antiseptic, it is also used for treating wounds.

27 Salvia

Lamiaceae
Salvia – Sphacele chamaedryoides

Crushed leaves are rubbed on the skin to reduce facial paralysis.

28 Toronjil Cuyano

Lamiaceae
Toronjil Cuyano, **Waka Lawen**, Horehound – *Marrubium vulgare*

Leaves and flowers are steeped in hot water and taken for nerves, insomnia, headache, and menstrual pains, and as a poultice for insect bites. Recent research shows that its essential oil has potent antimicrobial, anticancer, antidiabetic, antiortherogenic, and anti-inflamatory properties. It is also used to make lozenges which aid digestion and sooth sore throat.

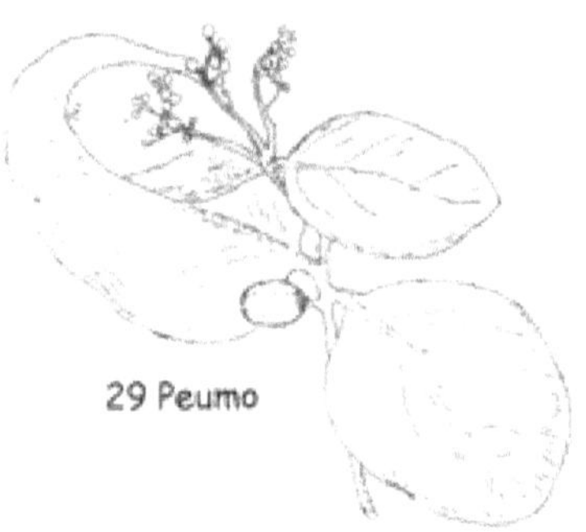

29 Peumo

Lauraceae
Peumo, **Penu** – *Cryptocarya alba*

Leaves and bark are steeped in boiling water and the cooled water taken to improve liver health. Its essential oil has antifungal properties.

30 Fui Fui

Juncaceae
Fui Fui, **Fui Fui** or **Kachu**, Rush – *Juncus* sp.

Stems are boiled and the cooled liquid is taken several times daily, to initiate the menstrual period, and reduce blood coagulation. Root extracts are taken to reduce chance of miscarriage.

Malvaceae
Huella – Corynabutilon vitifolium

Leaves are steeped in hot water and the cooled water taken several times daily for treatment of colds, and to initiate menstruation.

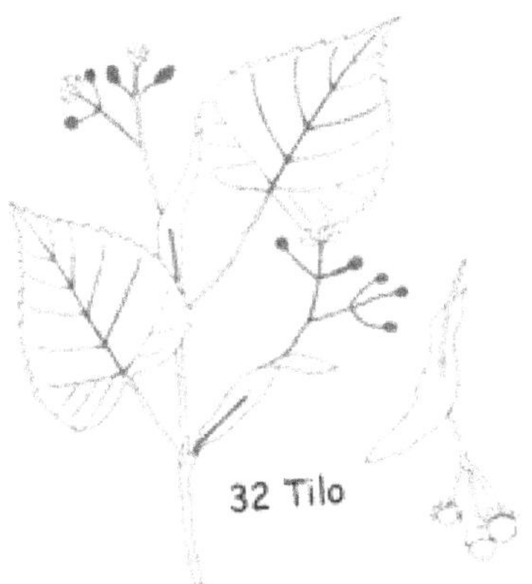

Malvaceae
Tilo, Bigleaf linden tree, lime tree – *Tilia platyphyllos*

Flowers are steeped in hot water and the cooled water taken to reduce discomfort of head colds. The bark is soaked in cold water until it becomes gelatinous and is then applied to treat burns.

Monimiaceae
Boldo, **Folo** *– Peumus boldus*

Infusion of leaves or ground leaves are prepared as capsules, tablets, or mixed with *yerba mate* to moderate its flavor. For traditional uses it should only incorporate aqueous extracts and not ethanolic extracts because of their high levels in the latter of the toxic ascaridole constituent. It is used to reduce liver and kidney stones. It also relaxes smooth muscles to prolong intestinal transit, serves as a diuretic and as a mild laxative. It can also work as an antiseptic, is hepatoprotective, is antioxidant, improves digestion, is a liver bile stimulant, is a vermifuge, is diuretic, and abortive, eliminates intestinal gas, reduces high blood sugar levels, and ensures a healthy menstruation. It is also known as the hangover drug as it alleviates the most distasteful symptoms resulting from imbibition of excessive alcohol.

34 Laurel de Campo

Monimiaceae
Laurel de Campo, **Triwe**, **Tihue**, Chilean laurel – *Laurelia sempervirens*

Leaves, flowers, and bark are boiled in water. The cooled water is a diuretic and is also used for treatment of indigestion, colds, headaches, venereal disease, and skin problems.

35 Eucalypto

Myrtaceae
Eucalipto, **Kalitro**, Eucalyptus – *Eucalyptus globulus*

Leaves are steeped in hot water for several minutes and the hot water is taken to reduce respiratory problems, sinusitus, and coughing. Its essential oil is famous for many other pharmaceutical uses.

36 Chilco

Onograceae
Chilco, fucsia, Evening primrose – *Fuchsia magellanica*

An infusion of leaves and small branches is prepared in hot water. The water is taken warm and is useful as a diuretic and for urinary problems.

37 Culle Colorado

Oxalidaceae
Culle colorado, **Kellu Kulle**, Annual pink-sorrel – *Oxalis rosea*

An infusion of the entire plant is taken several times daily and is an abortfacient and is used for inducing the menstrual period and to reduce bloody diarrhea.

38 Cardo blanco

Papaveraceae
> *Cardo Blanco*, **Troltro**, Mexican poppy – *Argemone mexicana*

The roots are used along with parts of other plants, such as *Hinojo* and *Poleo*, are boiled in water and used to treat liver pain. The plant is phytotoxic to many crop species (allelopathic) and is a possible nematocide.

39 Coralillo

Phytolaccaceae
> *Coralillo*, **Sinchull** or **Ivircun** – *Ercilla spicata*

An infusion of leaves is made in hot water and the cooled water taken to initiate the menstrual cycle.

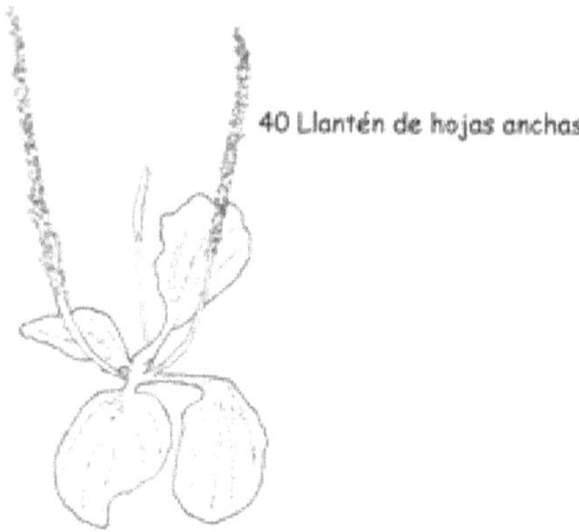

Plantaginaceae
Llantén de hojas anchas, Plantain – *Plantago major*

Leaves, either ground or steeped in hot water, are used for closure of injuries, treatment of earache, ulcers, hemorrhoids, diarrhea, and head cold.

Plantaginaceae
Siete Venas, **Trepú** or **Pilluñiweke**, Ribwort plantain – *Plantago lanceolata*

Same as for *Llantén de hojas anchas.*

42 Sanguinaria

Polygonaceae
Sanguinaria, **Lafquen kachu** – *Polygonum sanguinaria*

Leaves are steeped in boiling water and the cooled water is taken to eliminate kidney and gall bladder stones, purify blood, and as a diuretic.

43 Avellano

Proteaceae
Avellano, **Ngefün**, Chilean hazel – *Gevuina avellana*

An infusion of leaves in hot water is prepared and, when cooled, is taken for diarrhea, and with bark of *palo santo* and *trevol,* for internal injuries to lungs and kidneys.

44 Fosforito

Proteaceae
Notro, fosforito, Chilean fire tree – *Embothrium coccineum*

Bark and leaves are used to treat toothache, injuries, neuralgia, injuries, and as a bacterial antiseptic.

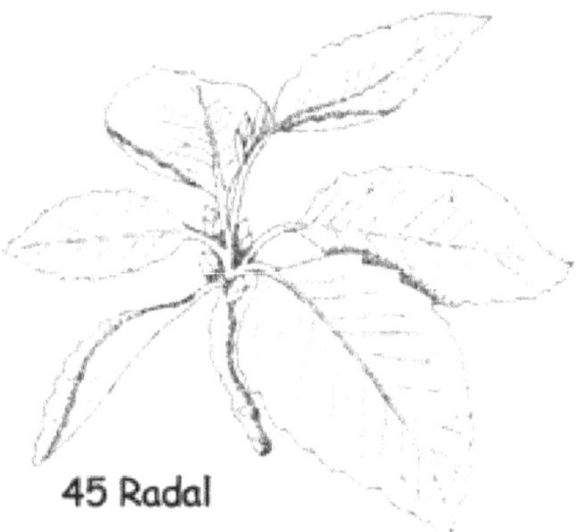

45 Radal

Proteaceae
Radal – Lomatia hirsuta

Leaves are steeped in hot water and the cooled water is taken to control head colds, coughing, bronchial troubles, and asthma.

Proteaceae
Fuinque *– Lomatia ferruginea*

The bark and leaves are used to cure injuries and is a purgative and diuretic.

Rosaceae
Amores secos, **Trun** *– Acaena argentea*

Entire plant is used to make tea that is then used against infections and to assist healing of wounds.

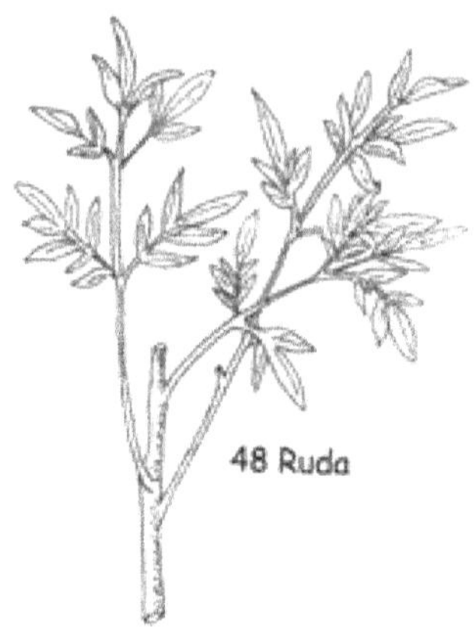

Rutaceae

Ruda, Rue – *Ruta bracteosa (chalepensis)*

Leaves are steeped in hot water and the cooled water is taken to relieve stomach and menstrual pains and is also used to treat neuromuscular problems. It is an aphrodisiac. Low dosages produce antispasmodic effects and must be taken with caution.

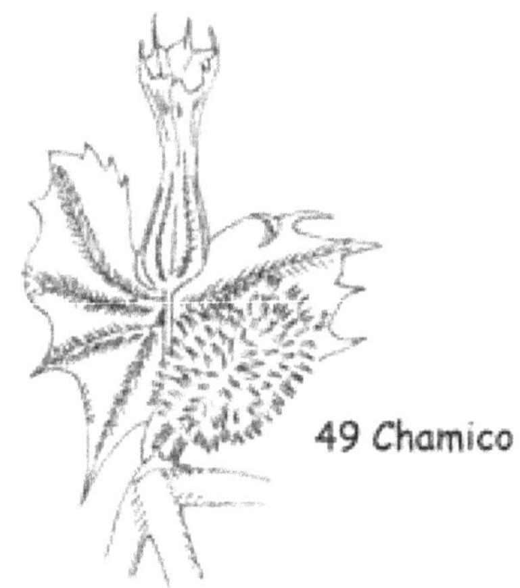

Solanaceae

Chamico, **Millalle**, Jimsonweed – *Datura stromonium*

Heated leaves are placed on areas where there is rheumatismal pain. Repeat each time after the leaves cool for several treatments. This plant has many toxic properties, probably due to the high levels of alkaloids it contains. These compounds block neurotransmitters in the brain and can produce vivid hallucinations and cause delirium. Its history of use goes back to Greek mythology where it is mentioned in Homer's *The Odyssey* in which the sorceress Circe made a potion in which she mixed what is believed to have been this plant. Its victims hallucinated and believed that they had been transformed into pigs.

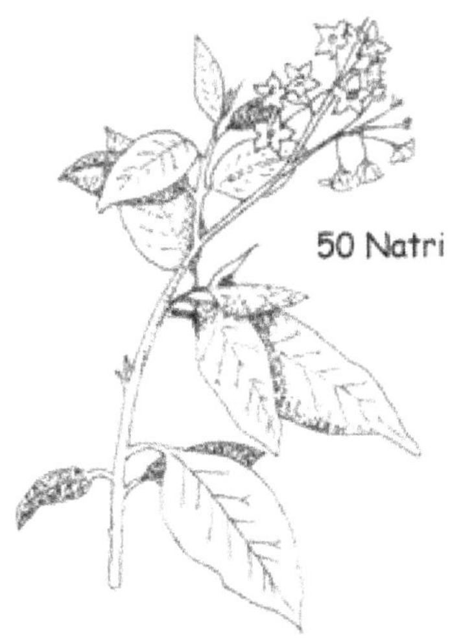

Solanaceae
Natri, **Natri** or **Natren**, Chilean nightshade – *Solanum crispum*

Leaves are steeped in hot water. The cooled water is taken for head cold and fever. It is very toxic.

Solanaceae
Palqui, Green cestrum or willow-leaved jasmine – *Cestrum parqui*

Leaves are steeped in hot water and the cooled water is taken for fever. All parts of the plant are toxic.

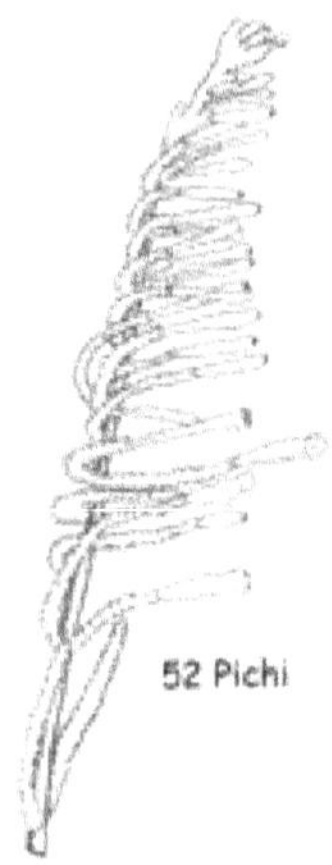

Solanaceae
Pichi – Fabiana imbracata

Shoots and leaves are used as a diuretic, for treatment of nasal catarrh, jaundice, dyspepsia, and to increase secretion of bile.

Urticaceae

Ortiga común, Stinging nettle – *Urtica urens*

Stem with leaves are ground into a pulp and applied to areas with joint pain and rheumatism. It also helps to reduce skin rash due to food allergies.

Verbenaceae

Cedrón, Lemon verbena – *Aloysia* sp.

Leaves are boiled in water and the water is taken while still very warm. It is useful for reducing stomach pain and to reduce intestinal spasms, relieve gas, and coughing. Recent research shows it to have antifungal, antibacterial, antioxidant, antiothrombic, and hepatoprotective activities.

Violaceae

Violeta azul, Sweet violet – *Viola odorata*

The entire plant is used. It has high salicylic acid content and is used for treatment of coughing, migraine headaches, insomnia, and cancer.

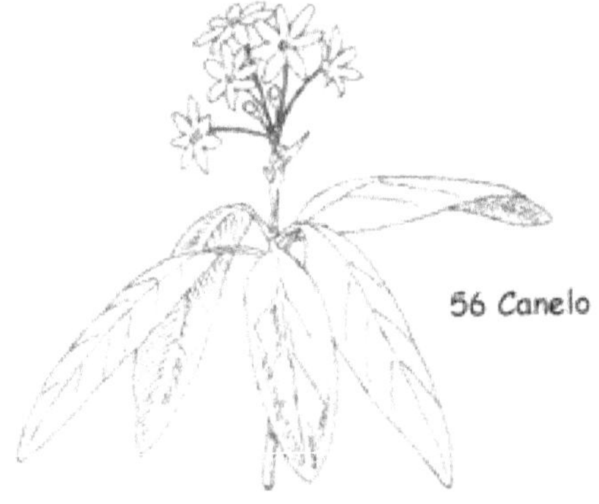

Winteraceae

Canelo, **Foye** – *Drymis winteri*

Infusion of leaves is placed on cuts to help clean and heal. It is also used for stomach problems and rheumatism. It has a high vitamin C content and was used historically to treat for scurvy. Recent research shows that essential oil extracted from the plant has insecticidal and fungicidal properties and is also useful for control of high arterial blood pressure.

Suggested additional reading

http://identidadyfuturo.cl/2013/08/la-tragedia-del-tunel-las-raices/

http://www.e-mas.co.cl/categorias/historia/guerrdelpaci.htm

http://en.wikipedia.org/wiki/Boldo

http://www.laguerradelpacifico.cl/campana%20terrestre/Sierra/

Sangrar.htm

http://www.mapuche-nation.org/espanol/html/articulos/art-59.htm

http://www.newworldencyclopedia.org/entry/Juan_Fernandez_Islands

https://en.wikipedia/org/wiki/Chagas_disease

https://en.wikipedia/Battle_of_Coronel

https://en.wikipedia/Battle_of_the_Falkland_Islands

http://www.victorianweb.org/science/darwin/massacre.html

http://en.wikipedia.org/wiki/Conquest_of_the_Desert

http://en.wikipedia.org/wiki/Machi_(shaman)

https://en.wikipedia.org/wiki/Mylodon

Anonymous. Undated. *Manual de Plantas Medicinales en la Medicina Casera. Sociedad de Campesino Mapuche.* 104 pp.

Anonymous. 2008. *Nuevo Manual de Medicina Natural. Ediciones FELC. Araucanía 1773. Santiago, Chile.* 154 pp.

Anonymous. 2013. *Diccionario Mapuche. Editorial Centro Gráfico Limitada, Colón 916, La Serena, Chile.* 251 pp.

Borrell, B. 2014. Seeds of a cure. Scientific American. June:65-69.

Bower, B. 2014. Bones offer insight into Clovis origins. Science News. June 14 :7.

Bower, B. 2019. Idaho site predates ice-free corridor. Science News. Sept. 28:13.

Echenique, A. and M. V. Legassa. 1999. La Flora Chilena en la Mirada de Marianne North – 1884. Pehuen Editores, Santiago, Chile. 132 pp.

Frias V., Francisco. 1969. Manual de Historia de Chile. Editorial Nascimento, Santiago, Chile. Segunda edición ilustrada. 527 pp.

Gaidos, S. 2014. T-Force. Science News. June 14: 22-25.

Garcia, M. A., S. Duk, G. Weigert, M. Silva, and M. Alarcón. 1993. Chromosome aberrations induced by Eumaitenine, a sesquiterpene isolated from *Maytenus boaria* Mol. in cultured CHO cells. Bull. Environ. Contam. Toxicol. 51: 803-897.

Gibbons, A. 2015. Humans may have reached Chile by 18,500 years ago. Science. 350:(Issue 6263):898.

Goldberg, A., A. M. Mychajliw, and E. A. Hadly. 2016. Post-invasion demography of prehistoric humans in South America. Nature. 532:232-235.

Grimm, D. 2015. Dawn of the dog. Science. 348 (Issue 6232): 274-279.

Hodges, G. 2015. The first American. National Geographic. 227 (1): 124-137.

Hoffmann J., A. E. 1994. Flora Silvestre de Chile - Zona Araucana. Tercera Edición Revisada. Ediciones Fundación Claudio Gay. Santiago, Chile. 257 pp.

Kaplan, M. 2015. Rooted in Truth. Discover. November: 52-55.

Kornbluh, P. 2003. The Pinochet File – A Declassified Dossier on Atrocity and Accountability. The New Press, New York, London. 551 pp.

Ledford, H. 2014. The killer within. Nature. 508: 23 – 26.

Maclean, N. 1992. Young Men and Fire. University of Chicago Press. 301 pp.

Marean, C. W. 2015. The most invasive species of all. Scientific American. 313 (No. 2): 32-39.

Marticorena, A., D. Alarcón, L. Abello y C. Atala. 2010. Plantas trepadoras, epífitas y parásitas nativas de Chile. Guía de Campo. Ed. Corporación de la Madera, Concepción, Chile. 291 pp.

Meiselas, S. (ed.) 1990. Chile From Within – 1973-1988. W. W. Norton & Company, New York and London. 58 pp.

Nickrent, D. L. 2002. Mistletoe phylogenetics: Current relationships gained from analysis of DNA sequences. Pp. 48-57 in: Proceedings of the Western International Forest Disease Work Conference, August 14-18, 2000. Waikoloa, Hawai'i. 253 pp.

Pizarro, Carlos Muñoz. 1966. Sinopsis de la Flora Chilena. Ediciones de la Universidad de Chile, Santiago, Chile. 500 pp.

Raff, J. A. and D. A. Bolnick. 2014. Genetic roots of the first Americans. Nature. 506: 162-163.

Rebolledo, R., J. Abarzua, A. Zavala, A. Quiroz, M. Alvear, and A. Aquilera.

2012. The effects of the essential oil and hydrolate of *canelo* (*Drimys winteri*) on adults of *Aegorhinus superciliosus* in the laboratory. *Cienc. Inv. Agr. 39(3): 481-488.*

Record, S. J. and R. W. Hess. 1943. Timbers of the New World. Yale University Press, New Haven. 640 pp.

Ruhlen, M. 1987. A Guide to the World's Languages. Volume 1: Classification. Stanford University Press, Stanford, California. 433 pp.

Saey, T. H. 2011. Lager's mystery ingredient found. Science News. Sept. 24:16.

Skinner, M. K, 2014. A new kind of inheritance. Scientific American. 311 (2): 45-51.

Sloan, R. E. 2005. Minnesota Fossils and Fossiliferous Rocks. Published privately in an edition of 1000. 218 pp.

Tainter, F. H. and F. A. Baker. 1996. Principles of Forest Pathology. John Wiley and Sons, Inc., New York. 805 pp.

Uliánova, O. 2003. Levantamiento Campesino de Lonquimay y La Internacional Comunista. Estudios Públicos. 89:173-223.

Urzua, A, R. Santander, J. Echeverria, C. Villalobos, S. M. Palacios, and Y. Rossi. 2010. Insecticidal properties of *Peumus boldus* Mol. essential oil on the house fly, *Musca domestica* L. *Boletin Latinoamericano y del Caribe de Plantas Medicinales y Aromaticas.* 9 (6): 465-469.

Watson, D. and M. Herring. 2012. For more than just kissing. Nature. 487:274.

Weise, G. A. 2013. Historia de Curacautín – "Testigo de mi Tiempo". Tomo Uno. Imprenta Wesaldi, Temuco, Chile. 418 pp.

Zin, J. S. and C. Weiss R. (no date). La Salud por Medio de las Plantas Medicinales. Editorial Don Bosco S. A., Santiago, Chile. 407 pp.

www.ingramcontent.com/pod-product-compliance
Lightning Source LLC
Chambersburg PA
CBHW041156150726
48006CB00016B/2006